Praise for *Work Like Any Other*

"Thoughtful, absorbing . . . In this engrossing, vividly drawn debut, Reeves delivers a dazzlingly authentic portrait of a restless, remorseful mind."

—*Publishers Weekly*

"Eloquent and acutely self-aware . . . Prose so lovely that it strains credulity . . . Elegant."

—*Kirkus Reviews*

"*Work Like Any Other* is addictive when it focuses on Roscoe's life behind bars, and the perils he suffers—a good man you can't help but have sympathy for, but one earmarked for suffering. . . . A book worth reading."

—*Missourian*

"A morally complicated ode to Alabama."

—*Jackson Free Press*

"The novel's great strength is that in showing so much in terms of race, our prison system, forgiveness, and labor, it never is heavy-handed. . . . Reeves's nuance for these people and this story is, indeed, quite powerful."

—*Minneapolis Star Tribune*

"Reeves's novel, with its strong sense of time and place and its interrelating cast of inmates and guards, calls to mind those Stephen King books set in prisons, *The Green Mile* and *The Shaw-*

shank Redemption, that were adapted into films. But it is Paul Harding's Pulitzer Prize–winning novel, *Tinkers*, that is perhaps a better comparison here because of its many bewitching passages of description of electricity. . . . Reeves is a fine wrangler of words, able to snake sentences of slithery charisma in and around each other. This is especially true in her depictions of time and place: her settings and the people in them stand firm and vivid in the mind's eye."

—*The Australian*

"Beautifully written, this is an unusual and moving debut."

—*The Sunday Times* (UK)

"There seems to be a hint of Steinbeck as well as early Annie Proulx. As a traditional story about human struggle in a now vanished America, this classic novel will appeal to admirers of Daniel Woodrell, whose finest books to date include *Winter's Bone* and *The Maid's Version*."

—*The Irish Times*

"In the era of instant gratification, Virginia Reeves's big triumph is the ambitious narrative arc she presents here: *Work Like Any Other* is a (timely) indictment of the racism and prison system of the United States. But it also uses the four walls of confinement to create a sharp portrait of a confined mind trying to sort out the debris of a life gone wrong."

—*Bangalore Mirror*

"How brilliantly Virginia Reeves brings to life her protagonist, Roscoe T Martin, with his hatred of farming, his love of electricity, and his long struggle to make amends to himself, his family, and his friends. *Work Like Any Other* is a novel of fierce beauty and hard-won redemption. A wonderful debut."

—Margot Livesey, author of *The Flight of Gemma Hardy*

"The world of this exquisite novel—1920s Alabama—hasn't let go of me since I finished it. It's gorgeous, painful, original, and so true in all its details. Reeves writes with incredibly intelligent compassion, and in Roscoe Martin has created an extraordinary man who more than earns his place among the complicated population of the literary South. Thick with dread and beauty, this is a stunning chronicle of a time, a place, and a mind."

—Fiona McFarlane, author of *The Night Guest*

"Virginia Reeves's assured and absorbing debut novel is a potent mix of icy honesty and heart-wrenching tenderness. It is certainly a work unlike any other, in that its humanity and optimism are salvaged from the darkest of places, from prison cells, from mining shafts, from decomposing marriages, and from the unforgiving workings of the land."

—Jim Crace, author of *Harvest*

"*Work Like Any Other* is a beautifully accomplished first novel. Reeves draws the reader in with such ease and plumbs the depths of her characters with such acuteness and care, I was totally won over."

—James Magnuson, author of *The Hounds of Winter*

"A riveting debut that oscillates between past and present, between the high price of hope and the betrayals of progress. Both an intimate family saga and a heartbreaking cautionary tale, *Work Like Any Other* is, above all, a starkly beautiful novel."

—Cristina García, author of *Dreaming in Cuban*

"Virginia Reeves has built her first novel with the craft and seriousness of purpose of a master carpenter. When the pieces come together, you're astonished at what a thing of beauty has appeared before your eyes."

—Anthony Giardina, author of *Norumbega Park*

WORK LIKE ANY OTHER

A NOVEL

VIRGINIA REEVES

SCRIBNER
New York   London   Toronto   Sydney   New Delhi

SCRIBNER
An Imprint of Simon & Schuster, Inc.
1230 Avenue of the Americas
New York, NY 10020

Copyright © 2016 by Virginia Reeves

First Scribner trade paperback edition March 2017

For information about special discounts for bulk purchases,
please contact Simon & Schuster Special Sales at 1-866-506-1949
or business@simonandschuster.com.

The Simon & Schuster Speakers Bureau can bring authors
to your live event. For more information or to book an event,
contact the Simon & Schuster Speakers Bureau at 1-866-248-3049
or visit our website at www.simonspeakers.com.

Interior design by Kyle Kabel

Manufactured in the United States of America

1   3   5   7   9   10   8   6   4   2

Library of Congress Control Number: 2015022240

ISBN 978-1-5011-1249-2
ISBN 978-1-5011-1250-8 (pbk)
ISBN 978-1-5011-1252-2 (ebook)

For my grandmother, Therese Reeves

Alabama does not mean "Here we rest." It never did.

—Mrs. L. B. Bush,
from "A Decade of Progress in Alabama," 1924

Kilby Prison marks the impending transfer of the State of Alabama from the rear ranks of prison management to the front ranks. Alabama is following the example of the State of New York and the State of Virginia in establishing a central distributing prison to which prisoners will be sent immediately upon their conviction, and where they will receive: first, a thorough study of their history; second, a most thorough examination, mental and physical, by trained experts; third, a thorough course of treatment to remove any remedial defects; fourth, assignment to that prison and employment for which the convict is best adapted; and fifth, a systematic course of reformatory treatment and training, in order that the prisoner may be restored to society, if possible, a self-respecting, upright, useful and productive citizen.

—Hastings H. Hart,
from *Social Progress of Alabama*, 1922

PART I

CHAPTER 1

The electrical transformers that would one day kill George Haskin sat high on a pole about ten yards off the northeast corner of the farm where Roscoe T Martin lived with his family. There were three transformers in all, and they stepped down electricity that belonged to Alabama Power, stepped it down to run on new lines along a farm fence, then on through the woods, then straight to the farmhouse and the barn. Roscoe built the transformers himself. He built the lines. He did not have permission.

The idea for running in power arrived nearly a year before the power itself. He should've been eating dinner with his family, but he'd hurt his son and made his wife cry, so he was walking the cursed land his wife had forced him to. He took the path through the north corn to bring him close to the new power lines along Old Hissup Road. The corn was to his hips, still young, and the giant grasses brushed his fingers, a sickly feeling that set him shaking out his hands as if to unseat an insect. Of all the crops on his wife's land, corn was Roscoe's least favorite, something obscene in its size and growth, in its stalks and blades and seeds—everything too big.

His wife and son had been reading together on the sofa, an oil lamp on the tall table behind them lighting the pages. When he'd first courted the boy's mother, Roscoe had read with her, but she shared books with their son now.

They hadn't looked up when Roscoe came into the room.

"What are you reading?" he asked.

"A book," his son mumbled, snuggling closer to his mother.

Roscoe peered at the cover. "*Parnassus on Wheels*, huh? What's it about?"

Annoyance showed on Marie's face. "It's about a woman who owns a traveling bookshop. She has a brother she's sick of caring for." Her voice was weary, as though she were talking to a troublesome child shirking his lessons. "The brother refuses to work the farm."

She seemed to recognize her overstep before Roscoe reacted, offering him some kind of conciliatory gesture, an uncertain stretch of her hand that he slapped away. Gerald sank deeper into her side.

"I am not the ugly one here," Roscoe said to her. "You knew I wasn't going to become a farmer."

She'd reached for his arm again, but the anger came quick, the way it did, pushing him taller, shooting him toward that ceiling her daddy had plastered himself. Roscoe wrenched the book from Marie's hands and threw it across the room, where it broke a ceramic plate that hung on the wall.

"Go upstairs, Gerald," Marie said.

But Roscoe leaned down into his son's face. "You reading about a lowlife like your pa? Some shiftless loaf-about who won't work his own farm?" The boy's eyes went wide, the whites of them showing all round, and he tucked his lips inside his mouth like a coward.

Roscoe put his hands on Gerald's arms and lifted him away from his mother. Marie grabbed hold of Gerald's shirt, but Roscoe had a firm grip. He held the boy in front of his face, squeezing his upper arms. He whispered, "I am smarter than you'll ever be."

Then Marie had appeared again in his vision, clawing at his arm and his face, screaming at Roscoe to stop, and he did—he dropped their son at his wife's feet and slammed himself out the front door to walk the ugly fields to the power lines he loved.

A farm was no place for an electrician. He'd said it enough times, and he'd wallowed away the past year tinkering with an old mechanical thresher and reading in his late father-in-law's library. Every day, Marie asked him what he was going to do, and every day, he said, "Anything but work this goddamned farm."

"You came," she replied. "You didn't have to."

Her resentment was as strong as his, stronger even, with what he'd just done. The boy's arms would be bruised.

Roscoe stood under the nearest of the power lines. The air was darkening around him, and the cicadas had started their crying, wiry and metallic. If Marie's father hadn't died, Roscoe would still be working in the powerhouse back at Lock 12. They'd be living in the village, and he would be doing the work he loved.

Roscoe had a letter from his old foreman—his job was open for him should he wish to come back.

He was considering exactly that option when the idea for the transformers came, a vision before him—two or three of them perched on a freshly raised pole, linked up to new lines he'd twist himself. He saw light fixtures in the farmhouse, the kitchen appliances Marie had loved back in the village. And he saw the farm saved. Surely, electricity had the power to do that.

Exhaustion finally sent him back toward the house, and in the midst of the cornfield he recognized exactly how electricity could save Marie's land. He would electrify that damn thresher—wasn't that what he was already trying to do?—and he'd have that great machine do the work of the men Marie hired every season with money they didn't have. The thresher would run for free on their pirated power, and the farm would see a profit, as it had only in the legends of Marie's childhood.

He chewed on the idea for a month before taking it to Wilson.

MARIE was on the front porch, drinking coffee and reading the almanac. She'd barely spoken to Roscoe since their fight before his walk in the corn, and she refused to acknowledge him when he came through the screen door.

The day was mild and green, everything growing in the April sun.

"Do you know where I can find Wilson?" Roscoe asked.

Marie didn't look up.

"Marie, do you know where Wilson is?"

She kept her eyes down. "He's working."

Roscoe wished he could tell her instead, that she were the person he'd go to with news or ideas. He wished for an invitation on her face, something welcoming, even just the hint of a smile. *Marie,* he wanted to say, *I have something for you to liken to your birds.* Marie was a birder—a thing he'd loved about her from the start—always catching a tune, a pattern, an errant flit of blue in the holly, and she defined people and ideas by the birds they typified. She'd called him a cedar waxwing early in their courtship, the two of them walking along the Coosa River. The waxwing is known for its bandit eyes and tips of yellow and orange. "Look," she'd said. "See that? They're eating the dried berries." She pointed out the birds' haphazard flight, wheeling and turning over the water. "They're drunk as beggars up there. The berries are all fermented now." She'd paused. "You're a waxwing. All this electricity getting you drunk." Later, she admitted that they were her favorite, these drunken birds, and Roscoe had taken it as a compliment that was both rough and tender.

Roscoe couldn't remember the last time Marie had pointed out a waxwing. He couldn't remember the last time anything had been tender between them.

"Where is Wilson working?" he asked.

"North field. He's mending rails on the far fence line. He could use your help." She was looking at her book again, her features cast in their resident fatigue, and Roscoe left her without saying goodbye. They were long past greetings and farewells.

The paint on the rungs of the porch steps was chipped and flaking, and Roscoe kicked bits free as he walked down. The steps had been white once, as the house had been white, but everything was gray now, the exposed boards and the remaining paint dulled by age. Roscoe glanced back at his wife, sitting under the roof of the porch, and he saw the sadness in her surroundings, the great failing of her father's house and land. Creepers had taken over the chimneys and lattice of the porch. The brick underneath crumbled in places, the mortar giving way to the vines. This was no longer the home of Marie's childhood, and Roscoe could understand—right here, for just this moment—his wife's disappointment. She had come here to save the place, to return it to the glory it had known under her father's care, but there had been no improvements since their arrival. They weren't even holding steady. Their yields and income continued to decline, the house to deteriorate, the land to fail them.

At one time in their lives Roscoe would have told her these thoughts, a time when his compassion would have helped.

He left Marie in her crumbling house and took a trail through a thicket of woods, veering right at its fork. Left led to a cottage where Wilson lived with his family. Right led to the cornfield, ending at the furrows.

Roscoe made so much noise that Wilson had his eyes on him before he'd fully cleared the crops.

"What brings you out here, Ross?"

Roscoe leaned his weight against the new rail Wilson had just hung. "I'm thinking about a project. Could use your help."

Wilson laughed the way he did over cards the nights Roscoe could convince him to play or over the fishing lines they strung out into the pond, begging for catfish or bass or bluegill. His was a light laugh, a whistle of breath through his nose.

"Can't imagine this project's got much to do with the farm." Wilson hammered a nail into a thick branch, recently cut, leaking sap.

"I figured out how to save the place." Roscoe believed it. And not just the place, but his life with Marie. The thought raised a yearning in his gut. He could fix things. He could make them right again.

"The place don't need saving, Ross."

These were Marie's words, and she spread them like the words of God. She had everyone, temporary hands included, thinking the place needed nothing more than its people. She was wrong. Her father had been wrong, too.

"I want to run lines in. Here along the edge of the field. It's the perfect spot. I can tap that pole right past the corner."

Wilson finished up with a second nail and jiggled the new timber, testing its strength. The wood didn't budge. "Those lines are bound for the city, Ross. What makes you think they'd run a line in here?"

"I wouldn't ask them."

Wilson laughed again and moved down a fence post. The next top rail was rotted through, broken in its middle. "You talking about stealing?"

Now, Roscoe laughed. "There's already so much current lost in line transmission—what we would take is nothing in comparison. A drop of water from a lake, Wilson. Nothing missed."

Wilson pried at the nails anchoring the rotted wood. "How are you going to tap those lines without killing yourself?"

"We'd knock out the power first, and anyway, I've been doing this kind of thing a long time."

Wilson looked at him. "Even if you could make it work, what's electricity going to do for the farm?"

Roscoe pounded his hands down on the solid rail in front of him, so good was the idea. "I've figured out how to convert a fuel-powered thresher to run off electricity. Think of it—all the shucking and picking we'd be rid of. We could get more fields of peanuts in. And then have the machine do the bulk of the labor. I know it'd make this place profitable, Wilson. I know it."

Wilson looked off into the neighboring property, its grasses grown tall while its resident cows worked the other side of the land. He had to be imagining the thresher. Roscoe willed it into his friend's mind, the giant machine squatting in the shop, churning out ears all plucked from their stalks, ready for market. *See it, Wilson.*

Wilson shook his head. "The farm don't need electricity, Ross. It needs more hands."

"Goddamn it, Wilson. That's Marie's pitch, and even I know we can't afford more hands. Growing up here doesn't make her an expert. You know that. Hell, you were here when she was a schoolgirl up in her father's library reading all day, and then gone to the university the first chance she got. She's a goddamned teacher, not a farmer."

"It's her land, Ross."

"It's mine, too."

Wilson shook his head again. "You gonna pull boss ranks on me, now?"

Roscoe kicked at the bunched grass near a fence post. He wasn't Wilson's boss. Marie wasn't either. Wilson had lived on this property since he was a boy, and he'd helped Marie's father tend it all through her childhood. He was the boss of the place, if anyone was, Roscoe coming to him for permission, a subordinate with a revolutionary idea. *Just give me a chance, boss! Let me try.*

"I'm not your goddamned boss. I'm an electrician, and if I'm going to stay here, I have to do something that's mine." Roscoe leaned his elbows on the rail. "I know how little I've done around here this past year. This is what I can do."

Wilson kept working.

"I got word from my old foreman at the powerhouse. Says there's a spot for me. Open door. If I don't do this, I think I'll have to go."

"You wouldn't leave Marie and Gerald."

"I would." Saying it, Roscoe fully understood its truth. If this didn't work—the transformers, the lines, the thresher—he would go back to that village at the Lock 12 dam on the banks of the Coosa River where he'd first met Marie. He'd move back into the single-employee apartment house and walk down the clay road to the dam each morning, all those wires and conduits awaiting him, all those new lines to run. He would leave his wife and son to get back to the drive and purpose of that work. He would.

Wilson set his pry bar into the gap between pole and crossbeam to wrench the broken rail loose. Roscoe watched, half hoping Wilson would refuse his proposal. He could walk back to the house and pack a small bag, kiss his son on the top of his head and Marie once more on her dry lips, and then start south. He would walk the whole way and never grow tired.

"What's my part?" Wilson asked.

"I'd need your help raising the poles and getting the lines strung."

"That's all?"

"That's all."

Roscoe saw himself walking through fields like this neighboring one, down lanes chalky with red dust, past farms worse off than Marie's.

"Is Marie gonna know about this?"

Roscoe saw himself turning around, walking back up those porch steps, gathering Marie into his arms. "She will know we have power."

"But she won't know how we're gettin' it."

"It will come from the power company, as far as she knows, and that will be enough."

"You gonna fake the bills?"

"If I have to. Alabama Power will bring in their own lines in the next five years or so. It'll work itself out."

"So I've only gotta lie to your wife for five years."

"Tops."

"What about Moa?"

Roscoe hadn't thought about Moa, though he should've. She had a place in every plan that unfolded on the farm. Moa was Wilson's wife, and she was the land's matriarch, her presence both firm and embracing. She was only eight years older than Marie, but when Marie's mother had passed away, Moa had taken up the role. She was tall and slender and coffee colored, much lighter than Wilson, and she rolled her hair under on each side in a shape like a wave. Roscoe knew she kept a soft spot for him, defending him most chances she got, but he knew, too, that she'd never lie to Marie. He didn't think Wilson could lie to Moa either. Their relationship was built of evening walks to the pond, their three children back at the house with Gerald. They were easy with one another, quick with smiles and gentle chiding.

"Would you be able to keep it from her?" Roscoe asked.

Wilson pried at the wood, the nail whining as it let go. "It'd probably be better if she didn't know. Should something go poorly, it'd be good she not be a part of it."

"Nothing will go poorly."

Wilson shook his head and lifted the old rail, tossing it into the neighbors' grasses. "Here"—he lifted up the new one—"think you can hold an end for me?"

It was the first farmwork Roscoe had helped Wilson with, and he didn't mind taking it on. He told himself he didn't need to go back to the powerhouse at Lock 12. He didn't need to leave. He would stay here and make this land successful. He would have his work back, a job of currents and wires, forces and reactions, and the farm would grow so strong that it could run itself. Marie could return to teaching, if she chose. She could set up a small school on the land, use the books in her father's library. They would reclaim something in their marriage, and Roscoe would figure out how to know his son. They would be all right.

OVER dinner, Moa remarked on his mood. "Goodness, Mr. Roscoe. You sure is fit this evening. What's got you so excited?"

Marie looked at him with her eyebrows raised, her face saying, *Yes, what exactly is this?* Judgment was in her expression, prickly as cornstalks.

"I received some fine news today."

Roscoe and Wilson each sat at one head of the table. Roscoe had Marie to one side and Gerald to the other, and Wilson's family flanked him, too—Moa and Charles to the left, Henry and Jenny to the right. They sat exactly that way for their weekly meals, their two families always coming together in the big house on Wednesdays.

"Well?" Moa pried.

"Alabama Power wants to electrify some rural properties, and we're one of the first on their list."

Curiosity seemed to be edging out the disappointment on Marie's face. "We'll get power here on the farm?"

"That's right, and they asked me to run the lines in—contract work."

"Does that mean we'll get lights, Pa?" Gerald asked.

"That's exactly what it means, Son, and what's more—we can get that old thresher running."

"You know we don't have the money for that," Marie said. "Let alone the fuel it'd take to make it run."

"That's it, though," Roscoe said. "I can convert it to run off electricity."

"Wouldn't the electricity be expensive, too?"

"Electricity won't run anywhere close to fuel prices."

Roscoe saw Marie wanting to smile, but she fought it, keeping her face in its rigid calm. "I thought farmwork was beneath you."

"It's just not mine. This is."

Roscoe followed Marie's eyes around the table. They stopped on Wilson, who sat still and quiet. "What do you think of this, Wilson?"

Wilson's face was as unreadable as his silence. "Well, Ms. Marie, Roscoe's discussed it plenty with me, and I think it's just what the farm needs."

Wilson's belief—genuine or feigned—was enough to make Marie believe, and Roscoe watched the faintest smile cross her face. "You'll do this work?"

Roscoe nodded, and the gesture set them apart. They were alone for a moment, as they had been before Gerald's birth, alone and young and hopeful, walking the banks of the Coosa River, watching the water make its way to the dam where it would build electricity. They were mesmerized by their future—all the light and power and change—filled with it, their own excitement rushing and flowing. Roscoe realized he missed those sensations. He missed his wife.

CHAPTER 2 / ROSCOE

The wall around Kilby Prison is twenty feet high, with four strands of barbed wire along the top. Every other strand is charged with sixty-six hundred volts of electricity. The other two are grounded, and so far as I know, the live ones have never been cut.

From the front Kilby looks like a redbrick school, a place for teachers like my wife. Shrubs line the front walk to the double doors, with globe lights on either side of the entrance. An eagle spreads its wings in a circle over the tall letters spelling out the prison's name.

The year is 1926, which seems as if it should mean something, more than a quarter of this century gone. I've been in this place for three years, and that, too, seems as if it should mean something. I just passed my thirty-third birthday, and my life has become only years before Kilby and years during. I hope for years after, but not too frequently. Hope makes disappointment that much harsher when it arrives.

Fall has come again, thin winded and tawny, and I've just finished my work tarring up the cracks between the thirty-foot sections of the wall that open up with the cold shift. The warden pieces together a crew to paint the gaps with tar, and I've been part of it since I came. I'm pulled from other work, and it's a good job to get for those few weeks. Out of the shirt factory and the cotton mill, out of the dairy. There's air to breathe along the wall, wafting in through the openings. Across Wetumpka–Montgomery Highway is the oak grove. Grazing pasture is to the east and fields of corn and beans and mustard, cotton to the north. Even the dirt and gravel in the pit to the west is something sweeter than the scent inside the wall. Stick your eye to those cracks and it's the world out there, a world we paint over with tar. The air gets sticky and black, and then we're closed back into Kilby. There'd never be the time nor the tools to make one of those cracks fit a man through, but we dream about it, think about excuses to get out to the yard alone. We may sneak a fork or two out of the mess hall. We may chip at those cracks with the rocks we find. We don't talk about it. We don't work together. Escape is solitary as confinement, or should be.

I was on the wall when Deputy Warden Taylor sought me out. "You've made a name for yourself. Bondurant and Chaplain—they're singing your praises. Best worker they've ever had and other such remarks. That true?"

"Can't speak for anyone else, sir, but I do my best with the work that's given me."

"Seems you might be a good fit at the pens. Come on out first thing tomorrow. I've sent word to your other foreseers so they won't be putting out the call."

"Yes, sir."

So today, I'm heading to the gate to meet him at the dog pens.

Beau's guarding the east side, and he spits his tobacco juice right at my feet. "Taylor making you one of his little bitches?"

"I don't know, sir."

"Won't win you any points with your cellmates—not that you've got many points as is." He laughs. "Bet you're thinking if you make dog boy, you'll make trustee, ain't ya? I'm sure Mason's told you it'll keep you safe, those trustee ranks, but I've seen plenty of trustees in the infirmary."

"I've no interest in working the dogs, sir."

"Shut your mouth."

He pounds on the metal door before unlocking his side. Another guard unlocks the outside gate and waves me through with his shotgun.

"Take him to Taylor. And keep that gun on his back." Beau's been gunning for me since I arrived. "Think you're better than all of us in here?" he asked me a couple months in. "All tidy mannered and educated. From what I'm told, you didn't even get your hands dirty when you killed that boy. Probably sitting in your well-lit house eating some fancy meal with your wife. That looks a hell of a lot like cowardice to me."

The guard on the other side of the gate settles the double barrels between my shoulder blades. "Walk."

There are nerves in me as we approach the pens. Deputy Taylor is at the closest run, a dog himself, snouted and whiskered and thick in the neck. His jowls shake as he yells at my escort, "What you doing pointing that gun on him?"

I hear the guard shifting behind me. "Was told to watch this one, sir. Was told he might run."

"You think I'd invite a runner out here? Jesus, boy, don't know that you're quick enough to be working this side of the wall."

The guard comes level with me, his gun hanging down next to his legs. "Just following Beau's orders, Deputy."

Taylor laughs and pitches his head toward the gate. "Get on back to your post, and stop taking orders from Beau. Man's a guard, same as you."

"Yes, sir."

When he's a ways off, Taylor yells, "And you best not bring any boys out here at gunpoint again, you hear?"

"Yes, sir!"

I take comfort in seeing a guard reprimanded.

"All right, Martin, let's see what these dogs think of you."

Taylor tugs gently on a dog's ears, then lets go and shouts, "Back!" His voice is hard and whiplike, and the dogs drop their paws off the top rails of their pens to the ground, expectant.

Two other men are farther in, mucking out the dogs' waste and filling their water buckets and food bowls. The smell here is worse than at the dairy, everything ripe and foul, and I want Taylor to see that I don't fit, that it's a mistake to assign me to these beasts.

"First thing we'll do is get you handling them. They'll learn you as a master when you're here and as a scent when they're chasing you. Dog boys is the practice, see. Got to get a belt on you and get you hooked up to one, see how they do at the end of that line.

"Jones!" he shouts to one of the other men. "Get me a belt and a lead."

"Yes, sir."

I watch Jones head toward a close-by barn. "Now, the belts we use are of my own making." Everything about Taylor is large—his belly, his voice, his hands. "Made 'em so that you boys could hook yourself up to nine dogs if you wanted to."

I do not want to.

He goes on about the leather leads, and in the middle of this talk the sirens start blaring, their whirl and pitch like some great bird descending from the sky. Every time I hear them, I think of Marie's knowledge of birdcalls, naming all those feathered bodies by their noise alone.

"Redtail," she might say of the siren. "Thick feathered and dusty. It's protecting its territory, warning off other birds."

The dogs have brought their paws to the top rails of their pens again, their voices joining the sirens.

"Jones!" Taylor is shouting. "Jackson! Get those dogs belted up!"

Jones runs from the barn, strapping a belt round his waist. He drops another at my feet.

"Put it on, boy," Taylor says. "Trial by fire on this one." To Jones, he says, "Bring out Ruthie. She don't care who she's belted to so long as she has a scent to track."

The belt is about two inches wide and thicker than any other I've ever worn. Two rings are on either side of the buckle, the base of them sewn over with extra patches. These must be what I could hook nine dogs to.

The guard who held his gun to my back comes running, a scrap of cloth in his hand.

I work to fasten the belt over my pants and shirt.

"Pick up that lead," Taylor says to me. He turns to the guard. "Solid scent?"

"Straight off his back."

I have the lead in my hand, and Jones is hauling a whining dog from the pen. "Strap one end to her collar, and the other to one of those rings on your belt."

"What's going on?"

"Taylor loves to throw new boys right in," Jones says. "Just follow the dog. She knows what she's doing."

"The man's still in sight," Taylor shouts at us. "Right in the close cotton. Get your dogs over here."

My dog pulls me to the piece of shirt in Taylor's hand. She buries her snout in the fabric, huffing and snorting, then lifts her head to the air and lets out a great howling siren of her own. "Follow along, Martin," Taylor says to me. The other two men are at the scrap now, too, their dogs digging into the smell, but I am going, my feet tripping me forward, this great beast hooked to my hips, tugging with a force I've not met before. She is a plow, an ox, an engine, cranking and turning and driving us on. I want reins attached to her muzzle, something to whoa her back.

The dog doesn't slow as she puts her nose to the ground, all her movements connected. I hear the others behind me, and the pounding of horse hooves, and then Taylor draws up, high on the saddle of a tall bay. It looks like Marie's horse once looked, back when they were both young. When I left for Kilby, that horse was nibbling the grasses around the farmhouse like a big, lazy dog, her back swaying deep between her withers and haunches, a great slump that could no longer support the weight of a person. I don't know if she's still alive.

The dog leads me into the cotton field, and we slow down. Cotton is a rough crop to move through. The plants let go of their moisture come harvest and turn their stems to twigs, hard and sharp. Taylor slips ahead. He has his Winchester across his lap. I still hear the yells of the other boys and dogs behind us.

"There!" Taylor shouts, and I see the escaping man, the great tear in his prison shirt that yielded the scrap for the dogs, such a fatal error in the running trade. He's still in the cotton, his back bright against the plants.

A field guard is after him, then Taylor and his horse, then this dog and me and the others.

"Boy!" I hear Taylor shout. "You stop!"

The man doesn't slow. He'll reach the woods in a moment, and I don't know what that means for me, whether I'll be forced to follow. If this great machine of a dog continues at her same speed, my body will collapse, a tethered anchor dragged through the undergrowth, my skin and clothes tearing against the ground and the brush.

Taylor draws his horse up short in front of us and slides down from the saddle. "Stop that dog!" he shouts to me.

I dig my heels in and hunker back, lowering myself into the cotton, down to the ground. The dog's head whips, and she lets loose the most mournful cry.

"Stop!" Taylor shouts to the escaping man.

The other men and dogs arrive on either side of me. Each holds a hand out to help me up.

"*Sit,*" Jones says to the dogs. "*Wait.*" All three of the beasts drop down, their snouts still turned toward Taylor.

Before us, Taylor aims his gun toward the sky. He pulls the trigger, and it fires a cannon's worth of shot. "The warning shot's enough to stop most runners," Jones whispers. "Nine out of ten, I'd say."

But the man is not stopping, even though the cotton keeps his movement slow. He presses on, ragged and halting, and then—he falls. I watch the crops swallow him.

"Want us to go on by you?" Jones asks.

"Wait," Taylor says, as though Jones were just another of his dogs.

Taylor moves ahead, his face trained on the spot where the man went down. I picture that escaping man still going, working his way woodward under the cover of the cotton, elbow-crawling along a furrow line.

How Taylor can move so quickly, I don't know. He's already yards away. The field guard before him has moved out of the line. Other men are around, too, working the field, all in stripes. Taylor's warning shot has brought them up tall, their hands paused in their picking, their eyes on the scene. They're all pulling for the downed man. I can see it. They are granting him a tunnel, a secret passage there, exactly where he's fallen, a corridor to the ocean where a ship waits. I want it for him, too.

But he returns to us, his body rising up through the cotton, pricked and ragged.

"Stop!" Taylor shouts once more. He levels his gun. I am close enough to hear him say, "All right, then. I'm gonna do this."

How is it that a shot fired across land can sound so much fiercer than one fired toward the sky? I have never heard anything so loud.

The man falls, and Taylor looks around. Shock is on his face, a little fear. He's sweating and pale, and he shouts at the men in the field, "Keep to your work!"

To me and the other two, he says, "Best bring those dogs on up here, just in case that didn't land where I think it did."

The other guard is there already, marking the spot, and Taylor's mumbling to himself as he walks. My dog is quiet, but still pulling. We level up with Taylor, and I hear that he's counting. "Nine," I hear him say. "Ten, eleven." He's counting his steps.

Nineteen, it turns out. He fired from nineteen steps away.

My dog brays when she sees the downed man, and he covers his face. "Don't put that dog on me. I'm not running. Please, just don't put no dog on me."

I pull the dog back, and Taylor tells her to sit.

The skin on the man's side is torn up, and when he moves his hands from his face, I nearly don't recognize him through the pain. His name is Jennings. We do a little business here and there—milk that I sneak from the dairy in exchange for cigarettes. It's another act of theft, I know, and I have stolen enough, but smoking is one of the only graces I have found here, one of the only familiar routines.

"We best get this boy to the hospital," Taylor says to the other guard. "Get some men. They can make a sling of their sacks. Come on, now. Boy's losing blood."

The men materialize, sprouting up out of the last of the cotton as though they'd always been there. A tall man with only one tooth—a front one—slides his sack under Jennings' head and shoulders. He takes one side and a short fellow takes the other. Two more are at Jennings's waist, two more at his feet. They lift him, and the sounds that come from his mouth are gut-shot and black, like the blood wetting the midway sack, like the blood spotting the plants. It's bright on the cotton, dark on the stems and ground. The crops are crushed down in a circle here, stamped out in a near-perfect ring.

"Put those dogs away," Taylor says to us as he goes.

We watch the men heave Jennings away. They move toward one of the wider row lines so they can walk easier. The fields are still stunned into disorder, the guards caught up in whispering, the men in clumps. If ever a dog boy was to run, this would be the time. We could push our dogs off toward the woods on some trail we'd contrived, deep into thick cover before anyone would notice we'd gone the wrong way. We could part and run our own directions, me with this dog at my waist, crossing creeks, scaling Montgomery, swimming rivers and lakes until we reached Marie's land. I could walk up the drive with this beast, both of us tired from our chase—"Rabbits," I could tell my wife and son. "We've been hunting rabbits."

"What the hell you still doing out here, boy?"

I don't know the guard who's turned his holler on me, but he's approaching. He's motioning with his gun. "Taylor told you to put that dog up," he shouts. "Go on, now."

"Sir," I say, and tug my dog back toward the pens, the other two men off ahead of me. They're quiet when I catch up.

"Lead that dog on into her run and then you can unhook," Jones says.

I'm nervous to enter the pen with the pushing throng of dogs, but I ease myself through the sagging gate anyway.

"Hell of a thing," Jones continues. He's staring at me when I look up. "Hell of a thing."

"Yeah." It is some sort of hell, this thing we've seen with its dogs and sirens, its cotton and striped men, its blasts and shots and blood.

"That's not what this job's about. Ain't never seen that before. Never seen Taylor shoot a man."

"Nope," the other dog boy, Jackson, says. "First for me, too, and I been out on these dogs since Taylor started the goddamn pack."

I set my dog loose among the thicket of bodies—snouts and tails pushing their way into other snouts and tails. They're not interested in me, all of the remaining dogs crowding round the one I brought back as though asking about her day. *What was the chase like?* I hear them asking with their eyes. *You get it?*

Taylor is away with Jennings, the other guards back at their posts. The three of us convicts are alone here with these dogs, and the itch to run takes me full by the shoulders, shaking me to standing tall and alert.

"There aren't any guards around," I venture.

Jones laughs. "You thinking about running? That your ticket?"

"Luck to you," Jackson says, joining in the laughter.

"What?" I ask them.

"This is the best there is," Jones says. "You get put out here on these dogs, and you're looking at trustee ranks, early parole, time outside the damn wall. But you run when you're out here? A broken trustee's the bottom of this ladder. You don't climb anywhere, and you sure as hell don't get paroled."

"That's right," Jackson says.

I know what Marie would counsel in this situation: "Patience, Roscoe. Do the work. Let the reward come later."

But I just saw a man shot, I would tell her. *I am an electrician. I should not be here.*

"Best thing for you to do is head over to the gate," Jones says. "Get yourself back inside that wall and wait to hear from Taylor." He gives me a leveled, honest stare. "These dogs are good. And your scent will be damn easy to track, starting at the pens as you are."

The image of these dogs after me melts the itch away—me as the runner and these men as the chasers tied to dogs. I can hear the men shouting and the beasts' whining behind me, their quick feet and their snuffling breaths. They suck in every speck of my scent, tiny bits of dust that fire a need in their brains. *Follow,* those bits say. *Find.*

I don't want to be chased.

So I leave the pens, Jones and Jackson there with the dogs. I head back to the guard at the outer gate who shoved his gun into my back earlier, and I look away from the smirk on his face.

Beau unlocks the interior door and shoves me through with the barrel of his gun. "Get on back to the dairy. Don't belong out here anyway."

"I'm going, sir." I'm glad of the gate and the door swinging shut behind me. I prefer the mulled quiet of the dairy barn to what I've seen and done today. I imagine Marie laughing at the irony of this—my wanting of a barn.

JENNINGS leaves the hospital the next morning.

"Wasn't so bad," he tells us in the yard. "They got all the shot out." The triumph in his voice doesn't match the blood in his eyes, or the shuffle in his walk, the way his hand goes to his side again and again, pressing. The next day, his back's bowed, a crease that never rights itself, and then he starts sweating, his face gone gray and dusky.

He seeks me out in the yard, wanting to hear the whole thing told again. "What's it like seeing someone shot down like that, Ross? Which way did I fall? I can't see it. It's all too quick for me."

"I don't know. You fell forward."

"What'd old Taylor do?"

"He walked over."

"Bastard counted his steps along the way, didn't he?"

I nod.

"Nineteen," Jennings says. Everyone knows the number, now, shooting through the fields and the cells like some secret we'd been trying to figure out for years—far enough away to miss and scatter that shot all over the field, but close enough to blow a man's side open should it land just right. *Nineteen.* We whisper the word like a curse.

Jennings is sweating too much, beads on his lips and forehead.

"You all right?" I ask.

"I'm feeling a little hot, tell you the truth. Think I've got myself a fever." He pushes at his side again and tries to straighten his back. It catches at an angle, keeping him bent, then he drops down to his knees.

One of the guards comes over. "What's this?"

Jennings doesn't speak.

"I think he needs to go to the hospital," I say.

"He that idiot got himself shot?"

"Yes, sir."

The guard laughs. "Hey, Buckshot. Come on. Let's get you to the infirmary." Jennings doesn't move, and the guard finally drags him to standing by one of his arms. "The hell you expect?"

The chapel is just past the hospital, and I know they'll be calling on Chaplain to come discuss Jennings's soul while he sits in his sickbed. Jennings is in on a liquor violation. He can't have more than a year or two left. But he's a damaged man walking next to that guard, not the same man to get me cigarettes, not even the man running through the fields just a few days ago. We change so quickly in here.

TAYLOR pulls me from the barn the next day, ordering me back through the east gate.

"Jesus Christ," Beau says.

He pushes me through, and the guard on the other side walks me to the pens, his gun pointed at the ground.

"You hear about Jennings?" Taylor asks as soon as I'm level with him. In the same breath, he says "Go on" to the guard.

"I was with him when he went back to the infirmary."

"Died this morning," Taylor says. "Blood poisoning. God-damned doctor didn't get all the shot out. X-rays showed a ball lodged there in the boy's kidney. Wasn't anything to be done then."

I have seen a man shot and killed from nineteen steps away.

"No sense in a death like that, Martin." I cannot tell whether Taylor's truly mournful for the loss of life or whether Jennings is just another lost prisoner to him, a man taking his release early. "No sense." Taylor shakes his head.

I can hear Marie's voice in the rustle of the dog bodies: *You know all about senseless deaths, don't you, dear?*

Taylor and Marie are both wrong to rely on sense as a measure-ment, though. Making sense is about logic, and logic follows in-structions, like electricity culled from water and transported along lines. If you point power somewhere—no matter the kind—it'll follow its course until it hits something. Perfect sense.

"How are you feeling about this work, Martin?" Taylor turns his face from the dogs to look at me. "Think it suits you?"

"Due respect, sir, but I don't know that it does."

Taylor almost smiles. "You're wrong, Martin, but it was a hell of an introduction, I'll give you that. You stick on the barn for a while yet."

"Thank you, sir."

"Ain't for you, Martin. Can't have a boy out here who's not ready for it. You best be next time."

"Yes, sir."

"Now, go on."

I glance once more at that pack of dogs, all red and black and needy, so different from the dairy cows in the barn.

"Go on," Taylor says.

I could run right now, take to the cotton like Jennings, crawl my way through its branches until I get to the woods. I do this again and again. I run. I escape. I return to my wife and son.

I don't know if they're still there.

CHAPTER 3

Roscoe used galvanized storage cylinders from the shop for the transformers' bodies, but he had to go into Rockford for the copper wire. The local mercantile was called Bean's, and Marie's family had been frequenting it since Edgar Bean opened its doors, a charge account still on file, though there wasn't money to cover the things charged.

Roscoe took the mules and wagon in. He left Wilson back, not wanting him to take part in this particular dishonesty.

When he walked in the door, Bean hollered, "Roscoe Martin! What brings you here?"

"I finally have some electrical work."

"You and your fancy electricity."

Bean was like Marie's father in his love of flames over bulbs. They'd both sworn that the country would never let itself get fully electrified, and if the country failed them, well, hell—they'd stay strong at least. "You'll never see a wired lamp in this store," Bean had told Roscoe once. "Fire needs to be out in the open, someplace we can keep an eye on it. Don't belong inside wires." Marie's father had conceded slightly since his son-in-law was in the trade. "Never my library, though. If you light up the house someday, that's one thing. But you stay out of my library. I want to know what's near my books."

"It's trapped," Roscoe tried to explain, both to Bean and to

Marie's father. "All that power is stored inside wires, which are stored inside rubber coatings. There's no threat to you. In fact, it's safer than flame. If you break a lamp bulb, the light just goes out. If you break a wicked lamp, you're likely to see your whole house go up."

"No, no, son," the men would reply, and Roscoe would keep at them until Marie laid a hand on his arm, or one of them forced the conversation in a new direction.

Roscoe couldn't understand their hesitancy and mistrust. He had only experienced fascination, intrigue, desire to know more. That first time he'd seen electrical streetlamps, in Birmingham, he'd thought he was seeing magic—something from the fairy tales he'd once told his sister. Those glowing bulbs belonged with princes who could be changed into toads and then back again with a kiss. They belonged with talking animals and flight for flightless creatures, rather than his father's world of coal and tunnels and prosperity at the expense of others' bent backs and widowed families. Then he'd found Faraday, and science had supplanted the magic—long descriptions of experiments that took Roscoe months and sometimes years to understand—and all while still working for his father in the mines, a candle's flame lighting the pages of the books he read every chance he could, trusted and esteemed narratives to which he could return. Electricity had freed him from his father's life.

He'd told as much to his father-in-law, and the man had listened, genuine care in his pale eyes.

"We find our own salvations, Son," he'd said. "You have your electricity, and I have my farm, and we both have my lovely daughter and a wagonload of books. We've more in common than not. You keep to your lines, and I'll keep to my land, and we'll meet over the supper table to talk about what we've been reading."

Marie's father had been a good man. Bean was a good man, too. Lying to him about this project felt like lying to Marie's father, and Roscoe disliked it. He'd make them both proud, though, distill their fears, prove the strength of his trade. A lie was worth that.

"I'll need quite a bit of copper wire," he told Bean. "The work's about midway between our place and the dam, and they've asked me to get the supplies up on this end. It's a first, for sure. They've always provided everything in the past, but it seems there's wire heading in every direction but this one. What's your spool count right now?"

Bean looked at a clipboard on the wall behind him. He flipped a few pages. "Looks like I got about ten rolls in the barn."

"I'll need all of them. My foreman will be coming through with the check soon as he can, and we'll guarantee it with our account."

"That's a lot of product, Roscoe."

"Yes, sir."

Bean rubbed at the peppered beard on his chin, holding his rheumy eyes low on Roscoe's face as if the answer were stored there, some sign to be trusted in Roscoe's lips or jaw.

"You don't make good on this, and I'll be forced to take the debt back any way I can. I could go after the land."

"Yes, sir."

"That's your father-in-law's land, son."

"Yes, sir."

Bean nodded, once, and then scribbled on a slip of paper. "Head on round back and give this to the boys. They'll help you get it all in the wagon."

"Thanks, Bean."

"Whatever this is, it makes me nervous, Roscoe."

"It's fine. You wait."

ROSCOE had Wilson weld the iron cores for the transformers, thick, ringlike creations about a foot wide and tall, squared at their corners.

"Whatever you say," Wilson said, given the instructions.

"Here." Roscoe flipped pages in the bound register he now kept. He found his drawing of the transformers, a plan deducted from

Faraday as much as from his own work with Alabama Power. "I'll wrap copper round the cores." He tapped at the page. "Iron is permeable to magnetic force, so it'll move the current from one side—the receiving side—over to the sparser secondary coil on the other side of the ring. What's not shot off through those secondary wires will return to the primary, and we'll be left with a twist of wires housing about half the original voltage. We'll feed those wires into the next ring, making the turns of the secondary coils even less, and then again, and after the voltage passes through three, we'll be down to a current close to safe. I'm going to leave it higher for the transmission from the road to the shop. If we stepped it down all the way up front, we'd lose too much over the distance and risk a weak current. I'll put one more transformer close in to step it down to two-twenty."

"You're talking another language, my friend."

"I'm not," Roscoe insisted, just as he had with Marie's father once, and Bean. "It's like—a windup toy. Think of those windup toys the kids have. It's like one of those as it winds down. Imagine that the strength of your hand stays the same, but the mechanism inside slows down. You're just changing the size of the spring."

Wilson cocked his head. "Why's it so important to you that I understand?"

"Don't you want to?"

Wilson smiled, the same slow, easy smile he brought to most things. "There's a lot I seek out, Ross. You've seen me on those trails—the likes of the crops on this land, all their stages of growth, all the things I might do to make them stronger and bigger. There's workings of music I'm right taken by. Even Moa's cooking calls my attention at times, all those leavenings and flavors. But this here"—Wilson tapped at the drawing—"this isn't my concern. Agreeing to help you was me agreeing to help this farm, not agreeing to be your student."

Roscoe clapped him on the back, glad of his honesty. "I hear you, but I won't stop the lessons."

"You want to holler at a deaf man, that's your concern."

They both laughed at that, and Roscoe found himself grateful for the camaraderie. He'd not worked with anyone since Marie had taken them away from the village, and he missed collaborative discipline and drive. He'd liked Wilson from the day they met—both for the man he was in person and for all the stories Marie had told—but only in this work had Roscoe felt friendship, loyalty, shared lives. He could see their families growing thick and comfortable, Roscoe and Wilson running the land and the wires, the wives and children happy, big meals and steady comfort. Maybe he and Wilson could even start their own electrical business installing transformers for the other farms, a marriage of their separate work.

He left Wilson to his welding and walked the line route again.

WITH the cores done, Roscoe started winding wire. Wilson checked in on him periodically, and Roscoe tried, again, to explain, holding up one of the iron rings. "See? The voltage will be doing laps."

Wilson shook his head. "When do we start raising poles? I'm readying to get some actual work done."

"Soon."

But the transformers took longer than that. A solid month had passed before Roscoe was confident enough to test them.

Together, Roscoe and Wilson raised their first pole, just nine yards from the original line. Then they hauled out wheelbarrows full of tools, those three transformers unrecognizable in their galvanized frames, all of the rods and coils hidden deep inside, along with levers to stop and start the current. The levers were in the off position, where they'd stay until Roscoe connected the first transformer to the live line, and then it to the other two.

Wilson helped Roscoe mount the transformers on the new pole, evenly distributed with the lowest one ten feet above the ground. Roscoe attached the first stretch of line that would lead to the house and the shop.

"You seem comfortable with this work," Roscoe noted.

"Only 'cause we're not hooked up to anything yet. You plug those wires into that live line and just see how fast I run out of here."

"You won't run." Roscoe knew it was for show, this disinterest. He'd seen the information seeping into Wilson's thoughts. He'd even found him winding wires around a core one day. "Just trying to keep this moving along," Wilson had said.

Roscoe had shown him a finished core, noting the differences in the sides, then left Wilson to finish the one he was working on.

IT was too dangerous to risk linking up to a ten-thousand-volt current, so Roscoe and Wilson set about temporarily halting the power on the main transmission line. Roscoe had already selected the pine they'd fell a couple miles toward the dam, just down from a crossroads where it'd be easy to locate—he didn't want linemen stomping around the fields searching for the outage. The past several weeks had seen heavy rains, and the water helped with the story Roscoe had built—just an old tree loosened by weather, ready to topple.

They left their supplies with the transformers and rode horses to the tree. "Even when it's down, we won't have that long of a window," Roscoe said. "They'll get this line running as quick as they can."

"So we'll ride like hell once the tree falls."

"That's right."

Wilson had spent a few days there already, and the tree swayed under the axes they took to its roots and the ground. They hitched their horses to long chains looped round the trunk and whipped them forward. The pine came easily, crashing against the lines, sparks and snapping branches spooking the horses into high-kneed gallops.

Roscoe and Wilson unhooked and wound the chains, swung into their saddles, drove their ankles into their horses' flanks. They raced along the trail slashed wide for the power line, and Roscoe found himself whooping like a boy, Wilson there with him, an adventure on their hands.

Back on their land, they tethered their horses to the fence and positioned the ladder against the pole that belonged to Alabama Power. Roscoe grabbed a wooden stick and climbed to line height. "If we failed, there will be sparks," he shouted to Wilson. "Best stand clear." A binder was on the line, coupling wires together. He needed to make the lines touch—different currents on different wires. If they touched quietly, the lines were cold. If not, Roscoe could be thrown from the ladder by the shock. He hesitated, knowing the power he might touch.

"Ross," Wilson called from below. "This is what you do."

Roscoe nodded. Camaraderie, companionship, a joint destination. This was what he did. These were his elements, his knowledge, his home.

He felt everything pause—the breeze, the birds, the trains on their tracks and the fish in their ponds. Even the great turbines back at Lock 12 stopped spinning, the water holding back its movement, the powerhouse winding down. The lines had gone cold.

"Clear?" Wilson said.

"Clear."

Now, Roscoe would work.

He strapped his tool belt round his waist. He looped the connecting line over his shoulder and climbed back up the ladder. Carefully, he removed the rubber coating from the binder, exposing the wires underneath. It was simply a matter of more weaving, more winding. The individual strands of copper from his new line were ready. He'd been doing this for a month, and then for years before that.

When his line was attached, he cut a new opening in the binder coating and replaced it over the coupled lines.

It was done.

"How long will it take them to clear that tree?" Wilson asked.

"Could be within the hour, and certainly no later than evening. We'll come back and test then."

Roscoe wasn't patient, but he didn't mind the long stretch of that afternoon, the prospect of power meeting him at the day's end. He was content to unsaddle the horses, brush them down, pump water into their trough. He found Gerald round the back of the house collecting ants, putting them in a jar with dirt to study their habits, and Roscoe knelt next to the boy to help pluck the small bodies from the hole they exited. Gerald was smart to choose small, black ants that didn't sting. He didn't tell his father to leave, and Roscoe took encouragement in that.

AT dusk, Wilson and Roscoe met at the fork in the trail and walked back to the transformers. Roscoe had made a small electric motor, a simple circle of coiled copper, bound together with rubber and mounted on small iron rods over a magnet. The current would probably be too strong for it, but if it was flowing, they would see a reaction.

Roscoe connected the last wires—smaller bundles—to the line from the last transformer. These, he connected to the iron rods of the motor.

"Time to flip the levers," he told Wilson.

They repositioned the ladder against their own pole, and Roscoe climbed to the transformers, lifting all three levers into their on positions. Then he was jumping to the ground to the sound of Wilson's shouts. The coil circle was a blur of hot, fiery proof. They stared at it like men bewitched by beauty or magic until the small wooden base of the motor caught fire, and then with more shouts from Wilson, Roscoe knocked the connecting wires away. They stamped out the small flames and shook hands over the trifling of smoke.

BUILDING the thresher's electric motor had moments of difficulty, but nothing compared to the initial acquisition of wire and tapping the line. Roscoe worked steadily, dividing his time between the thresher and the poles. He continued bundling wire to string along the ceramic insulators he'd brought from the village—boxes of them that were slightly flawed and given to him for nothing. Marie had insisted they stay behind when they moved to the farm, but he'd insisted they come, and it was one of the few standoffs in their years of marriage that he'd actually won. The boxes of insulators had followed them to the land, and here they were—being put to use.

Roscoe ran lines along the fence where he'd first told Wilson about the idea. They raised tall poles through the woods, one right at the fork toward Wilson and Moa's quarters—"We'll get you two power soon enough," Roscoe promised—and they kept the lines high all the way to the final pole between the barn and the house. The farmhouse still had to be wired, but Gerald was the only one itching for that particular luxury.

Marie stood by, showing an interest she hadn't shown since their courting times, back in the village. She visited Roscoe in the shop and walked with him out to the lines. "Tell me again how the transformers work."

He would take her to his drawings, saying, "As you remember, it all starts with dual attractions," explaining, again, how some bodies are graced with extraordinary attraction lurking below their surfaces. "You have to awaken the attraction, though, create it. You remember the Faraday experiment with the wax and the flannel?"

"No. Show me again."

He was sure she did remember, but he had no qualms demonstrating the base of electricity for her yet another time. "We've been seeing electricity forever," he said, taking a round stick of wax from a shelf, "in the shocks we feel when we've become charged." He rubbed the wax against his flannel shirt and held it close to Marie's head, his wife laughing as the thin threads of her hair rose to meet it.

"When you run the wax through your hand, the attraction will go away," Marie said, drawing a smile from her husband.

"You were paying attention to your lessons, weren't you?"

He could see her back in the village, young and eager and inquisitive, sitting across from him in the dining hall while he talked on and on. She'd once told him it was a poetry of sorts—his lectures on electricity.

"We can introduce attractions and remove them," he continued. "And Faraday took it further by showing how we can transfer the force, how we can harness and move it to other places."

"Through copper."

"And other materials. But copper is one of our best conductors, yes. That's why I've used it in these cores." Here, he'd take her to the guts of the transformers, showing her Wilson's ironwork and his own windings of wire.

WHEN Marie wasn't with Roscoe, she was educating Gerald, teaching him his geography and history, reading and writing, arithmetic, science. The two of them could be found in the front yard, studying more ants, or off in the fields taking notes on the crops. Marie felt like a teacher again—all this time with this one student—and Roscoe watched their son grow with his education, changing from the resentful boy he'd been into a young man ready to learn. They were all in their right roles—electrician, teacher, son.

Roscoe worried, at times, about Bean coming to call, looking for payment on his copper. Roscoe had sent in one small check, not enough to cover a quarter of one spool, along with a note promising the rest in full soon. Bean had sent a note back with clear numbers, Roscoe's token payment deducted. Roscoe needed just a few months. That time would see the corn ready for harvest, and a great surge of income not spent on temporary pickers. They'd knock the stalks down with the tractor and send them to the thresher. They'd be the first farm in the county to have corn, and the money would come. Roscoe knew it. He'd pay off Bean, and his family would settle into the comfort of prosperity—lamps blazing in the living room, Gerald reading one of his adventure books, Marie studying up on her birds, Roscoe returning to Faraday's words like a religious man to his Bible. Maybe, under those new bulbs, Gerald would take an interest, and Roscoe would be given the chance to be a father, explaining a part of the world to his boy.

CHAPTER 4 / ROSCOE

We are packed in tight, but they're always reminding us about Kilby's first-rate ventilation system. We have windows, more of them than walls, and they vent top and bottom. The cell house is cross-sectioned like a chimney, and its open-pitched roof holds a line of huge ventilators, squat cylinders that from the back edge of the yard look like side-lying tires. *Chimney effect,* our guards say, and *Enjoy the breeze, gentlemen.*

In the summer, they can run fans that flush the house with fresh air, but even though the guards have to suffer the heat and stink, too, those fans are one of their favorite things to withhold. Someone takes that fork from the mess, and we spend a day sweating ourselves out of our skin until it's found.

"Fork coming down," someone will shout from up top, and we'll listen to those tines hit the metal grates in the open floors, chiming their way to a sticking point, footsteps, and then the creak of belts and holsters as guards bend down. That fork will play its way along whatever row of bars it's near, and Beau or Henry or Stanley will say, "You boys hear that? That's a pretty noise, ain't it? Let's listen on it a while longer."

The fans are loud.

The guard towers are made of the same concrete aggregate as the wall, the same sand and gravel from the prison's own pit. The towers are on every corner, and they're lonely looking things, barely higher than the wall itself, slits for windows. The one out front is something else, though. A hexagon with a cement base and brick sides, its top stacked full of beautiful paned windows. The roof is a great turret, and the spotlight perched in its tower is more the beacon of a lighthouse than the glow of escape. I can see it from my cell.

"Why's the front tower look like a lighthouse?" I've asked.

"When have you ever seen a lighthouse?" the guard or foreman responds. "Get on back to your work."

The oaks in the grove across the highway are southern red oaks. Many of them were cut down to build the prison village, which stands just beyond the gravel pit. A community hall is over there in the village, and a hotel for the single employees. It sounds like our village at Lock 12, just drier without the Coosa flowing by.

The coffee here is stretched and weakened by ground acorns from the oaks. Even better than tarring the walls is gathering acorns. Few men get that job. They are short-timers with no risk of flight. Before anyone can resent them, they're gone.

Today is Sunday, and I am in church, sitting next to Ed. We share a cell, Ed and I, along with four other men, and he's the only person in here I'd call a friend. Ed Mason. He's a cabinetmaker by trade and a burglar by profession, serving a ten-year sentence for grand larceny. He got here ten months before me, right after Kilby first opened, and they assigned him to the woodshop, where he makes picture frames and cradles and baskets. The prison sells his work, and it does me some good thinking about those mothers settling their infants into one of Ed's cradles.

The warden came to him a few months ago, saying, "You think you could make us a certain type of chair, Ed? Following these designs?" The warden handed them over.

"This the kind of chair I think it is?"

Relaying it back, Ed said, "And you know what he told me? Bastard said, 'You're not making it for yourself, Mason.'"

Which is true. Ed's done nothing to earn him that seat, so when the warden was willing to throw in a month's furlough, Ed said all right. A month is a long time, and Ed's from London. He's confused as anyone as to how he got to Mobile, and then to Kilby. He's been looking for a way out since he arrived, and the warden gave him one.

The prison chapel is simple, like the one I occasionally attended with Marie and Gerald, and were it not for the men around me, I might well be in the same place. The windows are tall, but not colored, and the pews are plain pine, like the pulpit and the cross.

Today, Chaplain reads from Genesis. He reads to us about Joseph, which he does often. Why Joseph is our man, none of us know.

Chaplain doesn't mention Jennings, though his death is still fresh.

Because I am literate, Chaplain has made me one of his readers. At mealtimes, he stations a reader at each end of the long tables in the mess, a Bible in our hands. We must read at the start of dinner for five full minutes while the men wait with their food in front of them. It is the worst of the jobs I've received.

"You think Chaplain's getting any?" Ed whispers to me.

I shake my head.

"He's allowed to, isn't he?"

I nod.

"Not like them priests, who've got to hold out their whole lives. God'd have to promise a hell of a lot to get me to swear off that treat." I nod again. "That furlough is close. Going to find me a woman straightaway."

"Raise up your voices, brothers," Chaplain is shouting. It's the Lord's Prayer we're raising, and the men around me shout it loud. Ed stops his whispering.

"As though any woman would have you," I say, the voices draining off around us. "We ask in Jesus's name."

"I'm not above praying, brother."

Ed has told me that he doesn't plan to return. "You have the date set?"

"Nah. They have to be sure they don't need me anymore first. They're giving me a month, Ross. A month. Even Taylor's dogs couldn't catch a trail that cold."

The desire to run is something deep, I think. We had this boy Oscar—just a kid, really, barely eighteen—who'd drawn a four-week sentence. Some misdemeanor, we didn't know what. We'd had a recent opening in our cell, and they stuck him in with Ed and me and the others.

"I got a holdover," he told us. "They're going to come back with something that'll keep me here forever."

"Wait," we told him. Holdovers pan out, or they don't. Lots of times those other charges don't have legs. They don't stand up. But other times, they try you all over and give you everything they can, start you from scratch. It can go either way.

Being such a low-threat case, they sent Oscar over to the farm. He ran his first day. The dogs came back tired, Taylor saddle sore. Folks say Taylor puts the same effort into every escape, murderer or vagrant. Escaping is about pride, not sentence. A man walks off before he's done, it reflects badly on his overseer.

Six months went by after Oscar ran, and we forgot about him. Someone else took his bunk. Someone else took his job. Someone else was younger. And then—one day—Oscar came back. He walked right up to the front doors, saying, "I heard I don't have a holdover, so I thought I'd finish out my time."

The State doesn't have a sentence for escape, not anything official, so Oscar finished his sentence—those few weeks—and he walked out a free man.

"Why'd you come back?" Ed asked him in the mess.

Oscar was a funny-looking kid, big teeth and a tall forehead, hair that stood straight up, a big old birthmark down the right side of his jaw and neck. You could pick him out of a crowd.

"You ever tried being an outlaw?"

I laughed, but Ed said, "I'd take outlaw any day."

In church, Ed says, "They give me that furlough and I'm gone."

The men around stand from their pews, tired already by the jobs they'll return to. Chapel is full because it gives us a break from work, a spot to sit down. An hour of rest can make a believer out of any man.

"Your sentence is too long for them to forget," I tell Ed. I am embarrassed by the resentment in my voice, the envy I feel not just of my friend's furlough, but the work that's bought it. If they'd come to me with the wiring for the chair, I would eagerly have said yes.

They didn't come to me.

"You'll be all right, Ross," Ed is saying. We're standing, too. He'll go to the woodshop, and I'll go to the barn. "Early parole. I know it."

I shake my head.

"We're not the ones they're after."

But he's wrong there. We're exactly what Kilby wants. These prison guards can't do anything but shout and whip and run dogs. They don't know wire or wood. They're not skilled. They couldn't dig a stump out of the ground or sow a row of corn seed. They couldn't get the current going back through those strands of barbed wire along the wall should someone cut them. They couldn't build Ed's chair.

"They're going to paint it yellow," he tells me. "Highway yellow. They've got leftover paint. I asked them to keep it the natural grain. Made it out of maple and oak."

It only took him six days to build. Ed is a fine woodworker. I'm sure it's a hell of a chair.

"You get any word about that friend of yours in the mines?" Ed asks.

"Nah."

"Marie?"

"You know better than to ask." Ed knows about Marie's silence, that I haven't heard from my son. He knows my best guess to Wilson's whereabouts, that he's likely been leased to Sloss, sentenced to a dark life underground.

The sun is slanted sideways—winter light. It's a bit cold, this early in the day. I have always preferred winter to summer, Alabama's version of the season that is, mild and sun soaked. I have preferred mornings, too, the way they forgive a night's indiscretions or a yesterday's. Prison mornings are a different kind, but I cannot say it is an altogether awful thing to be walking across this dusty yard toward a barn where I'll work my back sore shoveling out stalls, my arms and legs aching from the pails and buckets I carry.

Ed veers toward the shop. "See you at meal. Think you can get me a glass of milk?"

This is the thing I barter—the sweet, creamy milk of Kilby cows. Their milk is too good for us. It's bottled and sold in Montgomery for profit, but sneaking it is not so different from sneaking electricity. When there's a surplus, it's easy to siphon off a bit.

Kilby trades its milk for money, and I trade mine for cigarettes and turned heads. The guards and employees aren't fed much better than we are, and I act as if I were just delivering what they're already entitled to when I bring them their milk. No one's entitled to a bottle of these Guernseys' milk unless they're paying royally, though. They're the best cows in the state.

"I'll get us some milk," I tell Ed, as I join the group of men heading toward the barn.

THE dairymen have different jobs, and we rotate through them. One day, I'm mucking stalls, scooping out the straw the moment the heifers soil it. Under the eyes of so many folks, the dairy can't stand for any contamination—no dirt or manure or any other foulness in the milk we ship off. Other days I'm tending calves, getting them ready for sale, weaning them from their mothers, who bawl as I lead them back to the milking bays. Then there's the milking. We're tasked with applying the milking cups, connecting the cup lines to the pail caps, and hanging those pails from leather straps we loop over the cows' backs. Foreman Bondurant's proud of those caps on his pails. "Latest invention," he tells every new man. "Our milk never touches human hands. Only time it comes in contact with the open air's when you pour it into the storage containers." Hanging the pails is another precaution, too. The cows can't kick over a hanging pail, can't spill that precious liquid out across the hard dirt floor.

As much as I'd hated farming, I don't so much mind the barn, with its tug and pull of noise, calves mewling and heifers lowing and the soft-piston grunt of the milking machines. There are raking sounds and the pitch of hay and straw, boots in the mud and boots on the hard dirt, the murmurs of men with animals: "Stop your bellowing. It's all right now. You're used to this show, old gal. Keep that tail out of my face." Bondurant walks through calling out orders we already know, and the barn guards keep their feet up on hay bales most of the day. We've never had a runner from the dairy. Maybe it's the animals that keep us here.

The barn makes me think about my father, who had always made it clear that we were not farmers. We had a respectable home on some land. My father made that distinction clear. "Not a farm," he reminded us, "a respectable home on a bit of land."

"We are not farmers," we repeated.

The barn makes me think of my sisters, too, all three of them. Three is not the number Marie knows. She knows me only as the older brother to Catherine, the girl who did as our father wanted— married a coal miner—and stayed in Alabama with that coalman long enough to see our father die. He only got a year with them, but my mother always said it was plenty. "Finally got a mining son," she loved to say. "It was all he wanted before he went."

My middle sisters died of pneumonia in late grammar school while our father was away working. He was gone a month that time, and he missed it all. My middle sisters were only ten months apart, and they shared everything, so it was fitting that they went together. When the two started their fierce coughing, my mother sent Catherine and me to the barn to live.

No cows lived in our barn, no pigs or sheep. A few laying hens perched in the coop along the back, but no animals lived inside. We had horses, but they were pastured, and they took their shelter under trees when sun or rain pushed them to hiding. My father allowed these animals to share our land only because their services were so easy and immediate.

"We use our horses for transportation," my father said. "And a man's got to have fresh eggs come morning."

"Yes, sir."

My father's barn was dusty with neglect. My sisters and I had grown out of playing there years before, so when Catherine and I found ourselves back among its stalls and loft, we set out in opposite directions to rediscover its corners. I found two dead doves in the hayloft, seven mice, and the remains of what must have been a cat. The doves were freshly dead, their bodies just starting to sink down. A few of the mice were powdered mummies, a few newly felled. The cat was well gone, nothing but a skull and ribs and a few final tufts of hair.

I used a rusted pitchfork to pile the bodies together, the noise of my steps and pitches bringing my sister up the ladder. She came to stand next to the pile, watching as I shook the last mouse on top.

"There's more of them in the stalls and tack room," she said.

"Should we sleep up here then?"

She nodded. I believe she was eight, then, and I was about to turn thirteen. I didn't know my time as a child was almost over, that I'd start working the mines in another year, and do that work until I couldn't stand a moment more of it.

I imagined our father as a hovering presence, a wisp of himself that arrived in the solid man's absence. I felt him watching me in the barn with my sister, collecting that pile of animals. He was there as I shoveled them out the hayloft door, onto the ground below, where they scattered and broke, dust and feathers and bone. Our mother brought us bedrolls and we laid them down on the rough boards of the loft, keeping close to each other for fear of the scratching and hoots and calls. Catherine didn't sleep well the first night, but I told her stories on the second, and she fell asleep in the midst of them. They were recycled stories—"Jack and the Beanstalk" and "The Fox and the Cat," and later "Cinderella" and "Snow White"—but she credited me their authorship and I didn't right her assumption. Let her think her brother was one of the Grimms. My father hovered nearby, judging my dishonesty, my stories, my willingness to comfort a small girl.

She's old enough to get herself to sleep, I could hear him saying.

And now look at you. My father laughs at me in this Kilby barn. *Hooking mechanical cups to these damn cows' teats. That electricity led you straight, now didn't it? Got you knee-deep in cream and dung, an abandoned wife and child, the death of a man on your shoulders. Straight as an arrow, I tell you.*

Just a wisp of him, but it's loud.

It'd've been bad enough if you'd worked your damn wife's farm, but now you're working a state farm, no better than the niggers in my shafts.

"Damn it. Stop."

My cow turns her head to peer at me, blinking her eyes. They are a pretty breed, honey colored and shining.

"Not you," I say, folding my words into a few more sounds for the barn. "You're doing fine. Let's get these cups attached. There we go."

I continued telling Catherine stories after our sisters died, but when our father returned, he came in person to tell me to stop: "Keep quiet. We're trying to get some damn sleep in this place." Catherine had taken to sleeping in my room, sneaking in after our parents had gone to sleep. My father found her there, and he pulled her from my bed, dragging her to her own room, rich with the emptiness of the sisters she'd shared it with.

"You're both too big for this," he shouted.

I waited for the house to settle itself down, then I snuck down the hall and knelt at the head of Catherine's bed, telling her again the whispered story of the cat who could jump high into the branches of a tree to escape the hunter and his dogs, while the fox with his bag of a hundred tricks died in their clutches. She liked this one best because the cat survived on its own.

Nearly three weeks after our sisters died, I found Catherine asleep when I came to her room. She was asleep again the next night, and I didn't come again.

Only once was that time in the barn mentioned after it had passed. I was meeting Catherine's husband at their wedding. He had the blackened hands of the mines and a towering height.

"Pleasure to meet you," he said when we shook hands. "Catherine told me about that time you two had to spend in the barn when your sisters took ill. I appreciate you looking after her."

Catherine had hold of his arm, and she smiled broadly. Those days in the barn were some of the last ones with any shared intention between us. She hadn't understood my leaving coal any better than my parents had.

"She looked after me, too," I told her husband.

Catherine laughed. "What could I have possibly done, Roscoe? I was a little girl!"

This got a laugh from her husband, too, and they took it as their parting jest, turning their attention to the other guests—mine foremen and owners and the elegant women standing alongside them. You'd never guess they were in the coal industry, clean and kempt as they all were. Only the men's hands gave them away, and even then rarely. These men had left the tunnels a long time back. My father was across the room, standing next to my mother. When I approached them, he walked away.

We are born with some things in our veins, coal for my father and farming for Marie's and a deep electrical current for me. My father's draw started from need, I suppose, and Marie's father's from land, and mine from glowing Birmingham streetlamps. I had stared at those bulbs the first time I saw them, the streets lit by a force greater than any I'd known—bigger than me, bigger than my father, bigger than his tunnels even.

"I want to work with electricity," I remember telling him.

"Them lights are burning because of coal, Son."

But digging up fuel wasn't what I meant.

When I left my father's mine, I went back to Birmingham, and I found an electrician named Wheeler who took me on as his apprentice. My mother answered my letters only occasionally, and my father's voice was never present. He's eleven years dead now, and my mother six. Catherine doesn't write, and I haven't seen her since her wedding.

My other sisters were named Anna and Margaret. I feel that's important to say.

CHAPTER 5

Years pass quickly in times of fortune. They fill up with kernels and furrows and sprouts, new fields and crops, beautiful glass-shaded lamps from Birmingham, and meals under wide chandeliers. There is always one more room to wire (never the library), and one more fixture to pick out, the thresher to clean, the lines to check. For two such years Roscoe found himself working the farm—electrical components, yes—but also ordering and oversight and sales. He liked to see the numbers in Marie's ledger, the productivity so easily measured and displayed.

Marie was a teacher again, and Roscoe was an electrician, and Gerald was a boy who loved his father. In addition to all that, the family farm was prosperous. The county talked about the prosperity, all those other people and farms full of envy at the family's acquisition of electricity, at Roscoe's connections with Alabama Power.

In Rockford, Marie tried to downplay their privileges, pointing instead to Roscoe's and Wilson's strengths as farmers. She watched Roscoe become respected in their small community. The murmurings about his laziness waned. Whispers about his incompetence ceased. Roscoe T Martin was a farmer. He'd given more to the farm than Marie's father even. The people remained envious, but they were in awe, as well.

WHEN the sheriff came, Roscoe was eating dinner with Marie and Gerald. They were eating a beef pie, one of Marie's specialties, with corn on the side.

Marie tilted her head in the direction of the sound. "Who would be calling at this time of day?" She folded her napkin into a rectangle before tucking it next to her plate. "You gentlemen keep eating. I'll see to whoever it is."

She put her hand on Roscoe's shoulder and leaned down to kiss his mouth. Roscoe watched their son look away. The boy had had to grow accustomed to his parents' intimacies over the past two years, foreign things before that. Roscoe had watched him stare at the first hands held and kisses exchanged, the first lengthy embraces, Marie's head tucked neatly under Roscoe's chin. Roscoe could see jealousy in Gerald, and he could also see confusion and betrayal. Marie had been Gerald's alone, her arms around him, her lips grazing his features, her voice drowning him in its love and care. Then she'd suddenly given her affections to someone else. Roscoe understood Gerald's need to look away. He'd suffered the same emotions in the years after Gerald's birth, and he now felt torn between empathy for his son and conquest over his competition.

They'd developed their own new bond as well, and Roscoe could see his son equally torn between hatred of his rival and love of his newfound father.

Roscoe squeezed Marie's hip as she took herself toward the door, then he tucked back into his meal, whispering through the food in his mouth, "Who do you think it is?"

Gerald was nine, bursting with tales of adventure. "A pirate," the boy whispered back. "He's missing an eye, and he's come for our gold."

"We'll have to fight him, then. You want to be the distraction or the sword fighter?"

"Sword," Gerald whispered, grabbing hold of his dinner knife.

Roscoe could hear the squeak of the door opening, then the

whine of the screen. There were voices—Marie's and a man's—but no words, something hushed and solemn in their tones. Roscoe worried about a neighbor in need of help he wasn't interested in giving, not because of laziness or lack of neighborly concern, but out of dislike for the tasks. Rural neighbors needed help hauling broken-legged horses and sick cows. They needed help raising barns and plowing fields. Back in the village the roles were different. Marie had delivered pies, and Roscoe had helped with electrical flukes. Marie had tutored children struggling with their letters, while he had taught husbands how to wire their sheds and shops. He preferred the village tasks.

The voices stopped.

"We may have missed our chance," Roscoe whispered.

Then Marie was in the dining room doorway. "It's Sheriff Eddings," she said quietly. "For you, love."

Roscoe looked at his son, whose face had gone taut with curiosity and fear. "Bet you didn't know Sheriff Eddings was a pirate, did you?"

Gerald grinned, and Roscoe tousled his son's hair before walking over to Marie.

"What's this about?"

"Nothing." Roscoe placed a hand on her shoulder, kissed her forehead. "It's nothing." Roscoe assumed the sheriff was there about the electricity—it was bound to happen sometime—but the offense was small, a negligible siphoning of power in exchange for such great progress. Roscoe saw the farm becoming the forerunner for rural electrification. The State would see their great success and make rural lines a priority.

Marie squeezed his hand, and he squeezed her shoulder, and then he pulled away.

"Finish up your supper. I'll be back before bedtime."

Sheriff Eddings stood on the newly painted porch, his hands clasped behind his back. He had the same bad scalp he'd always had, the same dander on his shoulders. His nostrils were plugged with the same brown hair, but the boil on his left temple had grown since Roscoe had last seen him.

"Roscoe."

"Sheriff."

He took hold of Roscoe's arm, just above the elbow, firmly, the way Marie's father had at their wedding. "You know why I'm here?"

"Imagine it's about the electricity we have running in."

"That's the start of it."

"It's so little we're taking, Sheriff." They were walking down the steps. "I can prove how little. We can easily pay it back."

"It's more than the electricity, Roscoe."

"How's that?"

They reached the drive and the sheriff's new car. The man's grip shifted and he reached for his handcuffs. "Would you put your hands out front for me?"

"Sheriff."

"I'm sorry, Ross, but I have to cuff you. No way around it."

Roscoe held his hands out. Even though Sheriff Eddings placed them loosely, the metal felt dense and tight round Roscoe's wrists.

"Go ahead and sit up front." Eddings opened the door, and Roscoe climbed in, his hands awkward and heavy. Eddings stood still, holding the door like a servant. "It's a goddamn shame," he said, looking at his feet.

"What am I missing, Sheriff?"

The man shook his head. "I'll give you the whole thing on our ride down to Montgomery."

"Not Rockford?" The county jail was in Rockford.

"It's out of my hands."

Roscoe watched the sheriff walk round the hood of the car. He took slow steps, worry cracking his forehead into deep lines. What piece of Roscoe's work could cause such deep concern? If a transformer had blown, every light in the house would've gone out. They'd have been eating under a dark chandelier, the dim shadows of evening getting the better of the room.

The sheriff opened his door and heaved himself into the vehicle. He drove them down the lane that connected Marie's property to Old Hissup Road, and they continued all the way to 22 before the sheriff spoke.

"Wish to hell it weren't me had to tell you this. And you'll be hearing it all again from the State boys soon as we arrive, but I figure you should have yourself prepared. See, I didn't want to cause too much commotion back there with Marie and your boy, and that's why I asked that they let me take you in myself. You're under arrest, Roscoe. This ain't about me asking you a few questions. And it ain't about the power, either. It is at its base, of course, but it's much more than that. You'd be right about it being a small thing should it've just been the taking of some electricity, but you're being charged with a man's death. That's the sum of it. Some fellow working for the power company was checking lines, and he came across your handiwork and electrocuted himself. I saw the poor bastard in person. Worst death I've witnessed in my life, Roscoe. Ugly as all hell."

Roscoe forced himself to meet the sheriff's eyes. He lifted his shackled hands, holding them chest level, unsure of his intentions. Maybe he was going to set his palms together, readying himself for a plea. Maybe he was making to form fists to pound on the dash of the car. His hands might be leaning toward the door handle, pulling it, that latch letting go, and then shifting to a push that pitched his whole body toward the roadway. He saw himself hit and bounce and roll, limbs loose and shuffling, rocks taking bites out of his skin. He saw himself dead there on the ground, half on the paving and half in the rough grasses along the side, the sheriff pressing hard on the brakes, jumping out before the car fully stopped, then running toward the mess that had been Roscoe T Martin.

"Now, I want you to stay calm, Ross. I got one more thing I've got to tell you. Set those hands down, son. You just sit there, calmlike."

Roscoe set his hands back in the gully of his legs. His shoulders were starting to ache.

"Wilson's already been taken in. He was right there when it happened."

Roscoe raised his hands again.

"Put those hands down, son."

He put them down. "Mind if I have a cigarette, Sheriff?"

"Not if you hand me one, too."

The cuffs made it difficult for Roscoe to fish his cigarettes from the chest pocket of his shirt, and more difficult still to handle the box. He ended up dumping its whole contents into his lap. Only six cigarettes were left, and he handed one to Eddings, tucked another in his mouth, then struck a match on the floorboards. He passed the flame to Eddings and cracked the vent window on his side.

"Wilson was just checking the fence line," Roscoe said. "He wasn't involved with the electricity."

"He was up on the ladder, Ross, getting the juice flowing again."

Then Wilson had been there to flip those levers back to on. That was why they hadn't noticed the short back at the house—the lights off during the day, and the thresher not in use. It wasn't Wilson's job to check the lines, not his job to clean up anything, but he did those jobs all the same. Roscoe breathed in his smoke, both his hands coming to retrieve the cigarette to knock its ashes outside, the left hand dragging along like something paralyzed.

"Wilson's a farmer," Roscoe said. "He's been working that land since Marie was a girl. He doesn't know a damn thing about electricity."

"But you do, son. And you likely needed someone's help with a project that big. The way I see it, it was either Wilson or Marie. You want me to turn around? Go get your wife?"

Roscoe turned his head to watch the woods blur by, the dogwoods standing out yellow against the bark of the tall loblollies. He thought the brown-leafed hardwoods were black oak, but they could've been chestnut oak, too. Those two were hard to tell apart in the fall. All the woods' undergrowth thinned out in these months—the beautyberry's leafless branches decorated with clumps of purple, the red buckeye left to twigs. In his time walking Marie's land, he'd found himself noticing the various sorts of shrubs and trees. An identification guide was in the library at the house, and Roscoe had started cutting clippings during his walks, bringing them back to match against the illustrations in the book. He'd been surprised at how many different species grew on Marie's land. Their memorization came easy to him, and he'd started telling Marie their names and habits the way she told him about birds.

Since the power had gone in, they'd started walking together in the evenings like Moa and Wilson.

"Summersweet clethra," he'd tell her. "See its spiky flowers? They'll all be gone in another week."

"Dwarf fothergilla. Those little white flowers will only last through the end of the month. It'll turn bright red in the fall."

Marie, Roscoe thought, there in Sheriff Eddings's car. *I did this for you.*

CHAPTER 6 / ROSCOE

Our librarian is a twig of a man named Ryan Rash. With a note of great accomplishment in his voice, he tells me that he's gotten me a standing Friday shift in the library. "Your foreman at the dairy isn't willing to let you go for more than a day a week, but it's something. And don't go thinking I'm doing you a favor, now. I need some kind of literary talk on occasion, and you're one of the only damn men who reads in this whole place, so it makes sense. The boys I have in here the rest of the week can barely keep the numbers straight."

Because compliments are so hard to get, I take Rash's words as one.

The Fridays are welcome, the library always dark and cool, something deep and musty about the place. The collection is small, but it takes time to sort and shelve. I enjoy wheeling Rash's creaky cart down the narrow aisles, stopping here and then there, slipping a book into its slot. The organization is comforting, a great structure that can catalog and number everything.

I prefer the numbers in Dewey's system to Rash's alphabetical sorting in the fiction. Dewey put literature in the 800s, but library folks like to give it a spot of its own, let the customers find their favorites by name. As though convicts have favorites. Taking the fiction away from the numbers breaks the rules of classification, and it bothers me like misplaced pails and caps in the barn. Any misplacement throws off the whole system, and the 800s are too small without their novels.

The use of electricity is in the 600s, applied science. Religion is in the 200s. If there were any books on the death penalty, they'd be in the 300s—social sciences—but we don't have any of those. Rash has a copy of the *Manual for Institutional Libraries* that warns prison librarians to ensure that their collections are "censored carefully. Nothing should be accepted which represents vice attractively, contains sensual suggestions, or deals with crime and punishment."

Rash finds the manual humorous and gave me that specific section to read. "Doesn't leave us with much, does it?"

"You have *Crime and Punishment* on the shelf."

Rash nodded. "I'd hoped the title might compel some of our men to actually read it." He showed me its card—checked out four times, returned a day later every time. "You've read it?"

"Yes."

"Why?"

"My wife's father had a large library in his home. The title caught my attention."

Rash laughs at this. "Ah! You see? *That's* why I need you around here." Rash is the only member of the prison staff who offers appreciation, and I believe it comes from his work. He's a trained librarian, and though he could've worked in any other library, he's told me he chose to work at Kilby. He believes in the prison's promise of rehabilitation, and he wants to be a part of it. At times I feel compelled to ask what the milk I occasionally steal for him is doing to rehabilitate me, but Rash is so good a man compared to his peers.

Our library has seven books on dairy farming—600s. Cotton is in there, too. All the agriculture. It's strange to me that electricity gets filed under the same number. Dewey must've seen the running of power through wires as the same as running shoots out of the ground, seeing them all as applications of science. If Rash can stand for electricity and agriculture to be lumped together under one number, there's no reason he can't let the fiction lie alongside the poetry.

I still miss the library in Marie's house, dark with its wood and heavy curtains. "Light breaks down the paper and the bindings," Marie told me the first time I came. "We keep the curtains drawn during the hours of high sun."

Marie's father was a farmer—yes, always—but he was also a reader. These were his two occupations, he told me.

"Are you a reader, son?" he asked early.

"Yes, sir."

"That's good. A heap of books is the only foundation a man needs."

Had my father lived to meet the man or chosen to meet the man given the chance, he would not have been impressed. "A solid occupation is the only foundation a man needs," I hear him saying. "It's those damn books that did you in."

Marie's father would be pleased with the section on fiction in Rash's manual, though. The last paragraph reads, "Let the prison library not only meet the recognized needs of the men, but inspire them in further efforts. The reading habit once firmly fixed is among the best safeguards for any man."

Rash appreciates this passage in the manual, too, and he uses it with the board to bolster his collection of fiction. To me, the passage isn't about fiction, though, but rather any book, regardless of its type. I want books full of information as well as stories, and I see this in the men around me, too. Roberts wants art books. Powers wants biographies on Alabama governors. The illiterate fellows want books full of etchings and photos. Somehow, there's a book in here about Yellowstone National Park. It's popular, all those hot bogs and steam vents. Maybe we just want to know the real pieces of the world now that we're so far from them.

Ed is always looking for books about ships. Rash has built up the maritime section solely for him.

"Why won't he read *Moby-Dick*?" Rash asks me. "He rotates

through the same seven books, and every eighth request, I slide it in there. Comes back in a day, just like *Crime and Punishment*."

I don't offer Rash a reason. He must already know that Ed isn't interested in literature. Hearing that truth aloud won't make Rash stop trying.

I hear footsteps, boots on the hard floor. It's Dean. He's in on the murder of his daughter's suitor, though some say it was more than that—a business dealing gone sour. Chaplain's teaching him to read.

"You got this?" he asks, setting a paper on top of the books on the cart. "Chaplain says the library's got it."

I recognize Chaplain's handwriting. It's dainty, neat as a lady's, and it reminds me a bit of Marie's. They make their *M*'s the same, and their *T*'s. He's written *The Old Tobacco Shop*, by William Bowen. It's a children's book, and I remember snatches of it, Marie reading it aloud to Gerald when it first came out. I can hear her voice.

"You got it?" Dean's asking.

"Yes." I lead him to the 800s. Rash stocks quite a few books for children, and he allows them to stay in among the few volumes of poetry we have.

I pull *The Old Tobacco Shop* from the shelf. Its cover is green, the corners rubbed tan. Dean flips a few pages. He stops at the first illustration. "What's this say, Roscoe?"

" 'Lord bless us!' cried the hunchback. 'Look at that!' "

"There's a hunchback in it?"

"Yes."

He nods and tucks it under his arm as though a hunchback were all he needed. Dean appreciates the Bible stories that deal with peculiarities and deformities. He's come up to me after services, his Bible in front of him: "Read me that bit, Roscoe, about those creatures with the four faces each."

And so I read the passage for him.

"How can they not turn when they go?" Dean asked.

"I don't know. You'll have to ask Chaplain."

That story was all Chaplain needed to convince Dean to start studying his letters, and now Dean is reading *The Old Tobacco Shop*. A copy of it is sitting in the farmhouse, on one of the many bookshelves in that dark library. I can see Gerald asking Marie to read it again. He has not outgrown it, because—in my mind—he has not grown.

I fear we don't grow, either, here in these walls. Instead, we go backward. So many of the men around me are boys, taken again with legends. All of us imagine new creatures in the dark of our cells. Four-headed beasts with calf hooves from our own new Guernseys, down in their fields.

I often wonder what Marie would say about this library, this glimmer of knowledge and learning tucked away in the walls of a prison, what she'd say of the things we still share—children's books, dictionaries, Bibles.

Dean is setting *The Old Tobacco Shop* down on Rash's desk, a green metal beast covered with papers and cards. "Let's see, let's see," Rash says. "Mr. Thomas. Did you return your last book?"

"Yes, sir."

I like the sound of the date stamp on the card, and again on the envelope inside the book's cover, heavy and permanent.

"D," Rash is saying, "E-A-N. That's good, Mr. Thomas. Your writing is coming along. T-H-O-M-A-S. No, not like that. Like a snake. It curves top and bottom."

The wheels on the library cart spin in circles instead of rolling forward. It's a hard contraption to maneuver, and over its insistent squeaks and moans, I listen for Marie's voice reading one of those books from her father's library. I listen for Gerald's breathy laugh at the funny parts.

They are silent though, both of them, not like that night I walked the fields, the night I thought of the transformers and the thresher.

They are so different now, Marie and Gerald, so formless and malleable.

I finish with the stacks and sit at one of the tables to help organize the cards. Rash has me looking for overdue books, and it takes hours to go through the small files. When I'm finished, I set a stack on Rash's desk. "Nothing recent," I tell him. "But these ones have been out at least a year. This one"—I tap the top card—"is going into its third."

Rash picks up the pile, looks through the titles, then dumps the cards into the waste bin. "These are convicts, Roscoe. This is a prison library. We have no misconceptions about our customers."

He waves his hand in the air, dismissing me. Even Rash isn't above these gestures, the ones that turn us into flies or gnats.

CHAPTER 7

Roscoe got a State-appointed lawyer who refused to listen to any of his explanations about electricity and current and how little he'd actually taken from Alabama Power.

"None of that matters, son," the man said. "We'll do best just talking about the hardships on the family—your father-in-law's death, the struggling farm."

"It isn't struggling now."

"Best keep that to yourself, son. We need the farm to be struggling."

"What about Wilson? How are you handling his case?"

"I'm not. He has his own representation. You'll be having separate trials."

Roscoe sent letters to Marie: *Are you covering Wilson's court fees? Why do we have separate lawyers? Please visit.* Marie didn't respond.

Roscoe's lawyer had no information about anyone outside the courtroom—nothing about Marie or Gerald or Wilson. Roscoe assumed Wilson was in the same jail, but the colored section was in a separate wing, so their paths never crossed. Roscoe had no connection with the life he'd come from, and he spent most of his time recalling specifics he didn't want to forget. He took tours of the house, walking slowly up the stairs. At the landing, he took a right and then entered the library. He walked its walls of books, shelves rising from floor to ceiling. He pulled a book out, flipped a few pages, read a passage, slid it back into place. He did this again and again. Sometimes Marie joined him, sometimes Gerald.

The trial came quickly, and the *Birmingham News* covered it. The guards at the jail passed Roscoe their newspapers when they were finished with them, teasing him about his prominence in the headlines. Roscoe read about himself like a stranger, his time in that city jail one of layered realities. There was his own memory and understanding of events, and then there was the prosecution's skewed and daggered account, and then the paper's version, slimmed down to the meatiest, most damning moments. At times Roscoe found himself nearly swayed by some of the information; at other times anger would grow in him as it had in those pre-electricity days on the farm.

In the courtroom, the prosecutor asked an expert from Alabama Power to explain how the company measured electricity: "In layman's terms, please. So we can all follow you."

"We measure electricity by kilowatt hours. A watt or kilowatt is a measure of voltage times current—one kilovolt at one amp of current dissipates one kilowatt of energy."

"I said layman's terms, please!" the prosecutor said, and the chamber filled with laughter.

The paper wrote, *The prosecutor played to the jury with his humor.*

The electrician on the stand smiled. "Just kilowatts, then."

"And what can you estimate about Mr. Martin's consumption?"

"Preliminary data tells us that the average urban household is using twenty kilowatts a day. Let us say that this farm with its fully electrified house and thresher used only fifty kilowatts a day." The man had made a chart, and he pointed to it with a long stick. "Alabama Power charges its customers eight cents per kilowatt hour, which puts Mr. Martin's consumption around four dollars a day."

The man was exaggerating, Roscoe knew, exaggerating if not outright lying. Nearly 10 percent of a line's voltage was lost every day in transmission, which made his consumption negligible. Anyone actually working the dam or the powerhouse knew that, but Roscoe could tell the company's man wasn't one to put his hands on the lines. Figures and theories were fine if physical evidence backed them up—Faraday always gave numerous demonstrations during every lecture—but the man on the stand had nothing to substantiate his claims.

"Four dollars a day!" the prosecutor was shouting. "Now, that sounds like a lot of money to me, sir, but I'm just a lowly attorney." Again, the room chuckled. The *News* wrote, *Again, the room murmured with joviality*. Joviality?

Roscoe saw the jury growing convinced. He saw their anger rising. *Four dollars a day.*

"Now, we believe Mr. Martin has been unlawfully routing electricity to his home for two years." The prosecutor paced in front of the jury. "According to your figures, how much is that voltage worth, sir?"

"Two thousand nine hundred twenty dollars."

The *News*: *There was a gasp from the jury and the audience.*

There was. They glanced at Roscoe with disdain, as though he'd been robbing their own reserves.

"This is a conservative estimate?"

"Yes. With the extent of his consumption, we feel that Mr. Martin could easily have acquired double that figure, if not more."

"Are you aware of the average household income in this country?"

"Yes, sir."

Roscoe's lawyer objected to this question as irrelevant, but was quickly overruled. In the whole trial, the judge only sustained two of the man's objections.

"Could you please tell the court the average household income in this country?" the prosecutor asked.

"One thousand two hundred and thirty-six dollars, sir."

The prosecutor stood motionless and quiet at this number, letting it bore down into the hearts of the modest jury members. After a long minute, he said, "Ladies and gentlemen, an innocent man paid his life for this greed." The paper quoted that, too.

ROSCOE'S lawyer called few witnesses. Edgar J. Bean was one of them. "He's a good character witness," the lawyer told Roscoe. "He'll show your integrity, how you make good on your promises."

Bean told the judge and the jury how Roscoe had paid his debt in full, with interest. "I didn't require no interest, but Roscoe included a good five percent." Bean looked over at him. "I'd do business with Roscoe any day."

Roscoe nodded in thanks.

In cross-examination, Bean fumbled some, and the prosecution made Roscoe out to be a dishonest crook who'd taken advantage of a small-town businessman. Still, Roscoe appreciated Bean's attempt.

MARIE and Gerald didn't attend the trial, and they didn't visit Roscoe in his Montgomery jail cell. Rationally, Roscoe told himself it was a significant trip for them, but in his gut, he knew they were making a choice, and he didn't understand why. How could Marie not be deeply embedded in everything? Roscoe could see her taking to his defense the way she took to teaching. She was impervious, and she would work until an answer came. He knew she'd do a better job representing him than the State lawyer. And there was that, as well—why the State lawyer? Why not hire an attorney who could actually make something come of this time in the courtroom? They had the money now.

But Marie wasn't there.

Roscoe felt the haunting of abandonment, as he had after Gerald's birth. Marie had left him then, in every way but appearance. They had shared a home, yes, but not a bed. They were parents of the same son, but they didn't raise him together.

In his jail cell, Roscoe thought about their courtship, how quickly they'd become inseparable, intertwined, rooted. They'd courted longer than people thought they should, neither of them in any hurry to change what they'd discovered. They would spend their time in the village dining hall talking over village food, or they would stroll together along the Coosa River, Marie pointing out birds. Roscoe visited Marie's schoolhouse, and Marie walked out over the dam with Roscoe as her guide. They married two years after they'd met, and they took their vows at a small ceremony on Marie's father's land with few in attendance—Marie's father, Wilson and Moa and their first two children, Roscoe's foreman, Marie's closest friend from college. A child didn't come for two years, though they tried regularly to create one, and Roscoe could see plainly now that those two years before Gerald were their best. They had been given a house in the village, a tiny home just down from the dam, but an immense step up from the single-employee apartments where they'd both been living before. They were able to share a bed, to sleep together every night, and to rise together every morning. They drank coffee and ate eggs and bread and ham before Roscoe walked Marie to school. She always finished work first, so she lingered near the powerhouse at the end of Roscoe's shift, waiting for his appearance.

They were better in isolation—the two of them away from Marie's family and the ghosts of Roscoe's family, no child between them.

In his jail cell with its high, barred windows and stone walls, Roscoe played back his son's birth, the place where his marriage to Marie shifted like a tree uprooted in a storm, tipped so that its roots spread out over air, rather than ground. Roscoe knew it was not the boy's fault, that he hadn't meant to loosen those roots in his flooding and swelling—storms don't know their cruelty—but still, Roscoe had assigned him blame. The tree that had been his marriage remained, made up of the same components, but it stood at odd angles, its parts misaligned, its growth stalled.

Maybe Roscoe was better with everyone in isolation, one person at a time. Maybe it was always going to be factions of two, one person on the outside circling round, waiting for a chance to break in. Possibly the mistake was simply one of numbers—they should've known three wouldn't work. If there'd been the potential for four or six or eight even—they had dreamed of so many children—then maybe they could've managed the odd-numbered days, their investment in the future enough to keep them connected.

Roscoe tried to see a life with his son. The two of them becoming the inseparable ones, intertwined, rooted, Marie looking for a way in.

And he'd had a piece of it—a small intimacy with Gerald. But he was after Marie, ultimately. He'd wanted most to disturb Gerald and Marie's knitted comfort and steal back his wife. And he had! He'd gone to Marie's land, and he'd installed the transformers, and he'd run the lines, and he'd electrified the thresher, and he'd fixed the damn farm. He'd righted the damn tree, shoved its roots back in the ground, pushed its branches toward the sky. His marriage had returned, and if it'd put Gerald slightly on the outside, what was the harm? The boy would be grown soon enough anyway, and searching for someone else to complete his pair.

It was Roscoe who was alone in a jail cell, though, far from the land he'd electrified and the wife he'd regained. Gerald was back in his place by his mother's side. Roscoe knew it.

THE trial continued, and the prosecution focused on George Haskin. Photos of him from before the accident showed a nose that hadn't formed right at birth, giving where it should've held. The ridge above his eyes stood out like a cliff, his eyebrows hugging it tight. He wore a troubled face, which made his death somehow worse in Roscoe's mind.

While the jury looked at his photos, the prosecution described him as a kind and decent boy, churchgoing and community minded. He'd lived in the single-worker apartments in the Lock 12 village, moving in about seven years after Roscoe and Marie had moved out. He owned a hound dog, and he was an avid duck hunter. Both George and Roscoe had made their livings off electricity. Like Roscoe, he'd worked as a topper on ridge-pin crews before being assigned to other work. George Haskin was said to have a good singing voice. Though he had no evidence to contradict the claim, Roscoe found this hard to believe. Maybe it was just the photos—a man with that sort of nose couldn't be a good singer.

Roscoe also believed that George must have been stupid, and that didn't mix well with singing either. All the beautiful-voiced people Roscoe had known were intelligent, and that made sense to him. Singing seemed like a physical puzzle, a challenge to the mind's ability to coach and command the body. George Haskin couldn't have been strong in those areas if he was stupid enough to get himself killed by his own livelihood.

The prosecutor described George Haskin's body after his death—hands burned beyond recognition, nubs of blackened fingers. His hair had caught fire and burned his whole face and head. The current had made a mess of his veins, great branching lines of red that spread across his skin like roots. The prosecutor hadn't made that comparison, but it was all Roscoe could see.

Roscoe's lawyer focused his argument around the farm's failings and Roscoe's heroic effort to alter that course. Marie and Gerald's absence was a crippling liability, though. "I've reached out innumerable times," the lawyer told Roscoe. "I can't subpoena her because she's your spouse—and I don't know that her testimony would help us that much anyway—but she refuses to attend. Is there something I can pass along? Some way I could convince her to sit behind you in the courtroom? It'd make a world of difference with the jury. They need to see your family, Roscoe."

Roscoe shook his head. He'd tried, too.

"My client was trying to save his farm," his lawyer said in his closing comments. "He was trying to save his family. He took so little electricity—truly a drop from a lake—and the last thing he wanted or expected was for a man to die. Mr. Haskin's death is a tragedy. It's a tragedy for everyone involved. But I ask you to see my client as he is—a deeply burdened man who wanted nothing more than to provide for his wife and son."

That wife and son were nowhere to be seen, however, and Roscoe was convicted of larceny and manslaughter. He was sentenced to twenty years' incarceration in a state penitentiary. He would leave for Kilby Prison the following day.

Even in that moment, Marie did not come.

CHAPTER 8 / ROSCOE

I'm up for my first parole hearing today, which means it's been four years since I came here. There isn't sense in this number. Four is the age Gerald was when he started reading. It's a number on a chart in Marie's old classroom. It's bars on my cell window and scratches in the dust in the yard and attempted escapes this year. I can picture those fours. But as years made up of weeks and days, I can't fit that number to my time in this place. It is both too much, and not nearly enough. I have always been here, but I have also just come.

Ed has had one hearing already, and the chair assignment and furlough happened soon after. I know his chair still hasn't been wired, and I'm hopeful it will be the job that grants my own furlough. I've told myself they didn't come to me with the wiring because they weren't ready, so I'm prepared to go to them now. I will trade those lives cut short by electrocution for my freedom. If Ed hadn't built the chair, someone else would've. If I don't wire it, they'll give it to someone else. The State will have their chair. We can't stop that.

The parole board meets in the administration building, and two guards lead me through a covered walkway that connects it to the main cell house. Other guards open and close gates and mesh doors for us as we pass.

"Another hopeful, huh?"

"What? No packed bags?"

The ones that know me call me by name.

"I bet the board'll let you go today, Martin!"

"No good-byes for me, Martin? We'll probably never see you again."

My escorts join in the laughter, but don't add their own comments.

We enter a diamond-shaped lobby, the front doors directly across from us. I know the lighthouse is just past them, and the oak grove past that.

The parole board meets in a room at the southwest corner of the diamond, its presence clearly announced by an etched placard on the wall. Frosted-glass doors close off the east end, and I can hear voices behind them amid the snap and click of typewriters. It's peculiar to be around such foreign noise, given off by secretaries in offices or clerks at a bank.

"This way," one of my guards says, nudging me forward.

He knocks on the door, and a mild voice tells us to enter. One of my guards stays outside, and the other accompanies me in.

The room is sparse, but the windows are tall, and they are not barred or screened. I can see the front guard tower, there in its nautical moorings. If these three men behind their long oak table grant me parole today or give me a furlough, I will go to the ocean. I am sure of it. I'll find a lighthouse like this one and become its occupant, lighting my lantern in the dark to keep ships from danger.

Or, if Marie would allow it, I'd go home.

"Sit down, please," one of the men says.

A single wooden chair faces them, vulnerable and open. I feel like a child as I sit, unsure of what to do with my hands. I start with them flat on my thighs and then shift to crossing them over my body.

"Roscoe T Martin," the man in the middle says. He is balding at his temples, and the hair he still has is a mustard yellow, thin and stringy. As though to compensate, his eyebrows run out from his brow in two great hedgerows. His suit is dark blue. The men on his sides are dressed in the same color. His voice is the same mild one that called us in. It sounds either patient or drained, but not both. "You are here for your first parole hearing?"

"Yes, sir."

"You understand that we are not here to determine your innocence or guilt, and that we accept as fact the guilty verdict imposed on you by the State of Alabama?"

"Yes, sir."

"The purpose of this parole hearing is to determine whether you can return to society without endangering public safety." He pauses as though he's asked another question, and I am readying to say, *Yes, sir,* when he continues, "We take several factors into consideration when making this decision, Mr. Martin, including your intake evaluations, behavior while incarcerated, vocational and educational accomplishments during incarceration, and plans you have were you to be released. Does this make sense to you, Mr. Martin?"

"Yes, sir."

"Very well." He opens a folder that's in front of him, and I think of everything it must say about me, all of the history they took when I came. "We will start with a review of your crime."

Ed told me this was where they would start. I have reviewed my crime many times. I review my crime every day.

"Mr. Martin, you were convicted on two separate counts—larceny and manslaughter. For larceny, you were given a sentence of ten years."

"Yes, sir."

"For the count of manslaughter, you were sentenced to twenty years. I see you were given concurrent sentences, which puts you at a combined sentence of ten to twenty years."

"Yes, sir."

"Gentlemen," the balding man says to the other two men, "anything else you'd like to add?"

They shake their heads.

"I'll start with my questions about the central file, then. Please contribute as you like."

The men nod, and I put my hands back on my legs, my back impossibly straight against the rungs of the chair.

The balding man says, "I see that you were assigned to the dairy. How is that?"

"Very good, sir."

"Do you feel well suited to the work?"

"Yes, sir."

The man on the left says, "Do you think you could carry on this work outside the prison?"

"I do, sir. My family has a farm, and I could increase its productivity by adding a small herd of dairy cows to the existing crops and livestock."

The man on the right says, "You wouldn't want to return to electrical work?"

I wait too long to answer, and the man in the middle marks something down in my folder.

"I'm trained as an electrician. If there was electrical work, I'd—"

"That's quite all right, Mr. Martin," the balding man says. "I see you're also doing some work in the library. Do you find that rewarding?"

"Yes, sir."

"Why?" asks the left.

"I enjoy reading, sir, and I like to be around the books."

"Can you see yourself carrying any of the skills you've acquired in the library to your civilian life?"

"Yes, sir. My father-in-law left us a large library, and I would like to organize it using the same system we use here."

"Yes, but can you see yourself gainfully employed in this field?" asks the right.

"If there was a position close by, sir."

Balding makes another note in my file. "Any other questions, gentlemen?"

The two others shake their heads again, no.

"If you were paroled now, Mr. Martin, what would your plans be for reentering society?"

"I would return to my family, sir, and help them work the farm."

"You wouldn't seek electrical work?"

"No, sir."

"Just a moment ago, you said you would return to electrical work if there was something available."

I think of those streetlamps, the dam, the turbines. Poles and crossarms, insulators and wires. And those are only the wrappings and containers. Inside them is that great electrical force I've spent so much of my life studying. I know that here in Kilby I have lost it, but how could I not at least try to return to that work once I escape these walls?

"Mr. Martin?"

I see Wilson standing on the ground below me while I connect our own wires to the binder on Alabama Power's lines. I think of what he said.

"It's what I do, sir—electrical work."

The balding man pinches his nose and closes my file. "Mr. Martin"—I hear that it is not patience in his voice, but a deep exhaustion—"let me be clear. With your history, you will never again be employed by an electrical company within the state of Alabama. Likely, you'll never be employed in the country. What we are trying to glean is whether you're willing to start anew as a productive member of society in a different line of work. Does this make sense?"

Of course it does, just like his explanation of the proceedings. Unlike the four years I've spent in Kilby, everything said in this room does nothing if not make sense.

"Mr. Martin, am I clear?"

I nod.

The guard who followed me in shouts, "Answer the man's question!"

"Yes, sir." I turn my attention to the rest of the board. "There's electrical work I could do *here* though, to assist the prison."

"Shut up, Martin," the guard says. "You're done."

But the man in the center says, "What work is that, Mr. Martin?"

"The wiring on the chair. The chair that Ed Mason's built. I've heard the parameters—twenty-two hundred volts, two or three points of contact. I can wire that easily."

The balding man looks at me questioningly. "Mr. Martin, I would not recommend that you lend your electrical expertise to any part of this prison, let alone a part as significant as the one you've just mentioned. You have succeeded in electrocuting a man, but you did so by accident. I'd hate to see what would become of the poor fellow you intentionally tried to kill."

The guard chuckles, but the balding man isn't smiling. The men on either side of him aren't either.

"I imagine I can speak for the board when I say that we are denying your parole, Mr. Martin," the balding man says. The others nod. "You will be eligible for a subsequent hearing in two years."

"Don't you need to deliberate?"

The man in the center writes in my folder. He doesn't answer my question, but says instead, "I'll hope for improvement in our next hearing, Mr. Martin." His voice is definitive, severing. The guard pulls me away. I turn my head for a last clear view of that tower, and I think of the lighthouse I'll never inhabit on the rocky coast I'll never see.

CHAPTER 9

Marie didn't hire a lawyer for Roscoe's defense. She told the court there weren't funds to pay an attorney, that he'd need a state defender. She made that choice, and Roscoe would be fine. She was sure because when a man was convicted in the state of Alabama in 1922, his prison assignment depended most on the color of his skin. White men were imprisoned in state-of-the-art facilities; Negro men were leased to private companies. Marie's father had followed the state's leasing system, and he'd spent much of his life fighting it—writing letters and petitioning state officials. The mining industry's voice was louder than his, though, and convict labor was still the cheapest available.

Marie knew that Wilson would be leased if he was convicted, and as much for her father as for Wilson, she fought in his defense. The lawyer she hired was good, but he couldn't get the charges dropped. Wilson had taken too much of the blame to walk away a free man. He was given ten years.

Marie thought of her father shouting on the courthouse steps, *This fine state leases its prisoners to private companies for rates lower than mules and plow horses!* She saw him walking next to Wilson. *Alabama condemns her convicts to a fate worse than slavery. This young man will be joining those ranks!*

"I'm so sorry," Marie whispered to Wilson as the guards led him from the courtroom. She whispered it to her father, as well, and to Moa and their children.

She envisioned Wilson's future—leased to a big coal company, one of the many in the state that she'd learned about with her father, and then more thoroughly with Roscoe, son of a Banner foreman. How could she have forgiven Roscoe that black past, a childhood raised in coal?

She remembered the night he'd admitted it, the two of them still courting, sitting in that awful mess hall in the village, some foul meal before them. She'd told him about her father, so he knew the stakes of his admission, knew that their families would never speak to one another.

"My father was a foreman at Banner," he'd said. "He lost most of his hearing in the 1911 explosion." He didn't regret his father's hearing loss, Marie remembered, but rather mentioned it like a curse the man had earned.

"I don't know about that incident," she'd lied, wanting to hear Roscoe's father's version.

"It was a Saturday morning in early April." Roscoe then told a story she'd heard as a girl, a story her father had read to her from the papers. Roscoe had known more.

John Wright was one of the only white convicts in the mine, and he was doing electrical work near a detonation site deep in a central tunnel. Four shooters were down there with him. No one—not even Roscoe or his father—knew exactly what spark lit that powder, but the blast was big when it went. "John was blown apart," Roscoe reported, "and the four shooters died instantly." Marie vaguely remembered these specifics.

The blast blew out the fan that kept fresh air flowing through the mine, and the auxiliary fan didn't come on. Roscoe's father was down in a shaft, but he was close enough to the surface to get out before the black damp consumed him, the unbreathable gases left after oxygen is sucked out of a tunnel. Even with the ringing in his head, he stayed at the site. Marie resented the pride that fought for space in Roscoe's voice. *He should've died*, Marie had found herself thinking. *He should've died with the men he forced into those mines.*

The first attempt at a rescue mission didn't happen until the next day, and the twelve-person rescue team all collapsed as soon as they entered the mine, knocked unconscious by the pent-up gases. The team was mostly doctors, and they were pulled out quick. No fatalities. Their close call put a stop to any additional attempts at rescue until the fans were up and running. Marie hadn't heard those parts. They made her hate Roscoe's father all the more.

When they'd finally flushed out the tunnels, rescue teams set out for the deeper guts of the mine. "They ran out car after car full of bodies," Roscoe told her. "My father got a group of convicts to dig a long trench in the convict cemetery."

"Your father? Your *father* assigned the digging?"

Roscoe had nodded. Marie hadn't been sure his head hung low enough for the weight it should carry. Marie had never swayed from her father's politics—from his view of right and wrong—so it was hard for her to conceive of a child so far from its father. Weren't we all, at heart, our parents? Wasn't Roscoe his father's disciple?

She'd swallowed her suspicions.

"Onlookers started gathering the day of the explosion, and more came through the weekend." Roscoe told her that no relatives were present, which Marie already knew. Convicts were shipped to Banner from all over the state; their families were far away and didn't know they were there. "The crowd got so big, they had to cordon off the scene with rope and armed guards.

"The mine decided to sell some food. The officials made a killing on tinned ham and crackers." Marie learned that the foremen got a good piece of the profits from the blind-tiger stalls, too, allowing them to sell their illegal liquor in exchange for a kickback.

"You're describing a sporting event," Marie had said, "something for entertainment."

"That's exactly how it was by the way my father described it."

The official body count was 128. Only 5 of those were free men.

The other 123 were convicts, like Wilson now. The mine suffered little damage and started back up ten days later. It would've been sooner, but they'd had to wait on another shipment of prisoners.

"How could you live with him?" Marie had asked Roscoe. How could *she* live with *him*? This murderous past, so deeply contrary to her own, should have been enough to stall their courtship.

"I was already set on leaving when my father came home with the story," Roscoe told her. "My apprenticeship with Wheeler was waiting for me in Birmingham."

So he'd escaped, and Marie had forgiven him his father. She'd been wrong, she could see now. Roscoe had ended up doing the exact same thing. He'd used Wilson to meet his own ends, without thinking of the consequences. He'd wanted his electricity so badly that he'd sacrificed Wilson to get it. And not just Wilson, but George Haskin. Marie had read the accounts in the papers, all the damage done to that poor boy's body. If Roscoe had been content to be a farmer, then none of this would have occurred. If he had shifted the narrative of his life, drawing his strength from his wife and son rather than his lines, then they could have quieted Roscoe's past completely and replaced it with Marie's, with Wilson and Moa and the kids, the farm and the library, big meals and long days.

She could have forgiven him the other pieces, too, the parts of her body that were lost, all those children they didn't have, those years in the village when he was so far away, so distant, so deeply committed to his lines and mechanisms and turbines while she clung to their son, their only child, dear Gerald, her boy.

Marie knew that some threads of their story weren't Roscoe's to own, just as she knew her resentment was rarely rational. At moments this had been clear, long stretches, even, such as these past couple years with the lines and the thresher and the farm's success. She had allowed herself to float on their prosperity, to hide her questions. She had kept quiet about the simple bills that varied so greatly from the figures the prosecution provided at Wilson's trial, never demanding to know why theirs was the only farm with electricity. She had allowed the secret, owned it, held it, and she'd done that in order to see her husband as a man she loved, a man who spent time in her father's library, identifying and pressing plant clippings, a man she chose. Her father had insisted that she choose the man she would marry. "None of this assigned nonsense. None of this stability and household order. You pick the man you want to spend your life with. That's what your mother did. God knows why she chose me, but it was her choice." Marie missed her father. She missed Roscoe, too, but only in isolated scenes—there along the Coosa River where they would walk, an afternoon here in the farmhouse in their shared bed, the kitchen of their village house, infant Gerald in his arms. When she thought of him whole, though, she cringed. As a whole man—full up of his past and his choices and his actions—she wanted nothing to do with him.

CHAPTER 10 / ROSCOE

April brings a stretch of heat that lingers so thick and hot even the cows complain. The early calves exchange their bucking and snorting for the low moans of their mothers, and the herd clumps together in the shade of the buildings and trees.

Ed's time is close. The warden and his men have finished their tests on his chair. It is painted its bright yellow. We even know the first man they're going to put in it. He has been here since January, and we don't know him except by his name and crime. Horace DeVaughn. The name is as famous as Taylor's nineteen steps, whispered and passed along the cell rows.

We have heard that DeVaughn is a murderer, that he killed two folks up in Birmingham.

DeVaughn has never left that first stop in the detention house. I wonder if they bothered to take his history, or if they assumed they already knew it. The men scheduled for execution have their own row in that house, a floor above the dark row of solitary cells. All of those are singles, so there is space, at least.

They will execute him sometime between midnight and daybreak, and if it all goes well, they will give Ed his furlough. I have drawn directions to Marie's land and tied up a bundle of letters I've refused to send after the first year's went unanswered. I want to know my words have been delivered, that Marie's silence isn't born of a delivery error or a negligent postmaster.

"You think a whole year's worth of letters got lost?" Ed asked once.

"No."

Ed clapped me on the back. "Just need the lie, then, don't you? I tell you what—let's make it a good lie, how 'bout? Let's put some villain in the mix, some bastard lying in wait for the post, intercepting every letter that comes through. See, he's got eyes for your lady, and he can't have your lofty words tickling her ear. He's gotta keep you quiet. Every day, he sits there, jumping that poor deliveryman, until the man tires of it and starts pitching your letters himself." Ed smiled. "Yeah? It's good, isn't it?"

"No."

"Hell"—he laughed—"you don't know." Then he got himself serious. "Honestly, Ross, I'm sorry for it all—whatever the reason. It's a bloody shame."

I thanked him.

"And I'm happy to deliver your letters. I'll beat the little bastard should he try to get at them before they've reached your wife's hands."

"I know you will."

For a moment here, waiting for the warden to come for Ed, I worry about my wife and my friend, alone there in the house that was once mine. Ed is tall and wide in the shoulders, thicker than me. I don't know if he's the sort Marie would be looking for, but his mere existence in my old home jars me. Just for a moment. Just now. Then, it is gone. Wherever Marie's mind is, Ed's is on the ocean. He will leave my letters and push himself east.

He's cleared his bunk of anything personal, and it is a sleepless night, this last of Horace DeVaughn's.

"Do you think we'll know?" he whispers to me. "Think we'll know when they do it?"

If every light in the cell house were blazing, we might see the bulbs weaken under the pull, but with dark on us and few other demands on the current, I don't know.

"Watch the outside lights," I tell Ed. "They may dim a bit."

Our windows face the oak grove and the front guard tower. The globes at the entrance glow all night, and the guard-tower lights its beam once every quarter hour to draw across the cell house and the wall, a flash through our windows, out the interior bars, across the well. Were it to linger, it could be the moon, this ghostly light, white-blue and pointed. It shines on quiet places. The outsides of these cells and walls are empty. We are never there. We do not escape from the cell house.

But tonight is different.

"Do you think I'll feel it?" Ed asks.

"You?"

It is not a question, though, because Ed is still talking. "I think I will. I think I'll know. I'm scared of it, Ross."

The light passes.

I imagine the current running through Ed's chair, running through Horace DeVaughn, all that voltage pushing through his body, his blood and muscles becoming reluctant conductors. His veins go dark, like George Haskin's, his heart and brain trying to quiet the current, everything lit like a filament, a bulb about to burst. I see the current knocking out the power all round the perimeter, deadening the heat in those lines at the top of the wall, silencing the siren. We would pry loose the metal grates at our windows and shimmy down the brick sides of the house, men pouring out like roaches and mice, our fingers in the cracks like claws in bark. We'd build steps out of tar, using them to climb. We'd be down and over and out before anyone knew. The tower light would trace paths in the leaves overhead, shining on the same brick and cement, unaware. Everyone would be looking at Horace DeVaughn, no one left to catch us.

"There," Ed says. "Do you feel that, Ross?"

I look out the window, trying to catch a change in the glow of the bulbs. Are they weaker? Quieter? They are unchanged.

"What are you feeling, Ed?"

"My feet." The bunk rattles. He shakes out his legs, kicking. Now, his hands. He's making too much sound for the hour. His arms and legs thunder.

We both have low bunks, and I am level with him, level with his noise. "Quiet, Ed. Hank's on row tonight." Hank is a night guard known to beat the noise right out of a man. He likes silent cells. If he doesn't get them, we are all rattled awake by his hammering and shouts.

I'm surprised the noise hasn't woken our cellmates.

Ed steadies his body. "What are the lights doing, Ross?"

"They're holding."

"You'd have done it, wouldn't you?"

He is asking whether I'd have made the chair. The question is an embarrassment. I didn't tell him about my offer to the parole board.

"Yes. I would have done it."

The light from the guard tower passes again.

Before dawn, the warden and a guard come for Ed. Not a bit of light is in the east. We haven't slept. The light has passed eleven times since Ed's shaking. I don't know what to call this thing I watched in him. Nothing in my mind can explain the current that jumped from DeVaughn to Ed, that ran itself along the walkway from the detention house, into the main house, and up here to our sixth floor, to tap only Ed, not the man over him, not me next to him. Is it DeVaughn's blood calling?

"Mason," the warden says. "It's time, now."

"You kill him, sir?" Ed asks.

"Without a problem."

Ed is not moving. "How long did it take, Warden?"

"Don't see that that's any of your business, son. You want your furlough or don't you? I'm only offering once."

Ed swings his feet to the floor. He pulls my letters from under his pillow, taps them against his knee. "I'll let you know when they're delivered."

I nod.

"You'll get yourself out of here, Ross." He names all the ways like he does. My own furlough. Early parole. "You'll see Marie and Gerald, soon."

I don't believe him.

"Ross." Ed stands, his hand outstretched.

"Ed." I stand, too. We shake. He has been a good man to know.

"Let's go," the warden says. "Martin, back in your bunk."

I lie down and watch Ed's back. The keys in the cell door clang, and the bars swing out. It's a great sound, that of a cell door opening. Even though it's nearly identical, the sound of a cell door closing is as ugly and lonesome a sound as we get in here. The door settles with its clang. The guard bolts it shut, hangs his keys from his hip, and follows Ed and the warden. The men are quiet. It is still dark. The day Horace DeVaughn died has not yet started for them.

It has for me, though, and for Ed. I wonder if I would've felt the death if those wires had been mine. Would DeVaughn have run his last breaths through my veins, a throbbing rhythm that skewed my pulse?

I did not feel George Haskin. He does not call.

Ed holds Marie's letters in his hand. He will carry them out those front doors. He'll walk into Montgomery and hitch a ride down to Coosa County. I see him in the open bed of a pickup truck. The morning air will be cool, and he will love the sting of it on his face. Wind like we don't know in here, kicked up strong from moving fast down roads. He'll look at the map I've drawn him, recognize the turnoff at the pecan orchards, and tap on the cab of the truck. "This'll do," he'll tell the man driving. "I thank you, sir."

He'll carry those letters up the clay road to the farmhouse, Marie's house. He'll knock on the door, and Marie will answer. It's still early when Ed arrives. Marie and Gerald are just sitting down to a breakfast Moa cooked. Corn cakes and ham and rich, dark coffee.

"Oh," Marie says. "A friend of Roscoe's? Come in. And letters? Where have they been? We've been waiting."

Gerald shakes Ed's hand the way I once taught him, firm and strong.

Wilson is already fed. He is out on the farm. He is in the barn working on a plow. He is repairing fence along the north pasture. He is walking rows, looking for signs of pest or disease. He is there, having escaped the mines—a quick run one night from his bunk, his papers long lost so nobody could track him.

The farm has stalled, going back a decade. They've gotten plow horses and mules, and they are barely getting by. This is how it must be without electricity, without power.

Ed eats quick, and he does not stay. Marie and Gerald wave him good-bye from the porch. Marie sits down to read my letters—every one of them—then she picks up paper and pen to respond. She writes for days, stopping only to shove paper into envelope, and envelope into the hand of a boy she's hired for delivery. That boy brings them directly here. He walks into Kilby's front offices and says, "Mail for Roscoe T Martin. I have directions to deliver it in person."

"Right this way," the warden says.

They find me in the barn mucking and milking, or in the library shelving. I'll give the boy a few coins for his trouble, and Bondurant and Rash will lend me the afternoons for reading.

I will get my early parole, as Ed said I would, and I will go home to Marie and Gerald, and we will be as we never were—my time here in Kilby repairing us without our knowing.

Ed will catch a train to the Atlantic Ocean. "Atlantic Ocean," he'll say at the ticket window. "Quickest route you've got." He'll pay for his ticket with cash he earned in here. The man behind the glass will notice Ed's missing thumbnail. He'll notice the way Ed's fingers crack along their edges, how they crack but don't bleed. That man will never guess that those hands belong to Ed Mason, the man who built Alabama's first electric chair. He'll brush those hands, this ticket man in his booth. He'll touch Ed's hands as they make their exchange, and he won't know what he's touching.

I will never see Ed again, and it is still not morning.

IN the library, Rash says, "You sure are quiet today, Mr. Martin." The events of last night feel as though they occurred months ago, years.

"I couldn't find sleep."

"You weren't alone there."

I picture Rash unable to sleep in his tiny village home. Was he thinking about Horace DeVaughn's death, and with it, Ed's departure? Like me, was he searching for a flicker in the lights?

In answer, he says, "Mason will be back before you know it." His voice lulls as though to soothe a boy whose best friend's gone on holiday. Is my isolation that clear?

"Right," I say, wheeling away the shelving cart. I will suffer Ed's absence on my own.

Today's returned books are mostly fiction, barely read by the look of their date stamps. I slide them into their spots, something flimsy in their labels—that giant *F*, with the first three letters of the author's last name. They are missing the balance of numbers.

I've moved over to the nonfiction, the 000s with their reference books. All of the dictionaries have pages torn loose. I can't trace a pattern. Sometimes, it's a page from the *P*'s, other times from the *M*'s, the *A*'s, the *C*'s. There are words these men must know and love enough to possess, which is hopeful, I think. Every time I replace a dictionary, I flip through it, trying to find the page I'd tear out. It will come to me, I'm sure.

Rash doesn't seem to mind too much this destruction of library property. He includes new dictionaries with every book order.

I'm glancing through the *Q–R* section—*quiverer* (one that quivers), *quoin* (angle, corner), *quop* (throb), and on through *quota* and *quotation* and *quoz* (something queer or absurd); an interesting page, but not mine to tear out—when Rash's voice interrupts.

"Roscoe," he shouts. "Come on back to the desk."

The opposite page begins the *R*'s, and I take in enough of them to judge the page mine or not. *Rabbit* is here, and *rabble* and *rabies*. Not mine. I leave the cart where it is and walk the narrow aisle back to Rash's desk.

Taylor is standing there, the bulk of him at odds with the small spaces of the library. Here is the man of nineteen steps. He's left me alone so long, I'd assumed I was free of him.

"Sir," I say.

Rash speaks. "Deputy Taylor is looking for information about dogs. He needs someone to gather it together and dictate it to him. He's asked for you specifically."

Taylor looks me over like one of the calves at auction. "Martin, I'm looking for you to do the reading and then tell me the good bits. Think you can do that?"

"So long as I know what you're looking for."

"You being smart, boy?"

"No, sir."

He squints his eyes and looks over at Rash. "He being smart with me?"

"I don't believe so, Deputy."

"All right. You get all the information you can and report back the parts worth hearing. That clear enough for you?"

It isn't clear at all—what about dogs does he want to know?—but I nod my head for him anyway, hoping that Rash will help if the deputy doesn't provide anything else. Rash must have some idea.

"All right, then," Taylor says. "You're the one, then. Now, you listen clear, hear me? Deputy over at Atmore's something of a bastard, and he's quick to remind me how he's never lost a man—don't you repeat none of this, you hear?—his dogs have tracked every single one. Got a real solid brag going, old Mr. Atmore.

"We've got a tougher course over here, Martin. You see, there's thicker cover, more chances for the dogs to get called off on some other scent. You saw it that day you were out there. Lots of distractions. My dogs have done more than Atmore's, but they couldn't follow that Kelly stink, couldn't get themselves going. Can't let another man get by. You understand?"

"Yes, sir."

The convict he's talking about, this long-timer named Kelly, he'd gotten a tip from one of Taylor's dog boys a couple years back— get someone else's scent on you, and it'll throw off the dogs. Kelly enlisted a younger man named McCullers to be his accomplice, and the two of them made a run from the fields one day, taking off together in the same direction. Kelly had McCullers wearing his clothes. So when Taylor set the dogs on the two different scents, they got disoriented. Kelly and McCullers crisscrossed their paths until Kelly finally broke off and McCullers sat down, waiting patiently for the dogs to find him. Supposedly, those dogs stayed put once they came upon McCullers, sure that they'd found the right scent.

McCullers was all gloat back in the yard. "Got Kelly freed," he kept saying. "You bastards just wait. We've got ourselves a plan. I'll be gone before you know it."

"Kelly made you his slut," Ed told him. "And you didn't even ask for payment up front." Got a big laugh from the mess, and McCullers made a lunge across the table, but the guards already had their eyes on him, so he only got one swing in before they hauled him away. They put him in the doghouse for a day or two, and over the next month we watched the pride seep out of him slow.

"You still here, Cully?" someone would ask.

"Where's that friend of yours?"

"Hasn't dug that tunnel for you yet, huh?"

McCullers is still here.

I thought only he carried the shame of that escape, but I realize it's sitting heavy on Taylor, too. It's his failure, just as it's McCullers's mistake.

And now, Taylor wants guidance from books.

"Here." He pulls a scrap of paper out of his chest pocket. "Atmore spoke highly of this one." A title and an author are written in sloppy writing. "I want you reporting to me soon as you can. Tell Rash here when you've got something I can use, and I'll have him send you on out to the pens."

"Yes, sir." I don't want my Fridays in the library to turn into time with Taylor and his dogs, but I know better than to question these orders. Even Rash cowers before Taylor. We are all under his supervision.

Taylor nods and turns away, discarding us as he does any subordinate. *Back to work,* his back says.

When the door closes behind Taylor, Rash shakes his head. "You know why he needs someone to get his books, don't you?"

"Imagine he's busy."

"That may be, but think about it now. He's requesting books and *verbal* summaries. He wants you to *tell* him what you've found rather than give him a written report. Why's that?" Rash is telling me Taylor can't read. "Amazing, isn't it? I've known for a while. He came in here for something about horse care a few years ago and made me read half a book to him. Don't you go spreading this around, now. And you better never mention it to Taylor. I can't even imagine the punishment he'd think up for such an attack on his reputation."

I've watched any number of folks bluff their way into looking literate—both inside and outside these walls. Memory has a way of covering bases. People can get the look of a word without its letters making any sense, like Gerald with his early books. At first, all he was doing was reciting from memory the words his mother had read to him. He matched the words to the pictures. He didn't read. He *remembered.* Some folks never make it past that step, and most times they figure out how to get others to do the work for them, like Taylor. He can get someone in the library to pull information for him so long as he paints it like a matter of time he doesn't have. *I'm a busy man, see, got me these inmates to watch and these dogs to train, don't have the time to go reading.*

CHAPTER 11

Marie knew Roscoe's sentence. The newspapers reported it—such big news for their small county—but even before those inked words made their way into her hands, Sheriff Eddings came calling.

"It's long, Marie. He'll be gone awhile."

"I assumed that."

Eddings had rubbed at his wide neck. "You ought to see him off."

"Oh?"

"Come on, Marie. I've known your family my whole life. Hell, I've known you since the day you were born. You're not one to abandon your own."

Marie hadn't realized Eddings had been paying so close attention, or that he'd even had the mind and heart to make such observations. She tried to put herself at his vantage, watching over her family, its rises and dips. He had seen Marie's mother grow sick, stopping by the house once to pay his respects. He'd donned one of the cotton masks everyone had to wear when entering her sickroom, and he'd stood close by her bed. Marie had watched from her place in the hall, noting that he was the only person outside the family to have gone inside. Her mother was contagious, and because Marie was a child, she was not allowed past the threshold. Influenza had taken one of her classmates already, and the younger sister of another. Even in the hall, Marie had to wear the mask. She would stand guard until Moa or her father shooed her away. "Go on and play," they would tell her. "Your mother's going to be better very soon." They had to have known they were lying, but even as a child Marie had forgiven them. We mask what we don't want to see.

Did Eddings remember seeing her in that hallway, both of them so much younger?

When her mother had finally died—wheezy and thin and angular—Marie had helped Moa in the kitchen, the two of them preparing the food for the wake, Moa's most recent baby in a crib by the back door.

"You can talk to me, should you want to."

"I know."

Marie wasn't one to talk, though. Her mother had known it before she died, and her father knew it as well. Small losses had been met with silence since she was a babe—her parents had loved to tell the stories of her stoic eyes and stubborn lips—and a loss so grand as her mother only brought her deeper into those same mechanisms. Talking did little. Dwelling did less. Gloved and masked, Moa took the sheets to the burn pile out back, and when she returned, Marie was already remaking her mother's bed.

"Marie," Moa remonstrated.

"No one's going to want to see this stripped bare, and Father will want to sleep on a mattress again, anyway."

Moa had dropped her scolding to hold Marie close, and Marie had allowed herself some comfort in the thick smells of Moa's clothes, the ham and onions and biscuits, the sifty texture of flour entrenched in the fabric. Marie pulled away quickly though. There were still foods to cook, guests to welcome, hands to shake, condolences to accept. Her father was a mess. She would be strong. She was like her mother in that regard.

"I've volunteered to drive him myself," Sheriff Eddings said. "You could ride along. I can give you some time together before they take him inside."

"Time for what?"

"I don't know, Marie. There's an oak grove right there on the grounds. Maybe you'd want to take along a picnic? Maybe go for a walk?"

Marie pictured herself riding in Eddings's car, sitting in the back with Roscoe, the sheriff their driver, a picnic basket on the front passenger seat, a blanket folded neatly underneath it. She saw them pulling up to a formidable institution, gray and brooding, windowless and wide. She'd never seen a prison. She would step from the sheriff's car and pluck the basket from the front seat. Roscoe would take it from her hands because he was chivalrous. She would hold the blanket. They would walk into the trees—craggy, ancient oaks, shedding branches and leaves—until they found a place far from view, and there she'd spread the blanket. It would be the blue one from their bed.

"Come sit," she'd say, and Roscoe would join her.

What would she cook for that last meal? A whole chicken, her bacon-and-maple beans, corn bread, a peach pie. She would make coffee, and they would drink it out of tin mugs.

Would they hold each other, her hands seeking out an ankle or a wrist, clutching hold of him like something disappearing? The last time she'd touched him was the night Sheriff Eddings had come, her hand on his where it squeezed her shoulder. "It's nothing," he'd said. "I'll be right back."

It had been everything.

"A picnic?" Marie asked Eddings.

"Jesus, Marie, the hell if I know what married folks do before one of them heads off to prison. I just thought you'd have it in you to see him again before he goes." Eddings tugged again at his neck. "He's having a hard time."

"So are we."

Eddings held his hands up, something of a convict himself, caught out at the end of a chase. "It's your choice, Marie."

It was her choice, but then a voice startled them both. It came through the screen door from inside, wary and disappointed. "Dad's on his way to prison?"

"Yes, love."

"And we can go?"

"No, love," Marie replied. "We can't."

Marie had been honest with her son about Roscoe's crime. "There's one thing I need you to understand," she had said to him early. "All the hardship we're facing now—Wilson on trial and your father gone and the electricity cut off and the back payments we owe—it is your father's fault." She had held on to him, squeezing gently, willing the words into his mind. He'd been hers alone for so many years, trusting her, needing her, loving her—he must remember that time, the time before electricity, the time before they'd both opened their arms to the man she'd chosen to push away. "It was his fault," she repeated.

"We can't go see him?" Gerald asked through the screen door, his voice quiet and mistrusting.

"No."

"But it's like we're abandoning him."

There was that word again—*abandonment*. Marie hadn't heard Gerald use it before. Maybe he'd been listening in since Eddings arrived, ingesting that word as one of his own. But he didn't know that sometimes abandonment was right. It was necessary. Marie'd had to abandon the memory of her mother in order to survive the ensuing days. She'd had to abandon the farm for the university in order to get a job that could sustain her through poor growing seasons and a shortage of labor, bad seeds and too little rain. She'd had to abandon one thing in order to acquire something that would remain. Like her own marriage, she'd once thought, and her own children—they would preserve her.

She'd never intended to return to her father's land.

But then Gerald had been born.

"Your father is the one who abandoned us," she said to her son. "You'll see that."

"All right, Ma."

Gerald stared out at them through the screen door with his child's hooded eyes, his chapped lips, his mussed hair.

"Well, I did what I could," Eddings said. "I won't admit to knowing why you're holding the anger you're holding, but I suppose I can't judge it none. You let me know if you need anything, Marie."

"Thank you, Tom." Marie would have liked to have given him some explanation, should she have known how to explain it—this place where she found herself. She could trace it to her mother's strength and vibrancy, followed by her sickness. Isolation and austerity had bloomed in that hallway and then paused when Marie found herself in the Lock 12 village, Roscoe across from her in the mess hall, then a home of their own, and a belly. But it rekindled itself after Gerald's birth, and Marie returned to it like a hungry stray. When her father died, and the land became hers, she knew she would go back, even if Roscoe didn't follow. A part of her had wished he'd stayed behind at the dam, tinkering with his electrical currents, hunkering down in that seat of power. She would have known how to play the solitary woman. She would play it now.

But then a part of her had hoped they would be able to rebuild, that they could do this thing together—farming—while letting their other professions go. She'd brought them here for both their sakes, his as much as hers, and his failure to acclimate had delivered them to their current poor fortune—and the Grices' poor fortune. Wilson's arrest and incarceration rooted all the other veins of Marie's anger, Roscoe condemning him to the very life her father had helped him to avoid.

In truth, she couldn't give any one explanation to Eddings or anyone else. There wasn't one thing that was keeping her away from Roscoe—while he was in jail, at his trial, and now on his trip to prison. It wasn't one thing, but everything. All things. The things he'd been unfortunate enough to inherit when he married her, the things he'd brought along himself, his unremitting love of electricity, its stubborn practice, the laziness of the first year on the farm, the lies about the power, the exploitation of Wilson. All that ugliness, but somehow, too, the beauty she'd once seen in him—the strength to defy his own lineage, the circuits of his brain in their understanding of something so new and foreign as harnessed power, the cut of his face, the roughness of his hands, even the man he'd been in their bedroom, both tender and ardent. Every piece hurt. Every piece made her again that little girl standing outside her mother's sickroom, inert, meager, inconsequential. No, she could not ride with him in a car to the prison that would keep him for years and years. He was already gone.

CHAPTER 12 / ROSCOE

Yellow Mama is the new subject of myths swapped in the mess hall, the storytellers saying that something in the oak and maple Ed used, something about that wood, feeds off the electric current, breathing and swelling until those yellow legs grow strong enough to break from their metal stands and lumber away. The storytellers mimic the stomp of her wood-soled shoes in the open cell corridors at night. "She can climb stairs," they say. "She can slip keys from the belts of the guards. She can open cell doors without making a sound."

They say she speaks to you before she takes you away, and that her voice has a foreign accent like Ed's. I imagine he'd enjoy these stories.

The four other men left in my cell skirt by me in brooding silence. They resent Ed's freedom, and they turn their looks of anger and betrayal toward me now that he's gone. Ed was a trustee, which granted him the warden's protection. He knew the only thing keeping our cellmates from killing him in his sleep was the punishment they'd face come morning. Now, it's just me they have to despise, and my faults are too ridiculous for these men to act upon—the letters I write, the readings I give for Chaplain, the books I keep stacked near my bunk, the Fridays I spend in the library. They call me Books.

"All that reading didn't do you much good, now did it, Books?"

"Got you stuck right in here with us folks. Hell, I even got a shorter sentence."

"Hey, Books, go on and read us something."

"Yeah, Books—what new stories you got?"

Even when they ask me to read, derision is in their voices.

I don't think of myself as above these men. That's a hierarchy they've imposed.

Ed enjoyed his books, too, all those descriptions of ships read again and again.

It's hot in the cell house this evening, and I rise from my bunk to go to the window. It's impossible to see outside through the screen and bars, so it's only my reflection I take in. My face in the glass is abbreviated, shorn of its chin and mouth in one pane, my forehead gone in the next. This is a place of fragments.

I think about Marie out there, and Gerald. They may be sitting on the front porch, staving off the heat with a bit of breeze. They may have just finished dinner. Gerald is thirteen now, a year younger than I was when I went to work in my father's mines, but I see him as that seven-year-old he was when we first moved to the farm, a quiet boy in the corner with a book from his grandfather's library.

I see the other fights we had before the one that sent me to fields, fights between him and Marie and me, always the same—my explosive anger and their quiet victimhood.

I stayed away until morning, that night I dreamed up the transformers.

"What the hell you doing over there, Books? You're giving me the goddamned creeps." This is Fred Hicks talking.

Gil Boyd adds, "You pining for your husband, Books? Missing his arms round you in the warm night?"

The others laugh and Reed pats his bunk. "You want to crawl in here with me, pretty?"

This gets them going all the more. Our fourth cellmate, Vincent, lost his hearing in a mine explosion the same day he stabbed his overseer in the side. He loves to join in, but tonight he's facing the wall in his upper bunk, oblivious of the talk.

Ed was better at defending himself than I am.

"I'm missing my wife and boy," I tell these men, looking over my shoulder, "like you're missing your whores and bastards."

Reed is up on his feet. "What's that, Books? Your husband ain't here to protect you no more. Best not start trouble."

I know full well that Reed is married. I know he left his wife with four children to raise on her own. He's in on assault and sex crimes, and the words that go round this place say his children took the brunt of it.

Hicks and Boyd aren't moving, but the grins on their faces show their thirst for my injury.

I am tired of this place, so I say to Reed, "You're right. I have no business insulting your wife, being smart and strong enough to marry the likes of you. Brilliant woman I'm sure." I know that he will attack me, and I want him to be unmerciful, so I say, "Those kids though—they couldn't possibly be yours, so I stand by the bastard comment, if you take my meaning."

Hicks and Boyd both laugh—they find Reed as disgusting as I do and Ed did—but that doesn't forgive me my place inside this prison. They will always side against me.

Reed turns his back, and I think for just a moment that I've won this conflict, but he turns back fast, a knife in his hand, something homemade and ragged up to its point. There is no handle, just this great triangle of metal, and I don't even have the time to yell or turn or block before he drives it deep into my thigh.

The pain is a shard the same thickness as the blade, just as ragged and grubby. It doubles in width when he pulls the metal free.

Boyd is shouting and so is Hicks, and I see them clambering from their bunks, but before either of them gets to Reed, he's buried the metal in my stomach, and I am vaguely aware of the popping sound the point makes as it goes through my skin. Other sounds come from every direction—more yelling, running footsteps, the ever-present jangle of keys, clubs on bars, the demands of guards, and I'm on the floor of my cell, the cool concrete under me—how is it cool in this heat?

A man is leaning over me, and I hear the words he's saying, but part of my mind sticks in dreams, peculiar scenes that feel tilted and waffly.

I am in a pasture fighting with a man who's killed my grandchildren. He shot them in the chest, and I'm showing Marie their bodies. She looks at them indifferently before saying, "They never meant much to me." The man jumps between us. We both have rifles, but we fight with them as though they are swords. He pushes me away and fires in Marie's direction.

"Mr. Martin?"

Marie is gone, and the man is surrounded by small beasts with smashed, toothy muzzles and the ears of hounds. He points at me. "Put him back to sleep."

CONSCIOUSNESS breaks in briefly, coinciding most often with visits from Chaplain. I see him in patches of fog, a wavering crow there by my bed, flapping his black wings. He reads to me from Job. "We're all tested in different ways, Roscoe," but I am not Job. I may even deserve the infection that's taken over the bandaged wounds on my leg and stomach, pitching me into a fever this warm and prickly. I don't know whether this is Chaplain sitting at my side or, indeed, a big crow, set to devour me. His voice is a raspy caw, his mouth peaked and pointed.

He pecks at my sheets and then my arm, nipping at my clammy skin, then he opens a book with his black wings and reads, " 'And unto the married I command, yet not I, but the Lord, Let not the wife depart from her husband.' Where is your wife, Roscoe?"

I don't know which of us is asking this question.

"Listen, Roscoe." The crow reads more from his book. He reads, and the words eddy and swirl like the Coosa. They break and pitch like Ed's ocean. They are birdsong and wind, a field of corn, a bricked powerhouse. They are lines and insulators and poles. They are the branching veins of George Haskin.

"Is there a storm?"

"No."

"The wind," I say. "It's so loud, and the rain."

"It's a beautiful, sunny day."

"You brought the ocean, didn't you, Ed? Brought it right into Kilby like I thought you would. How'd the warden take it?"

"Nurse," the crow says. "Nurse."

And there is my nurse. Here she is.

"Is it raining?" I ask.

She turns to the man. "It may be time for a rest, Chaplain."

"Yes."

"Can't you hear it?"

"Mr. Martin," the nurse coos. "Open your eyes—it's a beautiful day."

She whispers something to the man who's now standing by my bed, but I cannot hear it. The man is wearing black. His face is familiar.

"Have we met?" I ask him, and I don't know why his face looks so desperate and caught. "I'm hot, and sick of lying on my back. Will you roll me over?"

But the man is gone and in his place is Nurse Hannah, this woman tells me, the prettiest little bird in her fluted hat. I have forgotten how lovely women are. Look at her: almond eyes and a tiny nose, and lips that would never peck or bite. They squeeze together, those lips, and then they say, "You can't roll over, Mr. Martin. Not onto your stomach. But we can arrange you on your left side, if you'd like."

"Yes," I croak, and I let my body fall into her hands—there at my knees, and again at my hips, and again at my ribs and back, and finally, here at my face. Her hands cradle it, one tiny palm against each of my rough cheeks, and I am sure that she will kiss me. I have never lived on Marie's father's land, or in his home vacated by his death. I never ran power lines that stretch across this state and out into the country and all the way to the sea. I have only ever been here, in this white bed, with this small bird's hands on my horrible face.

"Are you comfortable, Mr. Martin?" she asks.

"Does God not live high in the heavens?" Chaplain responds. Has he returned?

"Mr. Martin?"

"Roscoe?"

"Chaplain?" I whisper back.

"No, Roscoe, it's me."

And, again, I open my eyes to a stranger.

"Marie?"

She puts her hands on my right arm, where the nurse left it angling over my chest as though it were broken. "The doctors say you're mending."

I cannot focus my eyes on her face.

"You'll be all right. I spoke to the doctor, and he says you'll be just fine." Her hand is heavy on my arm, pushing through the muscle and tendons, deep into the bone.

Her voice is the same, and she's put something in my hand— one of her fingers to grip? I am an infant curling my fist round the pointer of my mother. The slight effort awakens something rigid in my stomach.

"Right here, dear Roscoe," and I am happy to be here with her, to hold this small bit of her. Where has she been?

Then Nurse Hannah is back, and I can see Marie there with her clearly, and the nurse is angry, viciously so, and Marie's finger in my grasp is gone, though her other hand remains on my arm.

My nurse bird squawks, and Marie screeches back. I try to understand, but there's only noise in the room, a strange chorus of sound, truncated and taut. The voices are clotted things, and they're all I hear.

Now, Marie is standing. Her hand is leaving the bone of my arm. The muscle and veins close the gap, stitching themselves back together. I reach for her, trying to sit up, but she's so far away already, down there by the sad iron foot of my bed, and I am stopped by the desperate torment in my stomach. The pain guts me, scoops a voice I don't know I have from the depths of my lungs, shoots it dark and gruesome into the air, where it strikes Marie full in her nearly familiar face.

Does she tell me she's sorry? Is that what I hear?

The nurse switches her tone, comforting now. "Oh, Mr. Martin. No, no, no. It's too early to sit up." I wait for Marie to say something more, but she is gone. There is only my nurse, this lovely thing. Marie's words feel as light and shifty as her presence did, her apology hanging there in the sick breath of this hospital wing.

"Everything in time, Mr. Martin," Nurse Hannah is saying. "Are you all right?"

Put your hands on my face, again. There. Like that. Keep talking. I am Gerald, quite possibly, a boy, under the hands of my mother.

My nurse is a full bird now, shiny jewel white, her fingers a feathery touch on my skin. In her bird voice, she speaks of forces and affinity, attraction and change.

We are in the pasture, standing over our dead grandchildren. The bird says, "They never meant much to me."

But she must be lying.

"THE warden's been asking after you," Nurse Hannah tells me one morning. I have no idea how long I've been in this bed, but I know it's more comfortable than the cot in my cell. I appreciate the pillow.

"Was my wife here?"

"Shush, now. Don't make yourself upset. You're finally getting past that infection. Goodness knows we don't need another fever."

I have not yet seen my stomach or leg.

"We'll have you out of here soon enough." Hannah's checking on the solutions that drip slowly into my arm. Her voice reminds me of Marie's.

"My wife."

The nurse cuts me off with a curt shake of her head. "You realize how special you are, don't you, Mr. Martin? What with the warden asking after you himself? He told me you work with Deputy Taylor on the dogs."

I don't work the dogs, I want to tell her. *That isn't my job. I collect milk and shelve books. Don't think of me as one of Taylor's boys.*

"I visit them sometimes, the dogs." Her thin fingers slide something up the tube that connects to the needle in my arm. "Deputy Taylor scolds me for being out there alone, but he always seems to be there when I come round, so I'm never actually on my own. It's such a short distance to the village from there."

This information shifts my attention, and instead of correcting her about my prison employment, I ask, "You live in the village?"

"Oh, I'm talking too much. You rest, and I'll be back in a bit to change those bandages. The doctor will be round shortly."

I am in a long room full of beds. Most of them are empty, except for a few men—one with a plastered leg up in a sling, another looking near dead against his pillow, another with a bandage round his forehead. That one whistles as Nurse Hannah walks by.

"Hush," she says.

"But I'm in pain, Miss Hannah."

"Don't be a pest, Mr. Daniels."

I don't know how many hours and minutes pass before a tall man arrives with Hannah alongside him.

"Well, well, well. Mr. Martin. Awake for the first time."

"I was awake before."

"I'm sure it felt that way. Now, let's have a look."

The man's hands go to my stomach, lifting the loose gown, peeling back the cloth tape. I raise my head to catch a glimpse, but

Nurse Hannah sets a hand on my shoulder to hold me down. "It's not good for you to engage those muscles, yet. You'll be able to see it in a moment."

I feel the air on my skin, a cool shock of pain.

"Now, this is more like it," the doctor says. "Well done, Mr. Martin. We might actually be able to let you go someday."

"How long have I been here?"

The doctor smiles. "About two weeks, I believe. Isn't that right, Hannah?"

She flips a few pages on her clipboard. "Yes, Doctor, it's been fifteen days."

"Going into week three, then." He turns to the nurse. "Let's bring the man's head up. See how he does with some elevation."

Nurse Hannah turns a crank on the left side of my bed, and I see my wound for the first time. The stomach I see does not fit with the stomach I know to be my own. A great swollen line is down the center, midrib to pelvis, and I can't make out the indention of the navel. It is lost in stitches and flesh. The skin seems puckered and weak, both red and yellow, something like decay, like a carcass, sour and putrid. This can't be the look of healing.

I feel the doctor's eyes on me. "We had to do some exploratory surgery to address the internal bleeding. And we had to open you up again when the infection got severe."

Again?

"The blade that your assailant used wasn't very sharp, you see. And wounds from dull instruments cause much more damage. This"—the doctor nods toward my stomach—"was more of a tear than a cut." He seems pleased with his analysis. "It's quite remarkable that you've recovered."

"You're very lucky," Nurse Hannah adds, "to have such an accomplished doctor."

I stare at the great mess my belly has become, at this mark I will surely carry forever.

"What about my leg?"

"Ah!" the doctor shouts. "The leg was nothing. It got infected, too, of course, but, hell—there's only muscle and tendons in your thigh. Easy enough to stitch up."

He pulls the sheets down, exposing my nakedness—the tube I haven't felt yet that must drain my bladder—and points at a rough, thick line on my left leg. "The stitches just came out. That'll heal nicely."

It is a disgusting mark.

The doctor pulls the sheet back up. I wonder if he's the same doctor who missed the ball in Jennings's kidney.

"We'll leave you up like this for a bit and get some real food into you. If it all holds, we'll send you back to your cell day after tomorrow." He turns to Hannah. "Easy foods."

"I'll bring some broth."

It has been so long since I've eaten, even plain broth sounds delicious.

There are no voices in the room while she's gone, the ticks and stutters of the building resounding loud and dogged, a great gray presence. Minutes pass, then my nurse returns with a steaming mug. I could weep at the sight of it, and still again at the warmth when I take it into my cupped hands.

Nurse Hannah smiles and leaves me to this joy.

I take a sip, and it is every bit as good as I want it to be. The second sip is, too, but halfway through the cup, pain starts in, red and barbed. It takes my breath, a great inward gust that must sound as though I'm drowning or suffocating. The broth wobbles in my hands, and try as I can to settle the mug, the hot liquid spills down my chest and wound. I am shouting and twisting, and I've pulled the needle from my arm in my panic.

"Nurse Hannah!" I scream with the last of my breath, the pain reaching its hands into my lungs. I can hear her running footsteps, and here she is—my girl. *Hello, sweet thing.* I see her, but everything is going gray round the edges, like the persistent sounds in the room. Her hair is gray and the skin of her face and hands; even her white uniform has dulled.

The doctor has returned, his voice mixing in. "To surgery. Get at the foot of the bed."

There is movement and breeze, the swinging of doors.

"Prepping left arm, Doctor," the nurse says. Something cool is at the inside of my elbow. "A poke," she says, and I feel a new needle enter my arm, and that is all I'm left with. The voice, the cold, the needle, the gray.

CHAPTER 13

The lawyer Marie hired to represent Wilson was able to trace him to the intake facility at Kilby, but from there, he disappeared.

"Leased, you can be sure," the lawyer said, "but to where, we just don't know, ma'am."

"How can they have no record of a man they convicted?"

"It's not uncommon. I'm sorry."

Marie believed he truly was.

Roscoe's letters continued to arrive, as they had since he'd first left with Sheriff Eddings that evening in the midst of supper. Marie could taste the meal. She could hear the easy conversation. She could feel the closeness of him—his hand on her leg, an intimacy she'd allowed him to regain.

At first, Marie refused to read the letters, focusing instead on Wilson's trial. But after Wilson's conviction, she went back to the small stack in the top left drawer of her dresser, finding herself hungry for a man's words.

She knew Roscoe had been convicted, too.

Dear Marie, he wrote. *Where are you?*

Even that was too much—too entitled, too expectant. She was wherever she wanted to be.

Do you know what's happened to Wilson?

Yes. She knew.

These questions only angered her, only forced Roscoe further away. Even the voice she heard through the writing sounded whiny and pitiful and indulgent. That voice didn't care what had happened to Wilson. It cared only about its own discomfort.

But then Roscoe described the small cell that held him in the Montgomery jail, and for possibly the first time Marie imagined him there. She saw him, Roscoe T Martin, sitting on a thin cot, the beard he'd grown in his time there, the rough shagginess of his hair. She knew he didn't belong in this foreign place, no matter how much he deserved the punishment.

In the next letter, he described his trial. He talked about the State lawyer who'd represented him. *He did a good job,* Roscoe wrote, and Marie knew instinctively that the man hadn't. He couldn't have. He wasn't equipped to do a good job. *I've been convicted of manslaughter and larceny. They're giving me twenty years, Marie. I'll be gone a long time. Please let me hear from you.*

It had already been months since he'd written those words, half a year almost.

The rest of his letters came from Kilby Prison. The same intake process that had lost Wilson had held Roscoe tight. Her anger rose again. Why did Roscoe deserve to stay? She'd read the newspaper articles about the facility when it opened—a new penitentiary designed for true rehabilitation with its own livestock and farms, shirt factory and mill. *We have a library. The librarian is an interesting fellow named Ryan Rash. I'm glad for the books, but there are less than in your father's library, and Rash doesn't stock any Faraday.*

How dare he mention Faraday, the father of all this electrical madness. She stopped reading. There were more letters, but she'd wait. She couldn't hear any more in one sitting.

"Are those from Pa?" Her son stood at the door, not little any longer.

"Yes."

"What do they say?" He took a step into the room.

Their conversations about Roscoe had been quick and simple since Eddings's last visit.

"Have you heard from Pa?"

"No, love."

"Do you know if he can get visitors?"

"No, love."

Now Gerald was here, a step inside her room, asking about his father's letters.

"He's in Kilby Prison, working in the dairy. He spends time in the library, too."

"There's a library?"

"Apparently."

"That's nice." Gerald lingered. "Will we ever go see him?"

"No. We won't."

Gerald nodded. He'd suddenly become so old. He was helping with the farm, working with Wilson's oldest son, Charlie, to keep things going.

"Moa wanted me to tell you that supper's served. That's why I came up."

"Tell her I'll be right down."

"Yes, ma'am."

She wanted him to come to her as he had as a boy, to bury his face in her skirts and cry or laugh or simply breathe out his warm little boy's breath. She wanted to twirl the curls of his hair round her finger and whisper stories to him. She wanted to teach him his letters and watch, again, the delight of figuring out words and then sentences and then books. She wanted him to invite her to share a book together after supper, to go for a walk, to do anything.

Gerald was already gone, down the stairs, across the sitting room to the dining table, then into the kitchen, offering to help Moa and Jenny bring out the plates.

Marie didn't know how to bring him back.

CHAPTER 14 / ROSCOE

It's growing dark when a guard escorts me from the hospital. Nearly a month has passed, though it could've been a year. My time away feels long. Boyd, Hicks, and Vincent keep their eyes away from me as I come through the cell door. Reed's bunk is empty, and a new fellow is in Ed's spot. He looks up briefly—long enough for me to see the great swells and bruises on his face—and then he returns to the children's book in his hands.

"Boy's a trustee, now," the guard says to my cellmates. "Hands off."

This is the first I've heard of my new rank, but I'm not interested in challenging it.

I sit down on my bunk.

"Hey, Books," Hicks says. "You hear that the warden sent Reed to a turpentine camp in the north? Worst camp you can get."

I don't respond.

"Listen, figure we might use this whole ordeal to all our gain."

Boyd is looking at me, and Vincent, too. The new boy has raised his head, but he lowers it quick when Hicks shouts, "This don't concern you, Fresh."

"Tried crawling into Hicks's bed his first night here," Boyd explains.

He won't last long, then.

"What sort of gain?" I ask.

Hicks smiles. "The simple sort. Just a little share of your trustee favors."

"Such as?"

"Cigarettes and liquor."

I smile this time. "Those aren't part of the package."

"But they turn their heads when it's a trustee doing the business."

"No." I know that I'm above their reach now—wounded, healing, a trustee of the prison.

"Roscoe," Hicks is saying, "you best—"

"No." My new scars are itchy against my uniform. "We know you can't touch me, which means there's nothing I owe you. Only gain I see for us in this cell is keeping clear of each other."

"Can't promise you safe passage through the yard," Hicks warns. "Or sound sleep."

"Yes, you can." I have been wounded and brought back—a reprieve, but not an escape. I will force these bastards to step around me.

Vincent is the first to lie down, turning his back on us. He has always been the easiest to pacify. Boyd abandons the fight next, and I am left with Hicks above me, feet dangling, our short-term cellmate a guarded witness to my right, his eyes pretending to read the words in his silly book.

"Get out of your bunk," I tell Hicks, pushing against his mattress from below. "I want this whole thing to myself."

Hicks's been sleeping over me since I arrived. I'm asking him to move above Fresh.

"Go to hell, Books."

"I know how to make my injuries look new again," I warn him. "All kinds of insults I could see you causing. Get me another stint in the hospital with my pretty nurse. Get you a stint in the doghouse. Maybe something else." Ed is here with me, his voice in my throat, his hands clenched at my sides. "Get," we say together, and Hicks jumps from his bunk, grabbing his linens, stomping like a fussy child the few steps it takes him to cross to his new bed. He uses Fresh's knees like a ladder, crushing the book, digging heels into the flesh above the man's kneecaps, deep enough to make him shout.

"Shut your fairy mouth," Hicks says, bringing the toe of one of his boots into Fresh's face, opening the cracks on his lips. A few drops of blood land on the pages of his book, and I think of those stains there forever, making their way into every new set of hands that checks out the book from the library. Fresh coughs and whimpers. I know that Hicks will deliver to Fresh the violence and anger he wants to deliver to me, that Fresh has become my surrogate, my dummy, my double, that I have chosen this for him, that it is as unfair as George Haskin's singed body.

I am not ashamed.

Contrary to Hicks's prediction, I sleep soundly that first night back in my cell, a new comfort lapping at me that I haven't known in Kilby before.

I'M given easy tasks in the dairy for the first few days, but Bondurant doesn't care for exceptions, and he has me back in regular rotation quick. On Friday, I return to the library.

"Good to see you, Martin," Rash says.

"Thank you, sir."

He taps a book on his desk. It's called *Hunting Dogs*, and it's written by a fellow named Oliver Hartley. "Taylor's getting impatient. You wouldn't believe how angry he was to hear the news. Injury or not, he's tired of waiting."

I roll my shelving cart away, Hartley's words open on top of the sorted books. There are chapters on hunting coon, opossum, skunk, mink, coyote, fox, squirrel, rabbit, and deer, but none on the hunting of men.

I learn that once a dog knows how to tree squirrels, I should take him to woodchuck country, and that once he can tree woodchuck, I "may rest assured that he will tree a 'coon if he finds a trail." If it's summertime, I should take my dog "where 'coons abide and turn him loose."

I shelve the dictionaries. I shelve the host of Bibles we store in the 200s and a few books about psychology in the 300s. Hartley tells me that a successful trainer in Minnesota feels strongly that pups should not start their training until they are twelve to fifteen months old. Here is one of Ed's books on sailing ships, filed in with the 300s—the ocean reaches far across Dewey's system—and I swear the book is water-warped at its edges. He has been gone about two months, but his books continue to surface throughout the prison. Rash said Chaplain brought in this last one. "He found it under a stack of Bibles. Isn't Mason back now?"

"No. No one can find him."

I can see him back in London, Yellow Mama shaking him as he slips the diamond bracelet from a noblewoman's wrist, there on his English street. The current is touching the soles of his feet, skittering up his legs, through his guts and his heart, out his arms, down into his hands. It flicks his fingers.

"Oh!" the woman yells. "Help! I'm being robbed!"

But Ed is gone. He's too quick to be caught in the streets. "Damn," he's saying, steadying his walk around some narrow corner.

I keep expecting his return. I see him rowing in on a wave that he's trained on the oak grove. He'll coast up to the front doors, pulling the oars into the small boat he fashioned himself, a wooden craft, shiny hulled, clear-lacquered to show the grain. "I was about halfway across that ocean when I decided I better turn around," he'll say. The guard in the tower will lean his head out the window and say, "Row on over the wall, Ed. They'll be happy to see you."

That wave will spill out around the tower. It'll slosh against the brick of the administration building and then against the cement of the wall. It'll loosen the tar, rattle those cracks, inch them wider. The fire in those wires will short, and Ed will come slipping over the top, poured out in a gush that dampens the dirt yard.

Because I've never seen it, the ocean I know is capable of these things.

"They still using my chair?" Ed will ask, stepping clear of his boat.

"Yes," we'll tell him. "All the time."

"I can't even feel it anymore." He'll hold his steady hands out for evidence.

Ed will go back to the woodshop. He'll start making those cradles again. We'll mount his boat from the rafters in the mess.

He has sent one letter. It was waiting for me when I left the hospital: *No one home. Left the letters on the porch. Nice place. Your friend.*

I picture that bundle of letters coming untied. The first envelope waves a bit. It opens and its pages shuffle loose. Then the next. And the next. The paper is like smoke. It curls and loops and makes for the sky, where it breaks apart and disappears. When Marie comes home from her day at the school (for she is teaching, again—I see her there), a boy version of Gerald at her side, only the twine is left, a loose, ratty cord. She'll tie it in a circle and slide it on the boy's wrist because he asks her to. Later, it will hold up her hair.

These are all imaginings. Marie has made her choice. Ed, too, and Gerald. They are all gone from me, and I have a report to conjure from this hunting book. There are no wires, no conduits, no dam. There aren't even cows, whose nature I have grown to know and predict. Here in my book, there are only the hunted and the pursuing, and I must plug men into one and prison dogs into the other.

Here is another ocean book, filed in the sciences of the 500s, a few poems for the 800s, a world atlas and a history of the state in the 900s.

"I don't know what to take from this book," I tell Rash at the end of the day. "It's all about hunting other animals."

"Just put a man in for the animals."

"All due respect, sir, but men don't act like coons and squirrels."

Rash laughs. "You want my advice, Roscoe? Just give Taylor a story. There's nothing in these books that's going to help him train his dogs any better. Tell the man about treeing coons, and he'll either think it's groundbreaking or a pile of rubbish, and he'll either commend you for the information or curse you for your ignorance.

It'll depend only on his understanding of the information. There's no sure route on this one."

I can imagine Taylor's disgust when I tell him to set his dogs loose on a man's summer scent. Strapping men to dogs is different from everything Hartley's talking about. His dogs are off lead, the hunters well behind.

Rash gives me the book to study in my cell. "Taylor will be back next Friday," he tells me as I'm leaving. "You'd best have something ready for him."

TAYLOR is already at the desk when I arrive in the library the following week.

"Deputy Taylor's ready for his report," Rash tells me.

"Come on, boy," Taylor says. "I got work to do at the pens."

I look to Rash, but he just nods. "You're free from your shelving as long as Deputy Taylor needs you."

I resent Rash's easy disposal of me. Maybe he knows Taylor will soon be over this want of knowledge, that I'll be dismissed before I've said much of anything.

Taylor is walking away. "I'm listening, boy!" he shouts over his shoulder. "What's it you got for me?"

Rash waves me on.

I follow Taylor out into the yard, drawing up level with him. He is quick-paced for such a large man, and it's a challenge to match his stride.

"That the book?" He pitches his head toward the book in my hands.

"Yes, sir."

"Well?"

I hesitate. "Due respect, but I don't know that I'm turning up much, sir. Hartley's methods are all about treeing coons."

"Men have been known to climb trees, Martin."

"His dogs are off lead, sir." I turn to the page I've marked and read, " 'We will go into the woods and walk slowly, giving the dog plenty of time to hunt and if we don't see him pretty soon, we will sit down on a log and wait a while.'

"That's the sort of advice I'm getting, sir, and I just don't know that it's much help to you."

I don't recognize the guard on the east gate, who asks, "New dog boy?"

"Not sure," Taylor replies, and we pass on through.

We go to the closest pen, the dogs leaping up at the sight of their master.

"They think they're going on a run," Taylor says. "Best not disappoint them."

"Sir?"

"Might be something to this off-lead business. We damn sure slow the dogs down."

Taylor rubs one of his thick earlobes between his thumb and pointer, pressing the color out of it. When he lets go, I watch it fill back in, red as his nose. He spits in the dirt. "Let's give it a shot."

"Sir?"

"You'll push out through the north fields and into the woods there. After a bit, you'll come to a creek. I want you to go ahead and cross that. On the opposite bank there's a big old possum oak—you can't miss it—and I want you to climb up in the canopy there. Kick up the soil at the trunk before you start climbing. Don't want it to be too difficult the first time. I'm going to set our girl Maggie on it, with two of the new pups."

"Sir?"

"Jesus, Martin. You've done the chasin' bit. Now's the time to be chased. It's the other side of the job."

Taylor had told me about this the first time with Jennings, but I hadn't swallowed down the actual practice of it. It's obvious, though, standing here now. Hartley trains his dogs on squirrel and woodchuck and finally the coons they'll keep after. Of course Taylor trains his dogs on men.

I can see excitement growing in him. "Off lead," he says again, the thrill shaking him, his cheeks wiggling along with his weighty chin. His fingers drum on the great ball of his belly, as though he were playing scales on a piano. "Bet that's Atmore's trick—setting the hounds loose." He claps his hands down still and flat on his stomach and shouts, "Go, Martin!"

I still have Hartley's book in my hands. Taylor sees it and grabs it. "North!" he shouts. "Across the creek and up into that possum oak." He shoves my shoulder, and I start walking north out of perplexity and fear.

"Martin!" he yells, and I turn. "You get it in your mind to run past that oak, and the rest of your time here will be painful as I can make it."

"Yes, sir."

"Now get a move on! Men don't usually walk when they're running! And leave a stitch of clothing at the edge of the corn. Nothing else though."

I run, and I am sure the guards in the cornfield will shoot me dead before Taylor's dogs are even free of their pens. The men on the rows are all in stripes, and they're sowing manure in among the hip-high stalks. Only trustees pick the ripe ears, high as the crops get during harvest time.

The men hoot as I go past.

"Where you going to in such a hurry?"

"You finally breaking out?"

"Martin!" I hear, a stronger voice. "You doing what it looks like you're doing?"

It's Beau. I wish they'd keep him in one spot—the southeast tower or the sixth-floor row or the yard or the corn—so I'd know where to expect his lurching face. He's leveling his rifle in my direction.

"Best stop!" he shouts.

I'm near to slowing when I hear Taylor. "Easy, Beau. We're just doing some dog work." Taylor has got himself up on a horse in what seems just a few seconds. "You pass it down the line," he shouts, then yells in my direction, "Call that running, Martin? Slow as a lame heifer."

The corn shakes with laughter, men in stripes and guards in their denim.

I'm ripping the cuff from my sleeve—is this what Taylor wants?—leaving it for a dog to sniff out. And then I'm pouring myself into woods that could easily be the woods of Marie's land, woods I've stamped through in my freedom. I'm running to a large possum oak on the far side of a creek so that I can be treed by dogs. I'm doing this because George Haskin was ignorant enough to get himself killed on the transformers I'd so carefully built to run current to a dying farm.

My scars throb, angered by the exertion. All the moisture is gone from my mouth, and I feel the sweat on my forehead gathering itself into drips down the sides of my face. My hands sting from scratches, these spiny-branched bushes and trees plucking at my skin and clothes as I push myself past. I know the names of these plants, but I can't name them now. Holly? Buckeye?

Here is the creek, high and muddy from the rains we've had. I splash into it gratefully, the water to my knees, soaking my boots and socks. I bend at the waist to scoop a handful of brown water into my mouth. I don't mind the silt, the rich-earth flavor, and I go to all fours to lap at the creek like a dog.

I am soaked now, my back wet from sweat, the water on my front climbing my sides. I could turn over, make my body a board, my hands behind my head, my feet pointing downstream. The current would spill me into the Alabama River, and I would ride that wide channel all the way to Mobile Bay. A ship could collect me, and I could say, "London," when the captain asked where I was heading.

I hear dogs behind me, and I crawl from the water, leaving prints of my hands and feet in the mud. The possum oak spreads itself wide over the creek, its branches forking with their spoon-shaped leaves, wide at the tips and narrow at the base. It's kind enough to offer a few low branches, and I pull myself up to them with a moan I can't contain. It's an old man's moan, and I'm worried to house it. I climb a bit higher and settle myself into the crook of a thick branch about twenty feet off the ground. My breathing is desperately hoarse, a racket for the dogs to catch, and water drips from my boots and cuffs. I can hear the drops hitting leaves, a tick loud enough to be heard over the creek's slosh and ripple. It's a warm summer day, but I am cold in these wet clothes, the heat from my race washed downstream. Only that part of me will make it to Mobile.

I take a breath and chance a look down. I'm startled by the girl I see, leaning against the trunk of my tree, her narrow shoulders spread wide against the puzzled bark. She plucks a leaf from the closest branch, peeling the green away from the tendons. She faces the woods, away from the prison, and her hair is a lovely dark brown, like Marie's when we met. I can't see her face, but she seems young.

"You listening, Roscoe?" she says.

"What?"

She looks up, then, and the face she shows bewilders me. It is Marie's face, or a version of hers, younger than I have ever known her to be. A drop of water from the soles of my boots wets the sleeve of her dress, light blue and thin. "Those hounds are so loud. They're scaring off the birds. There's a warbler or two in this tree of yours." My God—to hear Marie talk of birds. "A cerulean, from the sound of it. What I caught of its song, that is, before those dogs got close."

She picks at the bark, a long finger in a rough vein.

"What are you doing here?" I ask.

She smiles at me, and she is young and beautiful, low on the ground under my wet and dirty boots, her sleeve speckled now as if caught in its own small rainstorm.

"The farm is doing wonderfully, Roscoe."

"Why don't you write?"

"What would I say if I did?"

She starts moving away, waving as she goes. A dog is in the creek, two smaller ones behind it.

"Wait!" I yell, but Marie is only a rustle of shadows in the brush. A dog has taken her place near the trunk, its nose at the footprints I stomped firm in the ground. A drip taps the middle of its head, and it brings its neck up level with the ground and shakes its giant ears. The thing is slow to sniff the bark, slower still to look up. The other two sniff wildly around it, dashing from creek bank to trunk and back, ears in their faces to shepherd in the scent, as I've learned from Hartley. They're dashing in circles when the big one spots me. It lets out a piercing wail of sound, and the smaller ones chime in. They've found me quick it seems, but I don't know what Taylor expects to happen now. Hartley would have him sitting on some stump a ways back, waiting for a dog to return and lead him to this spot. But if the dogs left, and I were a real escapee, I'd be quick to take off running again.

The dogs have set themselves wide around the base of the tree, holding still as they've been taught. One of the pups tries to mimic the older dog's point, and it comes off-balanced, adolescent limbs outpacing its joints in their growth. The other pup lies down.

Why was Marie here? Why so young?

At least a quarter hour passes before the hooves of Taylor's horse clomp to a halt on the other side of the creek. He whoas his mare.

"What do you think of that, Martin?"

The big dog whines, and the standing pup copies.

"They found me, sir."

"Ha!" Taylor shouts, and he clucks his horse through the water. "And you thought your book didn't have a nose for this type of hunt."

I fear Taylor's sense is clouded by his want for answers. If he climbed off his horse and stepped off a few yards, he'd see how foolish the chase was. The hounds may have found me quick, but they left Taylor behind. Without that lead tying them together, he was just a man on a horse, heading toward the possum oak across the creek where he knew I'd be hiding. Untying the dogs from the waists of his boys just makes for more hunting. The dogs track the man, and Taylor's boys track the dogs, and Taylor tracks his boys.

It's clearly not my place to tell him this.

"Wait," he's saying to the dogs. "Come on down, Martin."

I climb down to low growls from the big dog and one pup. The other pup lunges toward me in excitement.

"Back," Taylor roars, swinging down from his saddle. I am taken again with his ease of maneuvering. He swats the pup on the head, thick-handed across the ears. "No," he shouts. The pup cowers and whimpers, tail tucked, haunches lowered. The other two keep their snouts turned on me. "Goddamn." Taylor gives the pup one more whack and spits in the soil by the dog's head. "That was the last chance on this one."

I want to defend this dog, to at least tell Taylor not to hit him in the ears—Hartley has taught me that dogs need their sense of hearing as much as they need their sense of smell.

Taylor wraps my hands with rope. "Come on then, Martin. We'll lead you in now. Hup!" he says to the dogs. "Maggie! Dagger! Hup!" I walk past the cowering pup and trudge into the creek. I'm no longer thirsty, and the mud-brown current puts me off. Taylor's mare splashes heavily into the creek behind me, and the dogs plunge in alongside the horse's strong-pillared legs.

"Get," Taylor says.

On the far side, I look back. The chastised pup stands belly deep in the water, whining. The tips of his ears flutter in the current.

"Hup," Taylor shouts.

The pup whines, and Taylor reins his mare to turn. The other dogs are milling on our side, their noses down, confusion in their snouts. They are losing interest in my capture.

"What do you think's wrong with that dog, Martin?"

"Fear."

"Hup," Taylor shouts at the dog, and slaps his wide thigh.

The pup whines more and dips his head lower, ears half-submerged.

Taylor drums the saddle horn as he did his belly and lets loose a great, painful sigh. "Goddamn it." He pulls a leather lead from one of his rear saddlebags. "Shake off your cuffs, Martin. You're gonna have to go get him."

"Sir."

I'm tired of this creek, its muddy water and stubborn wet.

"Hey, pup," I say as I approach the dog, the current sucking at my knees.

The pup turns his head in shame and cowardice. The last time he came toward me, Taylor whipped him. Now, I'm calling him in. Hartley wouldn't approve of any of this.

"Come here." I reach for his collar. A small growl is in his throat. "Think you can bite me?"

He answers by stopping his noise, and I clip the lead to the rusty ring in his collar. The other end holds a clip, too. "Fasten it to your belt loop," Taylor says to me. "It's strong enough to hold for now."

Taylor's dangling that scrap of my cuff from the side of his horse for the other dogs. They sniff it for a second, then run back and forth along the creek bank, whining and yipping, trying to find my old scent. When I climb from the water again, they are ginger in their approach, confused. The big one is Maggie, and she sticks her snout to the toe of one of my boots, lets out a yip, then turns her eyes to the pup, who stands proud and alert at my side. Maggie sticks her nose back to the ground, and the unleashed pup, Dagger, snaps suddenly to a point, singling out the creek for her attention, as though the hunt ends there, drowned in the water.

I can see that this hasn't been a successful training venture. The hunting of men aside, we've violated any number of Hartley's rules.

Taylor reluctantly slides from his horse and pulls a couple more leads from his bag to hook up the others. "Might as well strap them up with that junk dog. See if they'll fall in behind the horse."

I look away as he climbs into the saddle.

He digs his heels into his horse's flanks and clicks it forward. The mare starts into a quick walk, then a trot, then a gallop, and the dogs follow, pulling taut their leads. My wet clothes hang on me, leaden and demanding, and my lungs heave up coughs as soon as I start running. The pointed pain in my stomach returns, and the creek boils up in my mouth, silty and sharp. Again, the brush and branches swat at my face and arms, pricks that bead with blood. The dogs heave my hips forward, and my body follows of its own accord.

"Marie?" I say, my voice a lost thing amid the winded dogs and horse, the leads and chains.

"What're you saying back there, Martin?" Taylor turns his head over his shoulder.

"Talking to the dogs."

He chuckles. "I think you may just be cut out for this, now."

I don't know what it means if that is true.

THE day after the run to the possum oak, Taylor comes to the barn to announce that I am being reassigned to the dogs. "Martin's one of the best workers I have in this place," Bondurant says. "And he's my main trainer on the new men. Find someone else to run your dogs." Though I am a decent enough worker, I believe it's personal dislike that's fueling Bondurant's fight.

"You don't want to work the dogs, do you?" Bondurant asks once Taylor is gone.

"I have grown quite used to the barn, sir, but I don't imagine it's my choice."

TAYLOR'S back the next day with the warden himself.

"You'll keep Martin through the rest of the summer months," the warden says, Taylor a bucket of gloat at his side. "And then he'll move over to the dogs. He can do more good for the prison over there than in the barn."

"Yes, sir," Bondurant replies.

I continue with my milking and mucking, delivering jars of fresh milk to Rash every Friday, though I know he'd get me my reading requests without the favors now. I exchange other jars for cigarettes—a new supplier was not difficult to find after Jennings—which I smoke in the barn or the yard, the guards turning their heads. This is new, and I appreciate it. Some moments, in the barn especially, this feels like a real life—smoke in my lungs, a summer day outside, stalls to clean. I could be a farmer going about his daily work, Marie and Gerald waiting for me at home.

I think often of that young version of Marie I saw in the woods. I know she was from my imagination, running loose of its tethers, the strain on my body clouding rational thought, but still I want to see her again. Some days I pass over meals and take too many shifts in the sun in an attempt to bring her back, to get my brain to that same place. Though she refused to share it, I know she must have something to say to me, some message from the real Marie.

Ed is still missing. The warden had to know he'd never return, but we still hear him talking about the hope of Ed's capture.

I assume that Wilson is still in a coal mine, though I prefer to see him back on Marie's land. Maybe this is what the young version of Marie can tell me—that Wilson has escaped and come home. I see him with his family around the table in the big house, dining with Marie and Gerald, back where he belongs. I see him working the farm, as he should, that land more his than anyone else's. He'd worked so hard for himself and his family—Marie and her parents included—and he'd allowed a space for me in his life on that land when he had no reason to provide it. In return, I'd led him to the coal mines, feeding him all those electrical dreams, firing that interest, getting him caught with a dead body. I want my young Marie to give me word of Wilson. More than the real Marie or Gerald, Wilson's the person it would do me best to know is all right.

The young Marie doesn't visit me in the barn, though, and fall comes too fast. I say good-bye to Bondurant and the other men, good-bye to the milk and the cows, the smells and sounds. The loss feels similar to my departure from Lock 12 and Alabama Power, the shedding of a favored job for one I don't want.

I keep seeing Ed in his small boat on that big ocean. Some nights he's coming this way, those waves crashing through the oak grove to Kilby's front doors. Other nights, I see him rowing about the streets of London. Everyone knows him by name, though he's been gone from that city seventeen years. "Mason," they shout. "You building boats now?"

I see Wilson laying down his pick. I see him shaking off the coal dust, see the whites of his eyes. They're white still, not sallow like those of the men around him. He's walking home now. Moa is waiting for him. She'll have cooked a large meal. "Papa," his children will say, "where've you been?"

But then I tell myself to stop. I have already dreamed these dreams. Their futility is contemptible, loose and wicked as the roaches in the mess.

I report to the dogs in the morning.

CHAPTER 15

When Roscoe T Martin entered his first building on the grounds of Kilby Prison, he was ordered to strip down bare. The other men who'd arrived with him, making twelve in all, were given the same command. Upon losing their clothing, they put their hands instinctively to their genitals—cupping out of protection, covering out of dignity. They were marched to a tiled area and sprayed down with a hose of cold water, their hands forced away, every bit of them exposed. They were treated for all possible pests, then they were injected with a variety of needles.

"You'll be healthier here than you've ever been, boys."

Roscoe had always had good health, but he spent his first night in discomfort, waking every half hour to fits of dry coughs from the dust they'd sprinkled in his hair. He'd been issued a scratchy gray suit, and his bed was a thin mattress on a narrow, bottom bunk. Five other men were in the cell with him, and he hadn't learned any of their names. Through the night, they took turns telling him to shut his goddamned mouth.

"Shove your goddamned face into your cot if you have to make that much noise."

"Only thing I got going for me now is sleep, goddamn it."

"That's it. I'm gonna come down and smother it out of you myself."

Roscoe didn't respond to any of it. He coughed and he waited, a good part of him still expecting the admission of a mistake. George Haskin hadn't been electrocuted by Roscoe's lines, he'd simply died of a heart attack or some other malady with a quick onset. The jury had been swayed, the sentence suspended. He was home with Marie and Gerald and Wilson. They were working with Alabama Power to put in a meter for the power they were using. All was well.

He wouldn't have to fight off his cellmates.

Morning was a subtle creeping of gray light, and a guard came right afterward.

"Eaton!" he called, and the man on the bunk over Roscoe heaved himself down to the floor. He was a short, thick man with muscle through his torso. The right half of his face looked as though it'd been boiled.

"You get used to the dust they throw at ya," he said to Roscoe before heading to the cell door. "Once you been here awhile." The skin of his right cheek didn't move when he spoke, stretched and thick as leather. His voice didn't match any of the ones Roscoe had heard through the night, and he saw the man's words as the first decent thing the prison had offered him.

He nodded, trying to convey the gratitude he was feeling.

"Eaton!" the guard yelled again.

The man stepped to the gate.

"Rest of you stay put till we come for you," the guard said, pulling the gate open, its hinges singing. Then he clanged it back closed. "You'll be brought food soon. No fussin' till then."

One of Roscoe's cellmates spat on the floor.

The guard gave him a half-lipped smile, wry and laden with threat. He didn't say anything as he led Eaton away.

Roscoe stayed in his bunk as his cellmates rose from theirs. He was tired, and his cough had retreated, so he closed his eyes. He couldn't have slept long, but he felt rested when he woke to the calling of his name.

"Did I miss the food?" he asked the remaining men.

"Nah," one of them said.

"Martin!" the guard yelled. "Let's go!"

It was a different guard from the first, and he spoke less, the gate the only noise as it swung open and then closed.

Standing outside the cell didn't feel any freer than standing inside.

"Walk in front of me," the guard said. "I'll tell you when to turn."

Roscoe followed the man's curt instructions down the cell corridor, then into a hallway that looked more like a hospital's, then to a door that opened into a small room with a single table and two chairs. A man was seated in one of the chairs already, facing the door. He wore a white shirt and a red-and-blue-striped tie. His shirtsleeves were rolled up. His hair was greased and slicked to the side, and his glasses were thick. Behind him, an unbarred window looked out the side of the building toward fields and a line of trees.

"Take a seat," the man in the chair said.

The guard nudged Roscoe gently forward. He sat. Behind him, the door closed, and Roscoe looked over his shoulder to see that the guard was still there, guarding.

"Are you comfortable?" the white-shirted man asked.

"No."

The man smiled. "First honest reply I've gotten today. Still, do you need anything? A glass of water? A cigarette?"

"Who are you?"

"I'm an interviewer. I'm going to take down your history. I'd like you to be as comfortable as possible."

"I imagine you already have my history."

"We have your court records, Mr. Martin, but we're interested in more than that." The man looked down at the file and papers in front of him, and his voice switched to recitation, clearly reading from a text. " 'The State of Alabama has adopted a new convict intake process, where convicts will receive a thorough study of their history, a mental and physical examination, a course of treatment to remove any remedial defects, assignment to the prison and employment for which the convict is best adapted, and a systematic course of reformatory treatment and training, in order that the prisoner may be restored to society, if possible, a self-respecting, upright, useful and productive citizen.' "

The man looked up.

"I'll take a cigarette." Roscoe had had few since Sheriff Eddings first came to the house, and the taste sat warm and thick on his tongue, the smoke clearing the last of the dust from his lungs.

The man watched him smoke for a moment. "Your name is Roscoe T Martin, is that right?"

"Does everyone come through here?"

"This is the central distributing prison, so yes."

"Did a black man come through named Wilson Grice?"

The man looked at the folder again. "I didn't conduct his interview."

"Can you find out who did?"

"No."

Roscoe took another drag.

"What does the *T* stand for?"

Roscoe shook his head. "Nothing. My father liked the look of the letter."

The man wrote something in the folder. "Your parents. Can you tell me about your parents?"

"They're dead."

"And before that?"

"My father was a foreman at a coal mine."

"You're married?"

"Yes."

"And does your wife have a vocation?"

"She was a schoolteacher."

The man flipped a page. "Did she continue teaching once you moved to the farm?"

"No."

The man flipped back. "How would you describe your profession at the time of your arrest?"

"I was an electrician."

"You weren't working for Alabama Power, though."

"I was working for our farm."

"Ah, yes, the farm you inherited from your wife's father." The man flipped again. "Is that right?"

"Yes."

"Tell me about your childhood."

"I'm sorry?"

"Your childhood?"

Roscoe thought immediately of his sisters, all of them—Anna, Margaret, and Catherine. He thought of the barn he'd shared with Catherine while Anna and Margaret died in the house, drowning in a room full of air. "Little to tell."

The man in the tie looked disappointed, but he moved past it, scratching something down in the folder before asking his next question. "You had a Negro family working for you, the Grices?"

"Yes."

"And Wilson Grice—who you were asking after earlier—he was your accomplice?"

"No."

"He was convicted."

"That was wrong."

The man pushed his glasses up his nose and wrote in the folder. "Were you angry with Alabama Power, Mr. Martin? Is that why you targeted the company?"

"No. I love that company."

The man made one more note, then flipped several pages ahead. "We're shifting gears here, Mr. Martin. These next questions aren't about your own life. Please answer them the best you can."

Roscoe's cigarette was down to his fingers.

The man noticed at the same time. "Help yourself to as many of those as you'd like." He nodded toward the box. "Now, Mr. Martin, if you had only one match and you entered a cold and dark room where there was an oil heater, an oil lamp, and a candle, which would you light first?"

Roscoe laughed. He was just pulling a match from its box, so he held it up for the man to see.

"The match, then?"

"Yes."

Roscoe lit his cigarette.

"Take two apples from three apples. What do you have?"

"Two."

"How many animals did Moses take on the ark?"

"Is this an intelligence test?"

The man smiled. "You're full of new responses, aren't you, Mr. Martin." He shook his head. "How do you know what this is?"

"I don't. How can you measure my intelligence by my knowledge of the Bible?"

"What's your answer?"

"Moses didn't take any animals on the ark."

"I'm sorry?"

"Zero is my answer."

The questions continued. Divide 30 by half and add 10. Numbers were easy for Roscoe. That was 70. Dividing by half was the same as multiplying by 2. They were games, those questions. Tricks.

The man in the tie stood when they were finished. "I'm sorry you're here, Mr. Martin."

"Me, too."

Roscoe shook the man's hand.

CHAPTER 16 / ROSCOE

Taylor has given me back my Fridays in the library, and Rash is the one to tell me about the end of convict leasing, a newspaper spread on his desk when I arrive.

"Governor Bibb Graves finally bowed to the pressure," Rash says, pointing to the front page. "He signed in new legislation that makes it 'unlawful to work any convict, State or County, in any coal mine in Alabama.'" It's been seventeen years since that Banner mine explosion, long enough for a child to be born and grow to age, get taken in, and sent off to a mine. That's a life we've let pass before making any changes.

What's become of this state? I hear my father lamenting, and his voice makes me wonder—for the first time in years—about my little sister and her coalman.

I didn't realize I was working alongside convicts when I was down in my father's tunnels. He only told me later, after I'd left. There wasn't any difference in our appearances, anyway, and I imagine it's always been the same—just a host of men covered in coal dust, black and blacker. I know the mines. I know the life Wilson must have been living there.

I can see him, deep in the guts of the earth, his skin grown darker with the dust. Wilson is a farmer. He belongs aboveground, sprayed clean by the sun and air. He needs soil and growing things, seedlings just coming up in their furrows, the great blades of corn grass slipping out of their first sheaths. If either of us should've been assigned to the mines, it's me with my mining history and my electrical experience. They could've made me a shooter, like those men who set off the Banner explosion, one of the few whites in the shaft, running the wires in, escaping back to fresh air before things blew. Though it hadn't worked that way for the shooters in Banner. It might not have for me, either. But that fate seems fitting, too—blown to bits belowground, a death I was primed for.

Rash has stacks of newspapers and articles about the lease system—his own fascination, he's explained, men's twisted desire to own other men—and I sift through them as I shelve. Photos show the offices at one mine, the brick rising into a triangle of a point above the main doors. Some eight hundred men block out the rest of the building, lining up with their shovels and lamps. One shot captures the growing pile of tools, all those handles and scoops, a jumble of elbows. I look for Wilson in the crowds, but few faces are showing. Just backs, bent, dark backs. I'd like to think I'd know the pieces of him anywhere, but I don't. The back of Wilson is the back of every man.

THE yard is overrun with newcomers, all these men to back up the papers in the library. They're coming from mines all over the state—Banner and Flat Top, Warner and Sipsey and Pratt. Kilby needs to process them and reassign them, but for now, they're stuck.

I seek out the miners by their black nails and skin, and I ask after Wilson. "Nah," they all say. "Never heard of no Wilson Grice."

Others ask me questions. "You know the secrets of this place?"

"Tell me what I've got to do to get put out on the fields."

I tell them I have no secrets, but one man reminds me of myself when I first came—pointedly out of place—and I want to give him an answer. I may even want to see him run, to do the thing I'm too cowardly to do, escaping for us both.

When he asks me what he can do to get a job out of eyesight, I tell him to go to the chapel. We're in the yard, enough inmates and guards around us to grant a sense of anonymity. "Get Chaplain on your side," I say.

The man smiles, but it drops quick, his expression moving toward fear as Beau springs up between us, his weasel's face slippery with excitement at what it's about to do.

"Hell you say, boy? Sounds to me like you're putting Chaplain in harm's way."

"Jesus, Beau," I say, sick of him enough to let my *Yes, sir* slip away, regretting it immediately.

His face shifts. "You talking back to me, you little son of a bitch?"

"Yes, sir," I say, trying to bring it back in balance, realizing too late it's *No* I should've said. Beau's club comes out and up and then down before I can correct myself. Something gives at my collarbone, and I am on my knees, sound roaring from my mouth. It is the bray of the dogs in their pens, needy and pitted.

The yard has quieted around us, and my hollering fills in the empty air. Then Beau joins in. "Shut your goddamned mouth," he yells. He repeats himself again and again, one of his hands yanking at the elbow on my good side, trying to get me up. "Get the hell off your knees, and shut your goddamned mouth. I didn't whack you but a bit. Get the hell up."

I can't speak, can't even move my lips. They are stuck half-open, slack and dumb.

Beau pulls on my arm, another guard appearing from the cluster of inmates to take my other side. Together the two of them drag me to my feet. The second guard's hands on my elbow make the pain bloom in my shoulder, a ripping apart, the limb leaving my body thread by thread.

I let out a sound of resistance, something drowned and gurgling.

They're pulling me in opposite directions.

"Jesus," Beau says. "This way."

My thoughts are not clear, nor is my vision, but I recognize the direction Beau points me. We're going toward the detention house, to Yellow Mama and the confinement cells.

Beau knocks on the exterior door, and another guard unlocks it from the inside. My thoughts are graying, quiet and slack as my lips. I can feel my feet shuffling, as though they're shackled, and the throbbing in my shoulder burrows deeper, knocking against bones and muscles and veins. The pain is a rusted saw blade, its teeth varied in length, turning and cutting of their own accord. Beau is talking to another guard at a wooden desk and they're laughing, and the desk guard says, "We're not picky," and they're laughing more and the saw plumbs deeper and there is another door opening, another corridor, a little sun to my left, and dim quiet to my right that swallows me in its evening tone, then another door, heavy and metal and dark, and a great heaving shove that sends my fumbling feet into themselves, where they betray me and send me to the floor. The saw explodes in my shoulder, a hundred small beasts eating away.

I don't know how long I've been lying here. Years, I imagine, years I spend pulling down my trousers and shitting in a hole in the middle of the room that I locate by groping in the dark. For years I feel the floor dampen with the contents of that hole when the guards choose to flush it. I sit in sewage in the dark for years. Water and bread come through a small slit at the bottom of the door, and I hunger for that meager thread of light as much as I hunger for the food.

The dark is thick and palpable, pressing up against my face, my hands and arms. It's moist and warm at times, cold at others, though it could be my body that's changing temperature through its fevered sweating and shaking. After a time, I no longer need to use the hole, my systems slowing. I can feel all those workings hunkering down into hibernation, only my mind spinning at its regular speed, possibly even faster, frantic. My name is Roscoe T Martin. My wife is Marie, my son, Gerald. My friend is Wilson, and I've condemned him to my father's coal mines. "Thanks for the extra hands," my father says. "Came around to my side, after all, didn't you, Son?" Catherine asks for a story: "Tell me the one about the cat and the fox." Marie and I are walking the village streets, the dam so close, the water loud and rushing. Our village has a church, an infirmary, Marie's one-room school with its double doors and windows, its clapboard painted a dirty red. The streets are dusty clay. Near the water, old claw-rooted cypress trees are draped with Spanish moss, cottonwoods tuft their seeds, boulders and shelved rock croppings offer seats. I am twenty. I am eighteen. I am an electrician. A laundress courts me and a nurse, but I only have eyes for the teacher.

"You're the teacher," I say, startling her in the dining hall.

"Yes."

"Why do you do it?"

"Teach?"

I nod.

"When they disobey, I hit them on the hand with a yardstick."

I laugh and tell her I'll have lots of children. We will have so many, I know it. Sons and daughters.

Faraday speaks in my ear: "Chemical affinity depends entirely upon the energy with which particles of *different* kinds attract each other."

I know, I tell him. I know. But there are forces here in the dark I don't recognize, their attractions great mysteries. I don't know what I should awaken and what should stay hidden. *Help me, Faraday. Give me a spark.*

"Hah!" laughs my father. "Electricity doesn't reach down here."

But then the door opens, and the light bleeds through my eyes quickly, shuttering them closed.

"Son of a bitch!" I hear someone shout. "Who the hell approved this without an order?"

There is no answer.

"Martin!" the voice shouts. "Come on out of there!"

I have my back to one of the walls, my legs angled out in front, just a foot from the hole that is my toilet. The lids of my eyes allow themselves to lift into a slit, and I see the warden himself is here to save me. I tell my feet to move toward my body, to prepare for standing. *Come,* I tell them. *We will gather this body into a small thing and push it up the length of this wall.* My feet are slow to respond, and before my knees have fully bent, the warden shouts, "Jesus, pull him out of there."

Hands are under my shoulders, and I do everything to force my mouth into speech, but they are pulling before the words can come, and the sound that escapes me is black and wet.

The guards put hands on their clubs, and the motion makes the noise louder and louder until it finally breaks into the sound of an actual word.

"Please."

I am a coward.

"Please," I say again, my voice thick. I cradle my right arm like the dead thing it is. "No clubs."

The guards look to the warden.

The warden looks to me. "Watch him close. Now come on out into the corridor, Martin."

I pull myself forward into the brilliant light. I know it's dim, the bulbs dampened and covered, but it's a cloudless sky to me, sun on water. I breathe it in.

"That's it," the warden says. "Now, it stinks like hell in here. Do you think you can let these gentlemen lead you to my office without making any more of those damn noises?"

"Yes, sir."

I don't know if it is good to have my voice back.

I should tell the warden that the stink will follow us, my clothes and skin thick with the contents of that hole.

We're able to get to the administration building through hallways and doors, never stepping outside, though I want a breath of air more than I want anything. I want the dirt of the yard under my feet.

I'm ashamed to enter the diamond-shaped lobby.

The guards from solitary accompany us to the warden's door, then he excuses them.

"Are you sure, sir?" one asks.

The warden doesn't answer, and I follow him into his office. The man's desk is wide and clean. The lamp on it has a green-glass shade, and the windows let in a heap of light. My eyes can't take it all in.

The warden leans against his desk, pulls a cigarette from a box, lights it. "Show me your shoulder, Martin."

"Sir?"

"I'm giving you an order, and you are to follow it. Show me your shoulder."

I set to unbuttoning my shirt, a slow endeavor. I have to shake my left arm loose before I can pull the sleeve from my right. The shirt is stiff in places, smeared and filthy. My undershirt stretches tight against the spot.

The warden smokes. "That one, too."

It's an impossible task.

"So long as you have one working arm, you can get a shirt over your head, Martin."

This isn't true. But I tell the warden my shoulder is fine. "It just needs a day or two."

"You don't think you'll need to shed that shirt before then? You're ripe, Martin. Worst-smelling man I've ever let into this room. Now pull your damn shirt off or I'll do it for you."

I take a breath and grab on to the fabric at the back of my neck, pulling it as quick as I can over my head. The right side of my body howls, ribs to pit to neck, then back down my arm to the pointed brown tips of my fingers.

"Good Jesus." The warden tucks the cigarette in his lips and leans in close to inspect. The smoke tastes good. "That's a hell of a shoulder, Martin." He's smiling. "Guard or inmate?"

"Corner. Corner of the cell house."

He keeps smiling. "Brick doesn't leave a mark like that. Have you gotten a look at it?"

"No."

He opens the closet to a length of mirror on the inside of the door. "All yours."

I can see his suits hanging inside, a few changes of shoes, a pair of work boots, a coat. A tan cowboy hat sits on the shelf overhead, and a couple of red and blue ties hang on hooks set into the wall.

I haven't looked myself in the eye for some time, and it's my face that scares me the most when I find it in the mirror. The time in solitary has given me a stubbly beard that does nothing to cover the bones jutting out of my face every place they can. The skin around my eyes is dark, and the eyes themselves seem to be sinking, as though I've slept every night with stones on them. My hair is rough and oily and strung with filth. The scar on my stomach stands raised against the skin, red still, and then, there is my shoulder—a great, contorted mass of purple and blue and red. The mark of Beau's club stands out clearly, a deep rut in the line of my body, deeply purpled with spiderwebs of burst blood vessels. The whole shoulder is shiny, the skin stretched tight over the pooling of liquids. It's a great blister, and I'm taken with the desire to slice it open and watch it drain here on the warden's floor.

"Guard or inmate?"

"Inmate. I won't name him."

The warden crushes out his cigarette in the ashtray on his desk. "I can make you tell me the truth, Martin. You have plenty of privileges I can revoke."

"I'll lose more than privileges if I tell."

He smiles again, then chuckles. "See, this is why you've gotten so far in here, Martin—you understand the place." He rubs at his jaw and looks out the windows. "I know it wasn't another inmate. Looks to me like a club did that, and I'll assume the guard of mine that took it upon himself had good reason. You want to tell me different?"

"No, sir."

"All right. Let's walk you on over to the infirmary. Doc will tell me when we can expect you back to work."

"Yes, sir."

I reach for my shirts.

"Best keep those off."

I ball them up in my left hand and let the warden lead me out of his office, through the lobby, down the corridor to the cell house, and then into the yard. It's hard to walk, my feet refusing to lift off the ground. The office folks stare. The guards stare. Outside in the yard, the men stare. My arm dangles. The sun is hot on my exposed skin. The warden is using me as an example, I'm just not certain of what. Maybe it's credit he wants. If the men think he's done this to me—one of his trustees—then he must be willing to do any sort of horror to them. I might be walking through here shirtless for the guards, a warning to keep their hands off me, or it could just as easily be an invitation to do the same, to make more of these marks.

The chapel is past the infirmary, and I am glad I don't have to face Chaplain. He has words for every occasion, and I am in no state to hear them.

Nurse Hannah is there to greet us. "My goodness. What's happened this time?"

"Got attacked, sure enough," the warden says. "And a misunderstanding got him a stint in solitary. I'd like him fully evaluated."

"Yes, sir."

"All right, then," the warden says. "Get yourself healed, Martin."

Hannah leads me back through the room of beds. I count four men, then five, a sixth toward the end. They all look sick, ravaged by some great disease.

"It's disappointing to see you back so soon," Hannah says, and I agree.

MY second parole hearing has arrived—second trip to the infirmary, second hearing. I am running a circuit, passing through the same points over and over. There is only one change. Unlike my first hearing, I have no expectations for this one. I will match my voice to that of the balding man. I will not hope.

Guards lead me through the same corridors, and the same guards heckle me on my way through.

"Been stripped of those trustee ranks, have ya, Martin?"

"You a threat, now?"

"Should I be scared?"

"Parole board," one of my guards says, and the others switch their tone. A few of them wish me luck.

"It's only his second one," the guard on my left says.

"Ah, well. Luck to you anyway, Martin."

My right arm is still bound to my body—I have orders from the doctor not to move the limb for a month—an obscene lump under my shirt, my right sleeve slack and empty.

The balding man is balder now. He still takes up the center seat at the table in the room, and the man on the right seems to be the same one as well. The man on the left is most certainly new, a great beast of a man with hair sprouting from his shirt collar, climbing his enormous neck. He, too, wears the customary dark blue suit.

"Please take a seat," the bald man says, and I lay my left hand flat on my thigh and sit up tall. The bald man delivers the same opening script, and I tell him—again—that it makes sense. I understand that this board does not doubt my guilt, that they are trying to assess only whether I am ready to return to society without endangering the public.

Again, they review my crime. I see George Haskin's face before and after his electrocution on the pirated lines I ran. I hear again the figures of money I stole. I see Sheriff Eddings on our porch.

"I'm sorry, Roscoe," he says, opening the car door for me.

"I see you've been working with Deputy Warden Taylor and the prison dogs, is that right?"

"Yes, sir."

"How do you like that work?"

"I find it enjoyable."

"Can you see yourself continuing it outside of Kilby?"

"No, sir."

"Why is that?" the new man asks.

"All due respect, sirs, I don't imagine there'll be much need for prison dogs outside of Kilby."

The large man laughs unexpectedly. "Right enough." He turns to the bald man. "What kind of outside training is dog work giving them?"

"Tracking skills," the bald man says. "And animal husbandry." He is defensive, and the large man looks skeptical.

"You're still working in the library as well?" the large man asks.

"Yes, sir."

"And do you see yourself continuing that work?"

Again, I tell them I will organize my father-in-law's books.

"You've suffered injuries since your last parole hearing," the large man says. "Do they have any lasting effects?"

I point to my right arm hidden away under my shirt. "The doctor doesn't know what the range of motion will be once it heals. I have a fourteen-inch scar up the center of my abdomen and another scar on my leg. Both of them still hurt when I run."

No one gets paroled their second time. There doesn't seem much point to try.

"What about psychologically?" the large man asks. He has taken over the bald man's job.

I find too many obvious questions here and have no idea what this large man would have me say in response. I'm unclear what constitutes a wholesome psychological reaction to physical violence. Had George Haskin lived, what would his psychological reaction be? Anger? Relief at having lived? Regret? I could tell these three men that my injuries have done little more than everything else in this place, that they are just one more piece, like the wall and the mess and the heat in the cell house. My injuries are not more or less than the dust in the yard and Yellow Mama and Ed's boat and that damn lighthouse. I did not expect the injuries, but they did not surprise me, and so, I could tell this board that they did nothing, that their impact was neutral, that they were a decent dinner one evening or a painful sermon one Sunday morning or the sounds of the dogs giving chase.

My scars ache and my shoulder, but that is a response to a question I've already answered.

"There's been no psychological effect, sir."

The large man starts to speak, but the bald man interrupts, "If we were to grant your parole today, what would you do to become an upright member of society?"

"I would go home and help my wife run the farm her father left us."

"You wouldn't seek out electrical work?"

"No, sir."

"Why not?"

"Because I couldn't get electrical work, sir." I don't know if he remembers giving me this answer in my first hearing.

"Any other questions, gentlemen?"

I expect something more from the large one, and at least one word from the silent fellow, but both of them decline. The guard leads me to the bench in the lobby, and I watch the clerks go about their filing and typing. The warden's office is directly across from us, and I picture him in there smoking.

They keep me out in the hall for at least ten minutes, but when I return to that unfortunate chair, their decision is the same.

"The board feels that you would benefit from more rehabilitation," the bald man says. "We are denying your parole. Your next hearing will be held in two years."

"Thank you." I go with my guards back through the corridors and gates and doors, back to the yard, where they will turn me loose.

CHAPTER 17

The prosecution hadn't been able to prove exactly when the transformers and the lines went in and finally settled for $1,000 in reparation. The farm carried the debt, and Marie had wanted it gone as soon as possible. Without the men and the thresher, the farm wasn't making enough money to cover its own expenses, let alone any additional payments, and so she'd sought out a teaching position in Rockford the following fall. Roscoe had been away nearly a year, and Wilson's sons were doing good work keeping the farm in order. Marie felt she could take herself away. She trusted her father's land in the hands of Wilson's family. Gerald came with her to the schoolhouse, though he kept his distance, his nose in his books and his thoughts on his father. Marie saw Roscoe there in the boy's eyes and his cheekbones and hair. She saw Roscoe in his desire to leave—a son wanting to run from his home. "Gerald!" she would call in class. "What is the answer?"

Only when she directly confronted him would he speak: "Columbus. The capital of Ohio is Columbus." He always knew.

Marie's salary was meager, but she was able to put most all of it toward the power debt, and by the spring she'd paid it in full.

Marie wasn't expecting the man from Alabama Power who arrived on her doorstep a little over a year later in mid-June, summer vacation stretching long and difficult for her and her son. Because the man's appearance was a surprise, it reminded her of when the sheriff came for Roscoe. She was bristly when she opened the door, stiff and curt.

She spoke through the screen, keeping the latch held tight. "May I help you?"

"Marie Martin?"

"Yes."

He explained his position with the power company, as well as his intent. "Do you have a moment?"

She didn't trust him. She didn't trust anyone with his hands or mind in electricity. The whole enterprise was slippery, dishonest, alternating. Here and then gone. She thought of Roscoe's explanations, all those passionate lectures he'd given her about forces and impulse—circulation, laps, and runs. All of it was ugly, now, a deeply channeled ugliness that was burned like the body of George Haskin. She saw the prosecutor's description—the blackened fingers and darkened veins. A book—*Parnassus on Wheels*—would join this image, and Marie would watch it fly over her head to hit one of her mother's ceramic plates that hung on the wall, the porcelain falling slowly to the floor, where it shattered against the wood her father had laid, board by board. Gerald came next, his arms bruised purple and blue, yellow tinged at the edge, marks the shapes of his father's fingers. There was so much to see.

"I have a moment," Marie told the man from Alabama Power.

The day was already warm, the night's chill burned away. The mockingbirds were loud in the pecan trees, and a solitary crow called out from the roof of the barn.

Marie sat down in one of the porch rockers.

"Is this a bad time, ma'am?"

"No worse than any other." She motioned to the chair across from her. "Please sit."

Marie knew that the girl who'd made her dead mother's bed had grown into the cold woman she was now. She hadn't meant to turn out this way, but once the push started, she'd been incapable of reversing it. She was not a welcoming woman, not kind. She was strong and reasonable and disciplined.

"Ma'am?"

She recognized the man's youth, a child really. What was he doing on this errand? So innocent-faced, rough-cheeked, haphazardly shaved, a bit of stubble near his ear and again under his nose. Marie couldn't tell whether he was handsome. "You want to bring power back in?"

"Yes, ma'am. The company's started a rural electrification program, and your property is high on the list."

Marie nodded.

"There's very little that needs to be done, really. We'll have a crew examine your existing lines, and then they'll put in a meter. From what I heard, your place was fully wired. Imagine it'd be nice to get back to that."

"I don't much care for electricity."

The young man looked perplexed. She could tell that he knew their story, knew her husband was a convict, far away in a prison somewhere, charged with the death of a man who'd held a job like his own. The young man clearly knew that they'd turned a nice profit in their time of electricity—the newspapers had reported as much—and that, were it not for the illegality of it, their experiment would've been lauded as revolutionary, the next great frontier of modern agriculture. His face asked her why she wouldn't want to return there. Why not retrace those steps?

"Ma'am? You don't *care* for electricity?"

"No. But it would probably do the farm good to have it back." Marie looked toward the stand of trees that stood between the main house and the Grices' quarters. Moa was still over there, tending to her family, crippled as it was without its father.

Marie had asked them to move into the big house—there was room enough—but Moa refused: "No, Miss Marie. No, no."

Marie wanted one of the boys to appear—Charles or Henry—so that she could tell the young man from Alabama Power that they were her land managers. She wanted to say that the decision was theirs. *Whatever they decide is fine.*

She was tired of decisions. There'd been so many in the past two years. "All right. Install your meter."

Relief pushed its way through the man's features. His ears were uneven on his head, and a slim, white scar ran its way across his chin. Marie noticed these pieces of him, letting herself stare. She was losing herself, she knew, sinking into something untenable, a deep well with madness at its bottom. The feel of it—slippery, cool, damp—hung on her like the wash she no longer helped Moa hang on the line, wrung to wrinkles and still dripping. Any previous version of herself would not stare so long at this young man's face, taking in the enlarged pores on his nose, the clump of hairs between his brows, the near absence of lower eyelashes, the irises like clay, muddy red.

She watched his lips say, "That's wonderful news, ma'am." The lips were chapped in places, dried to white. "We'll have a crew out within the week, and we'll send you rate details in the mail."

She recognized the words the man was saying, but she heard them for their sounds, not their meaning. *Like birdcalls,* she thought, *a detectable pattern.* She heard notes rise, pitches and drops. The combination equaled pleasure, contentment. She was sure she'd be able to identify this young man by his call alone, pin him as a company man, reaching completion on a difficult task. *Hear that lilt?* she would say. *That's self-satisfaction.*

The man stood. Marie could tell he wanted to go, get on with his other visits (were there other visits?). He wanted to be done with this strange woman who didn't care for electricity. "Do you have any questions?"

"No."

MARIE set to work in the kitchen. Peaches were ready for canning. Moa and Jenny would be over to help, and they would spend their day in orange-red flesh, steam, and heat. Though Jenny complained righteously, Marie didn't mind the discomfort—the dampness of her skin, sweat-beaded forehead, sticking cotton, heavy hair. She had always enjoyed physical work, and she could well have forgone the university and stayed home and tended the farm. She could've married one of the sweet boys from Rockford, raised on neighboring land, and they could've run their joined properties with ease and simplicity. Electricity would've been something far off and foreign until the day a young man knocked on the door to ask if they'd like to run some poles in. *Lovely,* she would say. *Let's try it.*

Moa and Jenny arrived through the back door, their faces shiny and their hair woven back. They said their good-mornings, Moa resting a hand on Marie's shoulder—weighty and kind.

They worked around the butcher-block table in the center of the kitchen, a great expanse of wood that Marie's father had made for her mother. Marie had grown up on that table, sitting on one of its edges to watch her mother build pies, chop meat, peel innumerable potatoes and carrots and turnips, tear greens, slice apples and peaches, crack pecans. She knew the table's cuts and burns, the knife marks and stains. Marie gave the table a thorough scrubbing every couple months, and she oiled it heavily after Christmas.

The women worked quietly, which had become their custom since Wilson and Roscoe went away.

The stone of the peach had always pleased Marie, its wrinkles like furrows in a newly plowed pasture or the deeply creased forehead of an old woman—like things soft to the touch. The stone was rough, though, nearly to scratching, and hard. Only a sick peach showed a weak stone, splitting with the flesh when cut, exposing the soft, flat seed inside. The fruit of those peaches clung to the sides of their stones, forcing her to hack away at the flesh in sloppy chunks. When the farm had been at its most prosperous, she'd allowed herself to throw those peaches out.

They filled huge bowls with slices, great heaping mounds of orange and pink and red, and then Marie added spices. She allowed only clove and cinnamon in her peaches—the sweet made subtly sharp in places, a small bite in the back of the throat—and she covered them with a light syrup mixture made from water and cane sugar.

It was hard not to think of Roscoe when she canned. He'd loved her peaches, exclaiming over their unique taste.

"What is that?" he'd asked the first time he tried one, forked from jar to mouth by Marie's own hand.

"Clove, and cinnamon. More cinnamon than clove." She'd fed him another.

He didn't know spices at all—his mother didn't use such things—and so she'd done something special for him the next Sunday. She'd baked shortbread, each flavored with one spice. They'd stood together in their small kitchen, there in the Lock 12 village, and she'd held a bottle to Roscoe's nose: "Clove. It has a bit of bite. Now try the shortbread." He'd grinned, that smile of his breaking his whole face into joy. "Now, compare it to nutmeg." She'd held the spice jar and then offered the cookie. "Do you taste the difference?"

He did, and there—after only two—he'd pulled her to him, burying his face in her hair, squeezing her back with his great hands. "Thank you."

"There are more."

"No. Not just this. It's more than the cookie lesson." He'd brought his hands to her face. "Thank you for being here with me. Thank you for living this life."

It wasn't the first time he'd said those words, offered the same general gratitude—it wouldn't be the last either—but Marie conflated every moment into this one. At times he had gotten specific, and so Marie knew the weight his words held, the reach of their meaning. He was grateful for his own profession, his escape from his father's mines, his chance to pursue electricity, grateful for their house and their conversations and their lovemaking. Roscoe attributed every positive aspect of his life to their marriage, even the ones that had come before. He attributed too much.

But that was before Gerald was born. Afterward, their marriage accounted for little, if any, of his pleasure.

Marie left Moa and Jenny to the slicing so that she could start on the syrup. She preferred to cold-pack her peaches, putting the fruit raw into the sterilized jars, rather than submerging the fruit in the boiling syrup first. The syrup went in once the jars were full, then the lids came, then the rings. The women all took turns during the boiling, spelling each other in exchange for moments outside in the sun, the summer heat cooler than the kitchen steam, drier, even though water held tight to the air, a great humid blanket wrapped round them all season. Marie took deep breaths during her turns on the back stoop, great lungfuls of the scent-tinged air—grass and cornstalks and peanut plants, mulch and dung and mule hide. She'd grown to prefer these smells to the chalk-and-paper scent of a classroom, the tidy cleanliness.

Moa pushed out through the back screen door. She dabbed at her neck with the hem of her apron, light touches up to her jaw and then to her lips and cheeks and forehead: "Hot."

Marie smiled.

"I'm worried about you, Miss Marie."

Marie looked up at her. Moa was taller by a good six inches. "Why?"

"You're quiet even for you, and what with this electricity coming back—I don't know. I worry it's too much. Might spark too great a memory in you. Too much of Mr. Roscoe." Moa squinted when she said Roscoe's name.

Marie reached for Moa's hand. "Don't you worry about me, Miss Moa. Your boys will know what to do with that power when it comes."

Moa squeezed. "All right. But you just tell me if there's something you need."

Marie nodded. She knew her times of going to Moa with worries were done, as gone as Wilson in his mine somewhere, lost like his paperwork. She could ask nothing of this woman who'd raised her, Moa's mother role yet one more thing Roscoe had taken.

CHAPTER 18 / ROSCOE

My shoulder has mended the best it can. There was nerve damage, the doctor explained, along with a break in the clavicle. When the doctor finally unbandaged my arm, we discovered that it wouldn't move much. I can operate my hand, now, in clumsy motions, and I've convinced my arm to hang along the side of my body, but the elbow is always bent, and the whole limb no longer moves from the shoulder. The only life in it resides below the elbow, and that life is limited.

In the mornings, I eat quietly in the mess, surrounded by men. They force their way into my silence, still talking about the incident.

"Shit, Martin, I saw Beau take that club to you."

"And then a stint in the doghouse! Goddamn."

"I didn't think the warden let that kind of thing happen to his pets."

"What's it like in the infirmary? Got yourself a pretty nurse, didn't you?"

Dean is nearby, a regular in the library now that he's reading on his own, exchanging books every week, and he edges his voice louder than the others. "Let him be. Man's had enough for now."

Rash says Dean doesn't come when I'm away, and I don't know what to make of his loyalty. I help him locate books that fit his interests, but he doesn't owe me this allegiance in the mess.

"You become a pet without us knowing?" someone asks him, but Dean doesn't take it up, and the rest of the table lets it alone. I know better than to acknowledge his help here, but I'll thank him when I see him on Friday.

I drop my tray at the dish line and request the bucket they keep for the dogs. "You back out there, Martin?" the man at the sink says, reaching below the basin to pull out a pail.

I nod.

This pail is more specific now—only meat goes in, raw or cooked—with other buckets for the chickens and the pigs. Ever since I read Taylor a passage about the dangers of rancid meat, the kitchen has been filling the dog pail with fresh scraps.

I make my way to the east gate. The yard is less crowded, the previously leased men trickling away to their new prisons and camps. There is nothing to keep me hoping for Wilson's life anymore—no papers, no sightings, no presence. I can only hope that his was a quick death in his mine, and that someone took note of his name so that Moa and the kids would stop their hoping, too.

Yet another new guard is on the gate, and he lets me through with few words. The guard on the other side has been here as long as I have, and he is cordial enough.

Taylor is staring off in the direction of a couple grackles, pathetic birds with their haunting insect noise. I wave to him and go directly to the barn to start on the dogs' feeding. My shoulder doesn't exempt me from the routine of this place.

The smell of the dog room hits me strong and foul as soon as I cross inside. Taylor's other boys don't tend it quite the way I do, letting the meat linger until it's fetid.

I make my rounds to the pens, then set to filling the water buckets. Other than Taylor, I'm the only one out here, and I prefer it that way. Jackson and Jones have been gone for years. Stevens came on six months before me, and working with him is a punishment, everything that comes out of his mouth either an insult or an idiocy. He loves to be the one hitched to the dogs while I'm the one running, pride flushing him as if it were a real run, and he were a real deputy warden.

Taylor's other men aren't much better. I imagine he agrees.

Taylor is at the fence when I finish. "I've made a decision, Martin. I'm retiring Maggie to the whelping trade."

"Sir?"

"You've seen how bad some of them pups from other places turn out. Figure we can at least do better than that." He's still blaming the ruined off-lead experiment on the dog rather than his own misuse of information. "Plus, the dog's not so quick as she once was. Falling behind. One of the best I've ever had, so I figure we might well get some good stock out of her."

Maggie is just on the other side of the fence, and I reach over to tug her ears. She's my favorite of the dogs, and motherhood doesn't seem a fitting retirement. Her eyes are reticent, as though she already knows.

TAYLOR hires out the stud from another friend of his in the industry—not Atmore—and I'm forced to listen to Maggie's cries while the male's in residence. She is locked in the smallest pen with him, and she does everything she can to climb the wire walls.

Soon enough, he is gone, though, and Maggie rounds larger by the day. This is Taylor's first litter, and he's jittery as any new pa. "Read, Martin," he shouts. "You best swallow down every word you can on the subject of breeding."

I put requests in to Rash. "Dog breeding? You think I'm stocking that subject in here?"

"You know it's for Taylor."

Rash still likes to chide me, though, and the first periodical to arrive is an old copy of the *Dog Fancier* out of Battle Creek, Michigan. Rash chuckles as he hands it over.

"Well?" Taylor asks, and I must tell him that Dr. O. P. Bennett recommends stewed sheep and calf heads once the pups are born, macaroni, spaghetti, and any other noodles.

"Good Lord, Martin," Taylor shouts. He's taken to only shouting during Maggie's pregnancy. "I don't have any goddamned macaroni. What the hell do I do when the pups *come*?"

"I haven't found anything yet, sir."

Taylor rubs his belly and looks at Maggie. "I paid a chunk for that stud, Martin. I have expectations of these pups."

"I'll keep looking." I want Maggie's pups to turn out as much as he does.

I take care of Maggie—bringing food and occupying her time. Taylor lets me walk her around the outside perimeter of the wall, all those guards watching, and I often wish young Marie would join us, barefoot and blue-dressed, her hair lighter from the regular days in the sun.

I see the excitement in you, she might say. *You can't wait for these puppies to come.*

I nod, thinking those same thoughts, my eyes on Maggie's growing belly.

DOGS don't take too long to grow inside their mothers. Sixty-two days, according to *The Complete Book of the Dog*. Around day sixty, we need to give her sloppy food and some salad oil.

Finally, I find a note about whelping for Taylor. "'No help is necessary,'" I read to him, "'and one may come down in the morning to find her with her litter comfortably nestling at her side.'"

"That's as unhelpful as the damn noodles," Taylor shouts. "What in the hell are you talking about, Martin?"

"It means Maggie'll do just fine all on her own."

Taylor looks out over his pack of dogs. Maggie lies near the north edge of her pen, barely the animal she was. Her stomach is a giant protrusion, spiked with her dropping nipples, and she waggles the way Marie did with Gerald.

"Is she close?" Taylor asks.

"By my count."

"We best separate her, then."

Her new pen has a shed in the back, a small protection from rain when it falls, built up on rough beams atop stone squares.

"She'll go in there to have them," Taylor says. "I'll get us some old blankets from the laundry."

But Maggie isn't answering her master's orders, now. Two days later, she's nowhere to be seen, and only the mewling gives her away. She's burrowed under the shed on the back side where we couldn't see her digging. When I squat low to peer in, I can see the rise of her head and back, bony shoulders and haunches. The rest of her lies deep in a curved bed, dirt and wood obscuring her body and the puppies she must have birthed overnight. I can't see even one of them, but they are noisy little things, bawling like kittens. Gerald sounded this way, only louder—bigger lungs and mouth.

"Hey there, girl," I say to Maggie.

When I lie on my side on the ground, right up next to the rough wood, my good arm is just long enough to reach her head. There's not room for my face under there, so I go by feel, trying to pet her, to give those dangling ears of hers a gentle tug. I'm wanting my hand to say, *You've done good work, here. You are a good dog.* I'm looking to comfort this new mother, to ease the terror she must be trembling under with all that need sucking at her belly.

"Martin! What in the hell you doing on the ground back there?"

My boots must be all Taylor can see, sticking out from the side of the shed, boots and ankles and dirty cuffs.

I run my fingers over Maggie's head once more and pull my hand out.

"You hear that?" I ask, coming round.

Taylor tips his ear to his shoulder and squints. His hands rest on the wooden rail of the fence, and I can see the blood sucking from his knuckles with the force of his squeezing. He is always pushing the red out of some part of him, gathering it back to his massive heart, extra reserves for the next run.

"That the pups?" he asks, but he does not need an answer. His wide mouth pushes out into a smile I've never seen, and he releases the wooden rail in favor of a few flat-palmed slaps, a child's joy in his hands and face. "How many are there? What's the bitch-to-male count? What's their color? All red like Maggie? Or some of that black and tan from the stud? They healthy? Any runts?"

"I've no idea, sir. She's dug herself under the shed there. I haven't gotten a look at the pups at all."

The mirth leaves him quick as it came. "Now, why'd she do that, the damn dog? Those blankets are good enough for you men, and she's turning her nose at 'em?" He lifts the sagging gate to get it clear of the dirt. The hinges are about done. I'm sure he'll have me framing out a new one any day. "Where's she at?"

I lead him round the back, and it's a worry to see him crouching down. I keep as much a distance as I can, but I can't close my ears to his grunts and curses, laboring to haul that body around.

"Well, goddamn," he finally says, belly balanced on one of his knees. "I can't see a goddamned thing." He lifts himself from the ground the way he pours himself into the saddle—fluid and easy. "You got to dig this out, Martin. Get us a line to those pups."

"From what I've read," I venture, "it'd be good to let them alone for a few days."

He points his eyes at me. "You running this show now, Martin? You the new deputy warden?"

I know not to answer, so we stand quiet for a bit, Maggie's pups keeping up their racket in their den.

"What's it we're supposed to do for the bitch?" Taylor asks.

"Broth. And sloppy food. Not too much at the start here. In a day or two, we need to get her a little exercise. Helps keep the milk up." I have been reading.

He looks down at the raw dirt under our feet, recently turned by Maggie's paws. He toes a clod, then kicks it toward the wire fencing. "Let her rest till tomorrow. Then you start digging this out. Be good for her to have an easy run in and out, too. You head over to the mess and get us some broth, now. Make her up a slew with the bonemeal and all."

"Sir," I say, and make toward the gate.

I start early. The days are long and sun-hot, the corn high. I'd like to have my digging done before noon. Taylor's good about giving me shade breaks with water and food, but there is no escaping a midday sun in early July. It drops closer to the land, these interminable days of summer, hovering just above our heads, a great round furnace. This low sun turns every lick of water to steam, even the fresh-pumped drinks in our mess-issued bottles. The sun bakes those metal canteens, boiling the liquid inside, and we chase our thirst with water so hot it burns our tongues.

This is the season Maggie's pups have been born into. They will learn how to pant before they open their eyes.

Maggie crawls out when I get there. There's still slop in the bowl I left her last night, and a bucket of water, and she goes after each with fury. She has transformed again, yet another dog I've never seen. Her spine ridges out of her back, jointed and sharp, and her ribs show through her skin. All that remains of her belly are the sagging red teats that hang from her like the Guernseys' udders. She curls her tail between her hind legs.

I set to work with the hoe, my left arm fronting the work. On my fourth drag, I wrest loose the hardened remains of a giant rat. Its body is still intact, the skin stretched tight and hard over the bones, something in the soil preserving it this way, rather than eating it back into dirt. The claws are long and yellowed, and the teeth are the same color, jagged extrusions from the sunken skull. The nose is a hard, blackened ball atop them, the whiskers like blackened string. The tail coils toward the hind legs, spiraling in on itself like a pig's.

Maggie comes to inspect. She brings her nose close to the body and huffs loudly, sending dust into the air. She raises her head to me, indifference on her face. The rat is so past life, it doesn't register as anything more than ground, something to dig loose in the making of a den. I scoop it up with its surrounding dirt and deposit it in the wheelbarrow.

Maggie paws at the ground. I've blocked her way in.

"Give me a minute, girl." I chain her while I finish. "Wait."

She won't listen, pulling against her chain.

Finally, I have the trench dug, and with one of Taylor's spurned blankets against my side, I belly-crawl my way under the shed. The ground is cool and rich as turned soil in the spring, the scent and lick of short winter days bound up in that dirt, seeping out with every fresh turning until the high-summer sun parches the rows dry.

The warmth of the puppies crowds my face.

It's difficult to bring an arm round the front of me, a hand to close round these small, whimpering beasts. A muscle near my right shoulder blade squeezes itself tight in protest, a stiff cramp that takes my breath. In the movement, my head strikes the sharp edge of a shed beam, hard enough to bring blood. There is no reason to remove these dogs from this space. But, still, I load them one by one onto the blanket, their round bellies and tiny ribs stirring the pain from my back and arm. I grope in the semidark to be sure I've collected them all, my hand running over the round nest, its edges gone dry with age. Maggie is a mess of noise by my feet.

"Here we come," I tell her.

The pups are tiny things, half the size of the rat I found, and lighter in color than their mother. Their heads are golden tan, their snouts dark and wrinkled. Their ears are the size of my thumbnails, small flaps on the sides of their heads, not even to their lips, though I know they will dangle to their shoulders once they've grown. They squirm and writhe in their pile, a crawling mass of need, hungry.

I carry them into the shed and set Maggie free. "They're right in here."

The doorway is large and open, the pups easy to see, but Maggie returns to the burrow, laying her body flat to edge back under. Marie once told me about particular birds that won't accept their offspring once they've taken on the scent of humans. This surely can't apply to bloodhounds, these animals we've bred to serve us, but I'm worried all the same.

Maggie scratches and paws under the shed. I hear her moving under there, the shuffle of her breath.

I know these pups won't hold without her. I think of the chapters—"Orphaned Pups," "Hand-Feeding Pups," "Whelping Your Own Pups"—we will need goat's milk and bottles. And even if we get them to eat, we will still lose several. That's what the books say. I will not be able to tell Taylor it's his fault, that we should've left the dogs alone. I'm fearing their deaths already, fearing the regret and guilt that is building in my stomach, in my back, in the cut on my head, the hardening blood in my hair.

But then Maggie emerges, the nape of a pup's neck held tight in her teeth. She passes me without care or notice, returning the lost pup to the others in their pile. She digs at the blankets and encircles the pups, a wall of a house. They crawl to her teats and settle into eating—all seven. Alive, and their mother, too, this dog in all her transformations, she is still there, whole, and the thought makes me ache for Marie, going again to that Saturday morning in March when Gerald was born in our marriage bed, in our village house, the resident doctor there to catch him.

The boy was slippery and bloody, and the doctor handed him directly to me. "He'll go to his mama soon enough. We just need to do a little cleanup here. Why don't you take the child out to the kitchen, Roscoe?"

The babe's eyes were squeezed shut and he was wrinkly as an old man. I dampened a rag at the sink and set to removing the junk from his face. It made him howl.

"Shush," I whispered, trying to rock him in my arms. I didn't know how to do it—how to soothe anything that small.

I worried about Marie hearing the noise and insisting on rushing through whatever the doctor had to do, so I took the baby outside into the clear spring day, a more fortunate time to be born than July. I stood on our small front porch, hoping for a woman to hear the baby's noise and come to my aid.

Nettie Williams, our next-door neighbor, came within minutes.

"Oh, Lord! The baby's come!" she shouted. "Let me see the little thing."

I was happy to settle him into her arms.

"Why he's not even cleaned up yet. Has something gone wrong?"

"No." The thought hadn't occurred to me at all.

But Nettie Williams gave the baby back quickly. "The babe's ruddy and loud, sure enough healthy. I'll go inside and see about that bride of yours."

In that moment, I wasn't concerned for Marie, only for this wailing thing in my arms, this sloppy infant in need. I settled into the one rocker we had, its joints squeaking under my weight, and I bent the pointer finger on my left hand so that his small mouth could close round the knuckle, far less dirty than the fingertip. As soon as my knuckle met his mouth, he stopped his fit and sucked away contentedly at my empty skin.

Marie was far from us then. And we were far from her.

And now Maggie is here in this shed with her seven pups, all of them in need of nothing from me.

"ONE of the females is missing," Taylor says to me on the pups' eighth day. He sets me to searching, and eventually I find it along the east side of the run where the grasses grow tall, winding their way through the wire, creeping along the edge of the dirt, hearty enough to thrive in this dog-heavy ground. Midway down, the dog's small head rises barely higher than the dirt, slightly covered by grass tufts. It's in a hole Maggie must have dug.

The warmth of the pup's body tells me it's not yet dead, and when I bring its head to my ear, I can make out its breath, weak and ratty. It is too light, and its head cocks to the side, something wrong in its jaw that I hadn't noticed before. It needs to die, so I press my palm against its snout, the shortest fight left, a tiny reach of the legs, a shake in the neck—not enough to constitute a struggle.

I return it to its hole and shout for Taylor.

"Maggie must've known," he says.

I dig the pup's grave right where Maggie started it, deep enough to keep out the scavengers.

Maggie walks outside into the sun, off to a corner to relieve herself. Her spine ridges out of her back in a notched line, her ribs tracing down her sides between deep furrows. Her tail is tucked between her legs, her ears dragging on the ground. Those long ears are dusty, all that silk gone gummy like horsehide under a saddle. Whelping doesn't suit her, and I wish I could free her from it. She should be tracking someone down. She should be tied to my waist, straining and braying, those ears scooping a convict's scent toward her nose. Ears like that have a job to do, and it has nothing to do with nursing pups.

Taylor tells me to spend the remainder of my day in the library. "Go on over to your books, Martin. Get your mind someplace else. That dirt'll be dry come tomorrow."

"I haven't worked the other dogs yet."

"Get." His hand finds its way to my good shoulder. "Go on. I'll expect you early tomorrow."

I leave the barn with its smells of bone and leather, and I walk that red dirt back to the wall, where I'm let through with little notice. The yard is quiet, every man off to his job, and I'm taken by the loneliness of the place. I pass the chapel on my way to the library, and Chaplain is out front. He's watering the flowers he's planted. I suppose we need flowers.

"Roscoe, what brings you here?" He is crouching down, the silliest watering can in his hand, a miniature thing, fit for a child.

"On my way to the library."

"Taylor gave you a day off?"

"We lost one of Maggie's pups."

Chaplain sighs, a deep, heavy breath that shakes his frame, then he holds the watering can out toward me, and like a fool, I take it. He goes inside his church without saying anything. He has disappeared before I realize he's going, and I'm alone with that dog in a hole behind me and this watering can in my hands and these unnamed flowers at my feet.

This is Kilby Prison. We exercise in a dusty yard. Around it, a high wall is strung with wire, and in that wire is electricity, enough electricity to kill me and George Haskin and anyone, more than they run through Yellow Mama. Listen. Electricity so strong, you can hear it. A chapel is here, and our chaplain has planted flowers. They are red and blue, and because I do not know their names, I feel that they are foreign. They are not Alabama's flowers. But they are ours.

CHAPTER 19

Nothing precipitated Wilson's arrival—no letter from the state that had sold him or the mining company that had leased him. Wilson was gone, and then one day he was standing on the front porch.

Marie and Gerald were returning from their lessons in Rockford.

"Who's that?" Gerald asked.

Marie squinted her eyes. "Charles?"

Gerald shook his head. "Too tall."

They kept walking, pecan shells under their feet. Marie's mind filled up with the crunching and cracking, the sharper moments when a shell caught the sole of her shoe in a way that nearly pierced the leather. She could almost feel the pain it would cause. A great hope was in her, something growing like a child in her stomach. She knew that frame and height, familiar as the land around her, familiar as her father's house. She wouldn't let herself look at the porch again, though, wouldn't allow herself another glance until her sight would be clear and solid.

Gerald started hollering when they were about ten yards from the house, his now-long legs sprinting him forward and up those peeling porch steps. Marie tried not to hear the name her son was shouting until she was there, right next to him.

"Wilson."

Gerald stepped away.

Marie saw Wilson's arm, but she brought herself forward first, letting herself ignore it for the moment of his holding her, brief and chaste. Marie had put her arms around Wilson on so few occasions—the birth of Charles, her own father's death—that they kept them light and quick. Maybe it was history pressing on them, the deep color-divided lines of their state, but maybe it was just their nature, neither of them in need of lengthy contact. Marie liked to assume the latter.

She stepped back to see Wilson fully. She closed her eyes, the picture sharp in her mind, projected against the backs of her eyelids. There was Wilson—tall and broad, a denim shirt tight across his shoulders, one sleeve of it flowing down to his right hand, the other sleeve cut short at the elbow. His left forearm was gone, the wrist and hand. Those fingers that he'd always had, capable of such work, gripping and turning and lifting—they no longer existed.

"It's all right." Wilson placed his one hand on Marie's shoulder. "I've made my peace with it."

"How?"

"It got me out of the mines."

"You shouldn't have been in the mines in the first place."

Wilson smiled. "That's a matter of opinion, Miss Marie."

Marie heard Moa's voice: "Wilson?" His name was a question, not that of a person standing there on the porch. His name was of a ghost, something as dead as his arm, something looking for its place. Moa didn't move from behind the screen, and Marie watched her eyes rove over her husband, taking in the hair cropped close to the scalp, the new scar lines on his neck and cheek and remaining hand, the same wide-open face, and then the sleeve rolled and pinned where his left arm used to hinge.

"Oh." Moa rushed from the house. She grabbed Wilson by the neck and covered his face with her lips, every centimeter, every ridge and dip—eyes, brows, nose, cheeks, lips, temples, forehead, lips again. And again. "Oh, Wilson." She gasped his name like air.

Then, Moa moved her attention to the remains of his arm. She gripped the biceps under its cotton, and Marie watched her fingers exploring whatever muscle and bone must be left there. Moa felt down to the pinned roll, and Marie found herself curious about what the flesh must feel like, puckered and swollen and scarred.

"I went to our place," Wilson was saying to Moa, "but no one was there, and I was trying to figure how to knock on this door when Gerald and Miss Marie came up the drive." It wasn't their place to have seen him first.

Moa put her hand on Wilson's shortened arm.

"This is Roscoe's fault," Marie said, already starting new blame, replacing the unconfirmed knowledge of Wilson in a dark mine shaft with this new, fragmented man in front of her. Roscoe had done this. He had employed Wilson in his crooked work, and he had left him to the destruction of greedy coal miners and foremen, to the self-serving hand of the State, selling off its convicted men for pennies. Roscoe was the new face of convict leasing, the new villain and perpetrator. He was the foreman, the owner, the coal itself, hunkering deep in the earth, hard to reach, tempting and tempted, looking for a fiery explosion to set it free.

"Now, Ms. Marie," Wilson said. "I knew what I was doing."

Moa spoke over them. "Come inside. Let's all go inside. I'll make us some coffee, and you can tell us what's happened. Oh, my love. Oh."

Gerald stepped forward—Marie had forgotten him for a moment, hidden back behind Wilson—and she caught him by the arm. "Go find Charles and Henry, and Jenny. Get them to come to the house."

"Yes, ma'am."

Marie trailed behind as Moa led Wilson to the kitchen. Moa held that shadowed arm as though the rest of it might disappear should she let go. Marie could see it—the slow disintegration of this incomplete man. First, that stranded biceps and its shoulder would go, then the chest and neck, the evaporation traveling down at a quicker rate, taking his stomach and hips, his thighs and knees and shins, his ankles and feet, and then his face would dissolve, one feature at a time: chin, lips, cheeks—all those places Moa had just kissed—gone. They wouldn't be able to tell whether he'd been there to begin with, or whether they'd simply wished him there, conjuring him out of their great need.

Wilson sat on a stool at the butcher-block table, and only then did Moa let loose of him. She went to get the percolator from the stove, and Marie stopped her before she made it to the sink. "Sit with Wilson. I'll make the coffee."

Moa relinquished the pot without a word, but didn't sit. Instead, she pulled his great head against her chest, the fingers of one hand turning small circles along his temple and forehead, up into his hairline and then back down. Her fingers had turned the same circles on Marie's back when Marie was a little girl, stranded in the dark of her room after her mother's death—night was the only time the hurt could control her. "There, there," Moa would say. "Hush, now." She'd coax young Marie back down to lying, then trace her long fingers in slow circles up and down Marie's small back. Marie had spent her childhood falling asleep to that touch, and she remembered it stronger than any specific intimacy she'd shared with her mother.

The Grice children came in while the water was heating, all three of them falling over themselves to get at their father, all three of them letting out the same remorseful wail upon seeing the missing arm. "No," they said, and "Papa." Marie watched Wilson's family encircle him, all of them pressing into him, their words split between joy and lamentation, excitement and anger.

Gerald came to stand next to Marie by the stove. She wanted him to lean against her shoulder or press himself against her as he once had. She wanted him to take her hand or link his arm through hers. Anything. Any small touch to help her feel the presence of her own family, to let her think she had some semblance of the scene in front of her, some bit of that same devotion. But Gerald kept a foot's distance between them, and when he spoke, his interest wasn't in her.

"Does this mean Pa's coming, too?"

"No."

"Why not?"

"He has a longer sentence."

"Wilson didn't have to stay for his whole sentence."

The Grices continued their praising and cursing, their holding and squeezing. They had become one mass, the children and Moa fusing Wilson to them, guaranteeing his place.

"Mama," Gerald said, "I want to visit him."

Marie shook her head.

"He's my father."

Marie turned to the percolator behind her, bubbling at its lid.

"I'm going to write to him," Gerald continued, "and tell him you're the reason I haven't written before. And you're going to let me read his letters."

Marie tried to find words, something to say to convince Gerald of his mistake. Her mouth was sticky, though, every word catching in the dry pull of her gums, the trap of her tongue. She couldn't say anything. She could only pour coffee into mugs.

"Mother," Gerald insisted. He was closer to her than he'd been in more than a year, his mouth next to her cheek, his breath on her skin. He had a boy's breath, still, a smell like autumn soil, dry and sweet, but he stood inches taller than her, his pants too short before they'd been broken in, his shirts too tight across his widening shoulders, his sleeves hanging silly inches above his wrists. He was nearly twelve.

"No." *Look at Wilson,* Marie wanted to say. *Look at what's left of his arm. Look at the scars on his one hand and the broken weight in his face. Your father did that. He is no one you want to know.*

Gerald brought his fists down on the countertop, rattling the mugs, sloshing coffee over their edges into shallow pools.

"Gerald, honey," Moa said. "What is it?"

"Nothing, Miss Moa." He ducked his head and went to the back door, stopping there to look at Wilson. "I'm glad you're back."

"Thank you, son."

"Gerald," Marie called. "Wait, love."

But Gerald was out the door.

"He missin' his father?" Wilson asked.

Marie pressed her hand against her eyes and tucked her chin. "Yes," she whispered.

"How often have you been to visit?"

Marie looked up to see Moa whispering in Wilson's ear. She was brief, and Marie watched Wilson take in his wife's words. What would he think of Marie's decision to stay away? She wanted Wilson to see the solidarity in it, the defense of his side, the anger and pain and resentment she felt for Roscoe. But he could just as easily see her as an angry, self-indulgent woman, flaunting her privilege to make that choice. Moa had been left with nothing—no information, no location, no letters—while Marie had been given everything. She knew Roscoe's employment at Kilby, his cellmates, his librarian and deputy warden and barn foreman. She knew how easy it would be to schedule a visit, and that they could even request an afternoon furlough because of Roscoe's good behavior. She could come with a picnic and they could eat together in the oak grove Roscoe had described in his letters, just as Eddings had suggested that day he took Roscoe away.

Would Wilson see her as petty and vindictive, worse, even, than the man who'd gotten them all there?

"Boy's missin' his father," Wilson said again. "How're you doing, Miss Marie?"

"I'm doing fine, Wilson, just fine." She appreciated his turning the subject away from her own guilt. "But you, can you talk about your time?"

Wilson brought his hand to the top of his head, rubbing the short bristles there, the black peppered with white. He'd always rubbed his head when confronted with a question he wasn't sure of answering, and Marie smiled at the habit, something familiar and comforting.

"What do you already know?" he asked, looking between Marie and Moa, asking them both.

"Nothing," they said together.

Marie continued, "You disappeared after Kilby. Our lawyer couldn't track down any records of where you went."

"Probably for the best. Visiting wasn't allowed in our camp, and those lost papers were what set me loose." Wilson kept his hand on his head, then he reached down for his cup of coffee, sipping at it delicately. "Ah. Missed that taste, sure enough." He kept the mug near his mouth and talked over the steam. "Intake was fast, there at Kilby. They're supposed to do this *thorough study*, they said, taking down our history and poking into our brains and getting at our deep thoughts, but for me, they just asked what it was I'd been doing for work, and then they said mining made the most sense. 'Flat Top's in need of men right now,' the fellow said. 'It'll keep you out of prison, keep you fit.'

"They shipped me out the next day. I got trained quick to be part of the crew that came in right after the first blast." Wilson set his mug down and set to rubbing his head again. "Suppose that's about it. I worked down in the tunnels until this happened"—he raised the stump of his left arm—"and then I spent time in the infirmary, and then they sent me home."

Moa had her hands on his shoulders while he talked, and Marie watched her fingers knead the muscle there. Their children flanked her. "That's enough," she said. She leaned down and kissed him on the head. "I'm so glad you're here."

Marie was frustrated with Moa's shushing. She wanted to know everything about Wilson's time in those tunnels. She needed the specifics—the sounds and textures and tastes, coal-dusted air and explosion-shattered rock, the damp floors and kerosene lanterns, the black-edged sky and housing and meals. "Wilson, what was it like?"

"He's said enough," Moa warned.

Their children stared at Marie, their eyes lit by Moa's same protection. *He's ours,* their faces said, their lips held firm, their eyes open wide. *You and yours have taken enough.*

Marie agreed.

Wilson set his mug down and looked over at Marie. "It was awful, Miss Marie. If you need more than that, you'll have to give me time."

Marie nodded, ashamed. "Of course."

Moa leaned her head down close to Wilson's ear and said gently, "Let's go on back to our place, dear."

Marie watched Jenny and Charles and Henry swarm their father, lifting him from his chair, floating him into standing. They moved as a unit, gliding across Marie's floor with the ease of birds—a flock of them, or a wing; they were like plovers moving over the sand, their steps smooth and fluid. They drifted out the door and out across the grass, disappearing from Marie's sight around the corner of the house. She imagined them taking flight just then, tucking their quick feet up against their soft stomachs, stretching their wings—Wilson's left would be back, a broad, feathered limb to replace that half-held arm—arching their necks to the clouds. They would fly over the hot-hearted power lines and the thick stand of longleaf pines and holly, glancing out at the fields, the patched grid of their land, and then they would slow their speed, dropping down to the small meadow outside their small house—everything small—and they would gather together in their clutch, moving as one toward the door.

Marie thought about her son, that small boy born into so much blood and wreckage, his own swaddling blanket more for mopping than for warmth. There he was, sticky with blood, passed over to Roscoe while the doctor focused on Marie, and Marie turned inward, a quiet taking over the room she shared with her husband. The quiet had been like fog, she remembered, creeping in at the edges of her hearing, muting it; the baby's crying was buffered and blanketed by flannel and cotton, thick sounds settling over everything—the doctor's hurried words, desperate and pleading, the metal-on-metal ringing of his instruments, the nurse he employed, her shoes on the floor, moving and clacking—all of it quieted down to a slow-drumming pulse, the like of river currents or tides, a rumbling, deeply tied rhythm.

She'd awoken days later in a Birmingham hospital room. Roscoe was there, but not the baby.

"Did we lose him?" she'd asked, reaching for her husband's hand.

"No, no. He's fine. Nettie's caring for him while you heal."

Marie had looked down her body then, the flattening of her waist. She felt the deep aching of her stomach, and her fingers went to the skin, tiptoeing their way under blanket and gown to spread over the great bandages there.

"What's happened?"

Roscoe had looked pained, a clotted hurt hanging on to his cheeks. "I'll get the doctor," he'd said, and though she'd argued, reaching for him, calling him back, he'd left her. He'd passed the burden of that news to someone else, and she'd taken the abandonment deep inside her, a crackly burden like the plants of peanuts or stalks of corn left alone to dry and harden in the absence of their fruit. She could still feel that place, dusty and brittle. It had never refilled.

Marie remembered the doctor's sallow complexion and tawny hair, his amber eyes and yellowed teeth. He was troubling to look at, and Marie had found her eyes roving far from his face—to the ceiling and then to the window, back to his white coat, a glance to his chin, and then away again.

"Mrs. Martin, your local doctor did great work. You were lucky to be in such qualified hands."

She'd looked at his chin, the bristles of his sun-dried beard.

"You're healing wonderfully."

"From what?"

He'd put a sickly hand on her forearm. "I'm sorry, Mrs. Martin, but there were complications with your son's birth—damage done to your uterus." His fingers squeezed her. "We had to remove it."

Marie felt the pressure of his touch, but couldn't register his words. Roscoe's desertion fluttered in her stomach, cornstalks in a breeze, the crisped, itchy dance of dried leaves. It grew wider, more furrows, a great stretch of field.

"What?"

He pressed down, then took his hand away completely. "You won't be able to have any more children. I'm very sorry. Would you like me to send your husband back in?"

Marie had trained her eyes on the window, the bright sky bleached nearly to white by the sun. "No," she'd whispered.

The loss of their future children had set them apart, moved them into their respective corners, far from each other's touch. They couldn't move together as Wilson's family did, even if they had tried. The brief years of ease when Roscoe had run his illegal electricity had been false. She had to have known they'd crumble in some way, their future torn from them again. She'd known, and she held this knowledge alongside her own part in it. Unlike Moa and Wilson, she was not innocent. They had taken pieces of each other—Marie and Roscoe—but now they had taken a piece of Wilson. They had taken a part of his family.

Sitting in the silence of her empty kitchen, Marie wanted to talk to Roscoe. She wanted to show him all they owed—to the Grices, to the land, to each other, to their son.

Here, she wanted to say to him, *tell me how we repay this.*

CHAPTER 20 / ROSCOE

I'm pacing the yard when the sirens start blazing, and I know to run to the pens. Taylor is there, and Stevens, and a fellow named Michaels.

"Those two," Taylor says, pointing to the far cage. Jack and Jesper.

"Hey, Jack," I say. "Hey, Jesper." To Taylor I say, "Where's the scent start?"

"Corn. Northwest corner. You boys start with the dogs. I'm getting my horse."

We set off. Taylor catches up just before we reach the first rows of corn. He whips his mount forward, and we chase after them— man and horse—until we get to the field guard. He holds the man's bushel bag, and those dogs settle their noses into the burlap, huffing their lips, flushing the scent, those big ears trapping it in their faces. My two lift their heads first and point toward the woods.

The dogs are faster than me, and they buck against my weight. Their voices pitch. They pause to recharge the scent. Here, in this bunch of grasses. There, on that twig. Here, in this fresh footfall in the muddy mess of ground near Cobbs Creek. The dogs try to break from each other, and from me, moving up and down the small bank, but then Jesper splashes into the shallow water, and we follow. The scent is right there, another footprint, and then just ghosting smells. My calves burn. My lungs heave. My emaciated shoulder and arm whine. All of this is too familiar.

We pass the possum oak, and a part of me wants to be chased again, to climb back into its branches, though I know I couldn't do it now, that I will never again climb a tree.

Stevens and his dogs are still with me.

Taylor's horse splashes through the water. "I'm following you two," Taylor shouts. "Michaels's dogs are heading a different way. Feels like we're close on this one."

The dogs don't tell me that, though. They change when they're close, their muscles tighter, something steep and tense in their steps. We have a ways to go, their bodies tell me now. Taylor is loud behind us, and suddenly that young Marie falls in at my right. She darts along quickly, her breath calm and even.

The dogs pause for new tastes, then run some more. The leather belt round my waist cuts into my back. The damp I feel could be sweat or blood, warm and cold.

Stevens falls back a bit, but Taylor's horse is in my ears, the soft felt of the thing's muzzle drenched in froth flying from its lips, drawn back against the bit and the breath it heaves. "Hup," Taylor shouts. "Hup, hup!" That breath goes sour, grasses rotting in its guts.

I hear a whisper to watch out. *Marie?*

"Hup!" Taylor shouts once more, before a great stumble of limbs crashes down, branches breaking under that fortress, sticks crumbling. The horse's chest hits the ground, then its neck, jaw, lips, nose. The body plows up the dirt, mulch and rubble hitting me. I pull the dogs to a stop, watching as Taylor picks himself up. A gash in his arm drains blood. Another guard comes up behind him, and I'm surprised to see that it's Beau. He's gotten here so quickly.

"Go," Taylor shouts at both of us. "I'm behind you. Go."

The dogs start pulling. They are disappointed to have stopped at all.

Beau runs next to me, and Marie is next to him, silent and intent. I can feel the nervousness in her, and I hope that Beau's desire to catch this man who's run trumps his desire to do me further harm.

Then we are there. We are here. It's nothing more than a shack, this structure, a forgotten still house, tired boards holding a rusty roof. The dogs are keen on the door. They're sure. I see it in them, that deep-pressured force.

There's snuffling behind us, and then Stevens appears behind his dogs.

"You!" Beau points to Stevens. "Give your dogs to Martin and go pound on that door."

Fear pales Stevens's face, but he unhooks his dogs' leads from his belt and helps fasten them to mine. I'm up to five beasts now, and it's too many. They'll kill me in their pursuit, I know.

"Get up there, boy," Beau hisses, slinking back toward the cover of the woods, his gun poised.

Stevens walks up to the shack and raises his fist, pounding it hard against the doorframe, the door too weak to sustain such a blow. Around me, the woods shake. We've made our way from the oaks into this thicket of pine, tall and red-barked.

"Boy!" Beau barks. "You best come on out without a stir." He is all but invisible in the undergrowth.

A scrambling comes from inside, a whine of metal, a scrape. Stevens is turning his head over his shoulder in Beau's direction when the door pulls back. A man named Hughes stands in the doorway. He's a regular in the library, like Dean, and he likes books about machines—the cotton gin, the engine, the letterpress. He's tall, thick in the shoulder and waist, with eyes too big for his face— fearful eyes that put a man to apology or confession, eyes fit for a leader, not a runner. He has a shotgun in his hands, held low at his hip. Before there's time enough to note its gauge, Stevens is on the ground, a great chunk gone from his right side.

The sound from him comes from everywhere at once: the suck and yaw of his body, the moan of skin and bone, of hidden guts meeting air, of a body draining. The sound from his mouth is a quiet whisper, barely more than breath.

Hughes looks down. "Shit. Didn't mean that for you, brother."

Stevens keeps at his noise, and Hughes looks up at me. I'm waiting for Beau's gun to fire.

"I'm not looking to shoot you, Books."

"I'm not looking to get shot."

The dogs are quiet, their eyes fixed on the barrel. Metal is a convincing master.

There's no movement, no sound from Beau's position.

"Where's the guard that's with you?" Hughes asks.

"Ran off," I say, buying Beau more time.

Hughes smiles. "They're all mice at heart." He looks down at Stevens. "What's he saying?"

I push through my dogs and crouch by Stevens's head, my ear close to his mouth. His side is so different from Jennings's, and I see clearly that he is dying. I know it by the sound and color. He won't make nightfall. He won't leave this spot of ground. He won't pass Taylor's horse a few miles back.

" 'Lord.' He's just saying, 'Lord,' over and over."

I'm more scared of my proximity to it than of the death itself.

Stevens is pale, the ground around him dark.

Where the hell is Beau?

My dogs don't know what to do. They're not so used to the smell of blood.

"I can't go back." Hughes steps over the mess of Stevens.

I move myself a few feet away from him, opening up a clean line for Beau to fire. He has to do it now.

Don't, I hear in a voice like Marie's—she's here again, among the trees.

Hughes's gun is back in its spot at his hip. "You best stay right there."

"They're going to catch you."

"That may be, but for now, I'm going. That all right with you, Books?"

I nod.

"You hold those dogs back."

"All right."

He runs then, sprinting his long legs in the opposite direction of Beau's hiding spot. The branches make a ruckus for a bit, snaps and shouts. He won't make it far.

"Beau!" I shout, but no sound answers me.

Don't you want him to escape? Marie asks, appearing now at my side.

"No," I tell her, realizing as I say it that it's true. Though I know him and have never wished him ill, I want Hughes caught. I want to see him fail in his flight. This is the closest I can come to freedom within the world of my confinement—seeing another man's freedom captured.

This isn't a great loss, Marie is saying of Stevens.

"I know." What does it say that I want Hughes apprehended and don't so much mind Stevens's harm? Have I finally and completely cast my lot with the prison, rather than the prisoners? Have I stitched my prison coat to my skin, the fibers fusing to my body, the two things blended so thoroughly they'll never come free of each other?

Where is Beau?

"Marie, I'm scared."

Her face is sad, and our woods are full of noise. Sounds arrive from the way we came, pounding feet and shouting voices, horse hooves, more dogs. My own start whining.

The warden himself makes our spot of land first, high up on his chestnut gelding, the handsomest of the prison herd. "Christ. Jesus Christ. What's this, Martin?"

Tell him it was you, Marie whispers.

"Martin!" the warden shouts.

Marie disappears, but I hear her words still, granting me guilt, handing me the burden of Stevens's body on the ground. If I take it, I sever my ties with the warden and Taylor, Chaplain and Rash. I become worse than Reed and his knife, than Hicks and Boyd and Vincent, worse than Beau even. If I claim this, I walk

myself to a single cell outside Yellow Mama's room, and I wait
to meet her.

Is that where I should go, Marie?

"Martin!" the warden shouts again. "Who the hell did this?"

Me. I did. Though everyone would know I'm lying, know I have
no gun, no motive, but still—it was me. Bind my wrists and walk
me back to prison. Strap me to Ed's chair. Bring me my electricity.

I will the words to my mouth. *Me. I did this. I'm working with
Hughes. We had it planned.* And then I say, "Hughes. He was hiding
inside. The dogs led us here. Beau had Stevens go to the door."

Just as I say it, Beau rises from the brush, leaves clinging to the
arms of his uniform. "Man turned his gun on me next, sir. It was
all I could do to dive out of its range."

The dogs whine.

"Hush your goddamned dogs," the warden says to me, and I do.

Beau has become a coward before us, shamed and disgraced.

The warden kneels at Stevens's white face. The man's lips still
move, but his body has grown quiet.

"You're not going to make this one," the warden says. "Take
your shirt off, Martin. Cover the man's insides, at least."

I pull off my shirt and lay it flat over the shiny mess of Stevens's
stomach. The fabric soaks up the blood, and mosquitoes make
quick for my exposed skin. The dog belt digs deeper into its rut in
my back. My ribs show too much, my stomach a caved thing under
its puckered scar. It feels disrespectful to be standing so naked in
front of a dying man.

Guards arrive, and Michaels, winded behind his leads. They
stare at Stevens and the warden. They're as lost as my dogs. Beau
still stands half in his bushes.

Taylor finally comes.

"Lucky your horse tripped, old man," the warden says. "Seeing
as you like to deliver the knock, would've been you lying here."

Taylor must know the truth in this; Beau, too.

"Let him lie here until he's gone," the warden says to the guards.

"Then put him on a horse. It was Hughes that did this. Big fellow. You guys know him. Start that chase again, fellows. Martin, you and this other one"—the warden points to Michaels—"get those dogs back on the scent. I'll be behind you." He signals out a young guard. "Head on back to the grounds and let them know what's going on. And fetch the chaplain, and a crew to take care of that horse."

"Sir," the man says.

My shirt has gone red.

Beau comes closer. "I'll go with the dogs, sir."

"You'll stay with this man," the warden booms. "And you'll escort his body back to the prison, and then you'll take a seat on one of those benches outside my office and wait as long as you have to until I'm done with this."

"Yes, sir."

Michaels and I step inside the shack to get the dogs' noses on the smell again—there on that rag, here on the floor. They catch and bray, yipping and pulling.

How is it I am running again? Stevens is dying or dead behind me, and Beau has been publicly shamed, but everything else is as it was. Men leave trails behind them. They run from dogs that only want a chase. Branches bend to our weight, sticks break under our boots. My legs ache and my back, yet I am still harnessed to these beasts, my own and Stevens's, all five of them. I have lost my stomach and leg to scars, my arm to ruin, my collarbone to a permanent cave.

No matter the changes in me, they will keep me running. Taylor will keep me searching through books for him. Rash will keep me shelving. Chaplain will keep me reading to his flock before their suppers. This place will take pieces of me, chunks and bites, until I am Stevens, filling someone else's shirt with blood.

IT'S dark by the time the dogs stop. They've led us to a weather-beaten house on the Alabama River, right near its start—the state's river flowing out of the marriage of the Coosa and the Tallapoosa. The house can't hold more than a room or two. Lamplight glows from its square windows. The warden climbs down from his horse and guards stake out their positions in the surrounding brush. Michaels and I are told to keep our dogs quiet and out of the way. We separate to keep them calmer, and I find myself alone in the trees.

The people inside must know we're there, but they're making no sign of it.

The warden steps up on the tilting, craggy porch to deliver that great Alabama Department of Corrections knock on the door, followed by the boom of his great voice. "We know Henry Hughes is in there. You just send him out without a fuss."

Scuffling and shouts come from inside, then the door opens to a man even larger than Hughes. The warden has his rifle aimed, along with three or four other barrels out there in the dark. The large man has hold of Hughes's arm, and he shoves him forward. Hughes trips on the threshold and goes down to his knees at the warden's feet.

"Oh, Henry," a woman sobs, coming to stand next to the huge man. "You told us you was out."

"That's not the case, ma'am," the warden says.

"Goddamned bastard," the man in the door shouts. "Goddamn you for bringing this down on your mama. You folks take his sorry ass back to that prison and you lock him up tight, you hear me?"

"Yes, sir." I've never before heard the warden call anyone *sir*.

Hughes's mama leans over him, tugging on his thick shoulders. "Why, Henry? Why'd you do this to us? You was s'pposed to do your time and come back home *for good*."

Hughes keeps his head low. "I was just so tired of it, Mama."

"You do your time and you come back home. To *stay*."

The warden doesn't tell her he's a murderer now, that this run will cost him the whole rest of his life. Hughes's original sentence was for liquor and larceny, and his max time would've been ten years. He told me once about the money he'd made, the corn he'd stolen. His still is back there with Stevens, the remains of a shack in the dark.

The warden lets him hug his mother before putting on the cuffs. The large man—Hughes's father, I assume—has already gone back inside. I want to tell Hughes that I've been renounced in the same way, and that the only way to live with it is to hate the man who hates you, to believe you hated him first.

There is a hand on my shoulder. Marie. *You could've saved him.*

"Marie."

He'll die now. You could've stopped that.

I don't know that I could have.

Marie's hand moves to my face, cupping my jaw. She's so beautiful.

"Why did you make me move?"

She brings her young lips to my old ones, roughened and coarse. *Why did you come?* Her lovely head nods toward Hughes, the cuffs on his wrists, the tears on his mother's face, the absence of his father. *Own this. It's yours.*

But I already own so much—our lost children and Wilson's death in a coal mine and George Haskin and all the anger I've dealt. I can't own this, too.

"Martin!" the warden shouts. "Michaels! Keep your dogs on him."

We nudge them toward Hughes, and they pull their leads tight to get at his scent. I will him an escape, a tunnel the likes of which I willed for Jennings, something deep that leads to the sea. Ed will meet him there on the beach, and they'll row back to London, banding together in their thievery. I was wrong to want him captured.

If I could, I would apologize.

A wagon arrives at dawn, and guards shepherd us into its bed. They encircle Hughes, and leave Michaels and me to settle our dogs. The eastern sky is a dusty pink, nearly orange, and the faint remains of a few stars are toward the west. I unhitch my belt, tell my dogs to lie down, then lie down myself.

They can't rouse me when we get back to Kilby, and I'm told

that it only takes one tall guard to heave me over his shoulder and drop me on the cot in my cell.

I sleep through the day and most of the night, waking to half dreams in the dark. The walls come in waves, like Ed's ocean, and I can almost make him out on the other side of the bars.

"What are you doing up so late, Ross?"

"Hughes will get your chair for killing that boy."

"That's not our concern." He starts humming the ballad that the men have made up as a prayer to Yellow Mama. "'I know I done wrong. I know I must pay. I sat in this jail one thousand days. The appeals run out. I will not win. I done did my time, and I've had my last feast. Yellow Mama have mercy on me.' She'll have mercy on Hughes, don't you worry."

I hear Marie again, telling me to take Hughes's place. "It's such a quiet way to go," she whispers. "All at once. They can't take any more pieces out of you."

Now, every man in Kilby is singing to Yellow Mama, a great ocean choir, and there's an organ, and Chaplain is up at the pulpit with his hands tented under his chin, and he's praying to Yellow Mama right along with us, and angels are singing with the men in the fields, and Ed's ocean crashes against Kilby's shore.

I don't feel rested come morning, and Taylor says I look like hell when I arrive at the pens with the dog pail.

"Shame," he says. "The whole damn thing. Loss of a good man, and now Hughes is a damn murderer. At least we lost Beau, huh?"

"Sir?"

"Warden let him go as soon as he got back from the chase. Man'll have a tough time working in corrections ever again, that's for damn sure." Taylor is breaking ranks to tell me this and he passes over it quick. "We're going to do some close-in training on the pups today. Go easy on you, all right? Head over to their pen when you're done with the feeding."

"Yes, sir."

I wish for my young Marie.

You best quit your ghosts, I hear my father saying. *Focus on what's here rather than what's in your head. Do your damn work, Roscoe.*

"All right, Pa."

I respect his words just now, a truth in them I couldn't catch before. Here in this barn with my hands bloodied by meat scraps and dusted with bonemeal, my nose stuffed up with the stink of it—here I can see why he took such comfort in those veins of coal. They were tangible, as were the coal cars and the mules and the men. They could be touched and moved, nothing like the slippery currents running through the wires I so admire. His coal was like the corn in the fields or the cows in the barn or the dogs in their pens—solid things we can feel with our hands and see with our eyes, smell and hear and taste. There's relief in that sort of integrity.

I'd like to tell him I understand.

PART II

PART II

I still see Kilby, all of it spread before me—the yard, the mess hall, the infirmary, the chapel, the toolshed, the dairy barn, the gates and wide stretches of wall, my own tar-black fingers. Then I see that truck in the dirt lot the day I walked free, its body a deep green like the leaves of the hackberry, wooden slats round its bed. It was a farm truck, a work truck, and I wanted Marie to be inside.

Hughes was on his way to meet Yellow Mama, and I had finally gotten parole. Hughes gave it to me, too, that run of his. While I was sitting on that same bench outside the parole room, waiting on the board's decision, the warden told me the news. "Hell of a run you did, carrying on after Hughes pulled that shotgun. We note that sort of thing in your file." The warden offered me a cigarette. "You'll be pleased with their call this time."

So I wasn't surprised when the large man, who'd taken the bald man's place, told me I was going free.

Chaplain sought me out to lay his hand on my shoulder. He read to me from Isaiah, a passage about trees clapping their hands at my return, and he gave me a Bible.

Rash gave me a dictionary and Hartley's book about dogs. "Damn it, I'm glad you've gotten paroled, but I hate that you're leaving."

I found Dean in the mess. "Keep going to the library. Even though I won't be there."

"Hell, Books. It won't be as good, but I'll give it a shot."

That was as close as I came to saying good-bye to a friend within those walls.

I sent one letter home, telling Marie the date of my release. *Please collect me from the prison on April 10. I'll be coming out the front doors around 3:00 p.m.* If that letter went unanswered like all the others and no one came, I was sure I would never go back to the land. I would go to the ocean, and I would find myself a lighthouse.

But a farm truck was in the parking lot, and I knew it was there for me. A rifle and fishing rod hung in the rear window, and they kept me from seeing the head of the driver.

"Martin!" I heard from behind me, Taylor's rough voice. "I got a send-off for you."

Maggie was at his side, her great nose to the sky, trying to find what she should sniff out.

"She's tired, and I don't think she's got another litter in her. Makes her no good to me. Figure you could take her to pasture." Taylor put a ratty length of rope in my hand, its other end tied to Maggie's collar. He'd never part with one of his leather leads.

"Thank you, sir." We shook hands.

"Best not see you back here."

"Yes, sir."

He tugged on one of Maggie's ears, then gave her a swat on the butt. "Go on, old mutt."

She looked back only once at her old master. "Come on, girl." I was grateful for the distraction, for something I could focus on rather than the hope of my real wife, there in the dirt lot of Kilby.

When we were a few yards away, the driver's door opened, and Marie did not step out.

I stopped, and Maggie tensed at my side. *Is this who I'm looking for?* her body asked. *Do you need me to point?*

"Wilson." His hair was short, and a few more lines were round his eyes, but his face didn't look much older than it had the last time I'd seen him. He walked toward me, coming round the back of the truck, and I saw his left arm then—gone from the elbow down.

My right arm hung tucked in its bend against my body, but my hand was there, my forearm, and I made good use of them. I still do.

Maggie growled.

"No. Sit."

"Got yourself a dog, Ross?" Wilson held out his right hand, and I shook it just as I had Taylor's a moment before. "Problem with your arm, there?"

"Shoulder injury. I don't have full use of it anymore."

Wilson raised the stump of his left arm. "Full use of what I have left."

"What happened?"

"Plenty of time for that. There's a meal cooking at home. Best get you back."

Maggie jumped in the truck bed with little prompting, and I tied her rope to one of the slats to keep her from diving out. I'd never ridden in a vehicle with Wilson. I'd never seen him drive, but he performed it with ease, his left limb propped against the wheel when his right needed to shift.

"Did Marie send you?"

Wilson eyed me, an old look I knew well. "When's the last time you heard from Marie, Ross?"

"Nine years ago."

"There's time for that, too. Kilby hand out pets to everyone they let go?"

"I worked the dogs."

"You a dog boy, then? Chasing down escapees?"

I nodded.

"That was a wanted job at the mine. Kept you aboveground, got you out in the woods. What'd it keep you out of?"

"The dairy."

"Dairy sounds good to me."

There are days the dairy sounds good to me, too. Days I picture myself back there even though I know it's nowhere I belong.

The truck rattled down the dirt lane to the highway, and there were the oaks. Kilby sat behind us, watching our dust through its many eyes.

"Where's Marie?"

"Mobile."

I didn't know how that could be true. I had always—only— seen her on her father's land. Marie moving us to that place set me to building those transformers and stringing those lines along the cornfield and electrifying that thresher. George Haskin wouldn't have had anything to explore if we hadn't been there. The time I'd served in Kilby grew from my time on that land, and there would have been no time on that land without Marie's insistence that we move there.

Electrical work could be come by in Mobile. Why not take us there directly?

"Mobile?"

"Moa's making you a fine meal, Ross. All the trimmings."

"Why is Marie in Mobile?"

Wilson had the stump of his arm up on the door now, alongside the open window. His right hand was scarred, raised strips thatching the skin, some pink, some black. "You were expecting her here? Thought she'd be waiting?"

I don't know if I thought that. "I didn't expect her to be in Mobile."

"There's plenty you didn't expect, Ross."

I thought he was referencing George Haskin and our sentences, but I know now he was talking about our new lives, the lives that were starting there in that truck.

The highway went on before us. Spring had come, the oaks bright with their new leaves. Hollies dotted green in the lower brush, some sprouting high enough to rival the trees. The road was smooth and newly painted, and it made me think of Ed's chair.

We passed into a stand of shortleaf pine, with its bunchy needles and clustered cones. The cones grow opposite one another on the branch, a reflection—that's how you can tell the tree apart from other pines.

Maggie held her head in the air, nose tipped high, ears flapping.

"What's Marie doing in Mobile?"

"Teaching."

"And Gerald? Where's he?"

"Tuscaloosa."

"Going to the university?"

"That's right."

Gerald made sense there, but Marie was a mystery I couldn't solve—not the young version of her or the grown one that might have come to see me in the infirmary. Nurse Hannah had never confirmed or denied that shifty presence.

"Did Marie visit the prison?"

"We got notice of you being laid up. Course Moa got no word about this." Wilson lifted the stump of his left arm. "They didn't even tell her where they sent me, probably had no record of it themselves. Just a list of numbers, you see, taking our shifts. You know their favorite saying about leased men? 'One dies, get another.'" Wilson thumped his damaged arm against the door. "See, I'm told I'm lucky, Ross. Would've been dead if they hadn't chopped this off and cauterized what was left. You ever smell flesh burning?"

"Not up close."

"From a distance, then."

"There's a smell when they use the chair at Kilby."

"The chair!" Wilson laughed. "They give you dogs when you get out. Infirmaries when you're hurt. Books to read. Even your executions get special treatment. At Sloss, it's either the mine or a guard that delivers that sentence." He shook his head and smiled as if it were the funniest thing he'd heard. "A chair! You get to consult on that, Ross? Lend your electrical expertise?"

"No."

"That's a shame."

I didn't tell him how close I'd been to its builder.

We eventually left the highway for a county road, the packed clay spinning into red dust behind us. The trees on the right had yielded to long stretches of peanuts just starting to spread. Small plots of spring crops were amongst them—lettuces and onions. It sent me back to the mess hall, some fellow from the fields talking about onion bulbs, yellow and red and white. "We've got two onion seasons," I heard him say. "You got to put the bulbs in the ground early February, pull that crop early June, then you're in with your winter bulbs late September."

The poles alongside us held the line I had tapped. They turned about two miles up to run along that far edge of the field.

In a quarter mile, we pulled onto the rutted drive that led to the house and the barn. The same pecans lined the way, their leaves full and green. The fields stretched out behind them. Everything I saw made me terrified to see the next. The pole fence still ran to the west end of the sling-backed barn, one new rail bright against the weathered others. There was the chicken coop, the chickens. Every piece was there, not much different from how I'd imagined it at Kilby. I'd seen myself walking up that drive, Maggie next to me. "We've been hunting rabbits," I'd heard myself say. I am just a hunter with my dog.

Maggie whined in the back loud enough for us to hear.

"Nice of her to do the speaking for you both," Wilson said.

Then the house emerged from the oaks. There was the white clapboard and the double porches—top and bottom, as Marie's father had insisted. The chimneys rose from their opposite sides, the brick seated in place with signs of fresh mortaring. The porches had not sunk with time like so many we'd driven past—an eastern corner sagging toward the ground, a post rotted through, the eave collapsing. The paint was fresh. The same two rockers sat on the lower porch, but they'd been sanded and varnished to look new.

They must have been made of strong wood, and I wished Ed were there to tell me the grain.

When I first saw Kilby, I thought it looked like a school with a lighthouse out front, strange things to me both, but that clean farmhouse was unfamiliar, too. We'd never polished the grounds quite that shiny. Even when the money was coming in, we'd left the creepers on the chimneys. Marie had liked them.

Her horse was nowhere to be seen, long dead, I supposed.

Wilson pulled up to the shop and reached across his body to open his door with his only hand. "You sit here a minute if you need to. Supper will be ready soon, and I know Moa's anxious to set eyes on you, but you get your bearings out here first." He stepped free of the cab. "You want me to let your dog out? She won't go after the chickens, will she?"

"No."

He slammed his door, and I watched him lift one of the wooden rails out to give Maggie leave of the truck bed. She was reluctant to jump down, and Wilson slid that stump of his arm under her waist, his right arm round her neck, lifting her to the ground gentle as a baby.

Wilson had been my friend. We had strung lines and seen crops turn to money and eaten dinners and watched our kids grow. Marie's father had always hired his help. Marie's grandfather hadn't had slaves. Wilson had been a free man his whole life until our arrest.

Maggie was sniffing at his one hand, unsure. She glanced toward the truck cab, and all I could give her was a nod before I looked back at the shop that held my thresher.

I don't know how long I sat in the truck, but it stretched long and vindictive like my time in solitary. I got out only when I heard a woman calling my name.

I so wanted it to be Marie. I wanted her to appear before me and tell me she'd needed all that time to think it through—nine years, she needed, all right. But she had realized that I'd acted for her and Gerald, for the farm, even for Moa and Wilson and their children, as much as I'd acted for myself. She realized that I had to have my hands in electricity, that I was driven by all those attractions that lay hidden until ignited. I saw her take me into her arms, letting me bury my face in the thick hair she'd let fall down her back. I could smell the cooking she'd been doing for my return—the maple-and-bacon beans I'd fallen in love with, bread, roast chicken, coffee. I could forgive her silence if she could forgive the work I'd done.

But it was Moa standing near the front door, her hands held tight over her apron. She'd aged more than Wilson—more lines at the corners of her eyes and around her mouth, her hair gone gray along the edges of her face. She was heavier, too, broader.

Maggie rose from where she'd been waiting near the back wheel and followed me to the porch steps.

"I didn't want him to collect you, you know," Moa said. "Told him to let you find your own way. Like he did his. Go get yourself a job in a coal mine. See how it suits you."

"You know I've spent time in a coal mine, Moa."

"With your own daddy as the foreman. You spent most of your time up top." Moa towered above me. "Wilson has his compassion for you, Mr. Roscoe, but it's hard for me to see why." She squeezed her hands tighter, then pulled them apart and slapped them against her thighs. "You took him right down with you, didn't you? Never even tried to help."

"I was in prison, Moa. What could I have done?"

"Told them it was your fault."

"I did that. They didn't listen."

Moa lowered her eyes. "He lost his arm, Roscoe."

"I'd change that if I could."

"You've said your piece, Moa," we both heard from inside, Wilson's voice coming through the screen. "Let's have some supper."

"That dog's not welcome in the house."

"She's never been in a house." I put my hand on Maggie's head as I told her, "Wait." She lay down on the brick walk, which had been hard-packed dirt before.

The porch was clean and the rockers even shinier up close. Electric lamps graced the sides of the door, and it didn't squeak when I opened it. Inside, everything was a greater version of itself, too. New wallpaper lined the foyer above the wainscoting, curving vines with starlike leaves and bright orange berries against a pale yellow background. Birds of all colors and shapes sat amid the branches, and in the middle of them, a yellow-orange squirrel held court. The old paper had been dark green and nothing more than an angular pattern.

A new electric chandelier dangled overhead, its crystals bright even when the bulbs weren't lit. "Marie felt like lightening things up in here," Moa said. "A while back, we took down all the old paper and put up new. You'll see on the way to the table. Hang your coat."

The stand was the same, tall oak with a box for umbrellas and a seat for putting on shoes. Its mirror reflected one of the squirrels just to the right of my head. My face had grown old and thin, and I looked preposterous against that wallpaper, like a tramp brought into a nursery.

"Come on through the sitting room," Moa said.

I didn't want to see any more.

The wallpaper in the sitting room was pink and light green, full of flowers and leaves. Gerald's reading chair in the corner was now rose colored, an electric lamp next to it.

"I would like to sit down." I went to that chair. I reached instinctively for a small book on the side table, a novel that Rash had forced on the other men, another Melville book about the sea. "It's about mutiny," Rash had demanded. "Isn't that enough to interest them?"

"No."

"You'll fall asleep in that chair if you don't get up," Moa said. "Come on. There's food to eat."

I set the book back on its table and followed them through the wide arch to the dining room. The pink flowers had bled across the walls in there, too.

Moa poured me coffee, which was every bit as good as I wanted it to be. She brought out a whole chicken, then a crock of beans, corn bread, and fresh butter. The canned peaches were brilliant orange in their jar. Moa had cooked up some chard and collards with crisp bits of pork fat. She'd outdone my imaginings, this woman who was not my wife. And on my other side, I didn't have my son, but rather a man whose arm I had helped to crush and cut loose from his body, whose skin I'd held a flame to in order to stanch the bleeding.

Moa recited from Deuteronomy, one of Chaplain's favorite passages: " 'For the Lord your God is God of gods and Lord of lords, a great God, a mighty, and a terrible, which regardeth not persons, nor taketh reward: He doth execute the judgment of the fatherless and widow, and loveth the stranger, in giving him food and raiment.' Thank you, Lord, for this food."

We said "Amen" together and worked through the meal without talking. I ate everything Moa put on my plate. I took second scoops and thirds. More, please. I had missed that food so much, and my mind could fix only on the plate and the fork and the knife, the meat dipped in the sweet-salty syrup of the beans, the moist corn bread spread thick with butter I had not tasted in years. Spices mixed with the peaches, clove and cinnamon, the greens bitter and sharp. The wallpaper didn't matter, nor the company, the whiteness of the clapboards outside, the absence of the creeper, the new brick walkway, not Maggie lying there, the shop and its thresher, the growing crops. I was just a man eating his dinner.

"Thank you, Moa."

"You are lucky I am a God-fearing woman, Mr. Roscoe. I'll get the pie."

It was peach, and she drizzled it with fresh cream.

"Another?" she asked when I finished my first piece.

"Please."

Neither Wilson nor Moa had seconds, and they watched me with caution and worry as I finished mine. I wanted to rest a minute more in that food before they told me what was drawing all those lines across their foreheads.

"We're living in this house now, Roscoe," Wilson said. Crust was still on my plate, a few slivers of peach, a pool of cream. "Marie set us up here when she went to Mobile."

It had never been my home—that big house. Not before, not then, certainly not now. "How often does she come back?"

"Infrequently," Moa answered.

Nothing was left for me to do with the last of my pie but to push it away. "Who's running the land?"

"We are," Wilson said.

"Yes, but who's paying you?"

"*We* are," Moa repeated. "It's been a while now."

"How long?"

"Five years."

I didn't know how to put Moa and Wilson in Marie's house and Marie in a school in Mobile. Did she have a view of the bay, gulls out the windows distracting her students?

"Where are your children?" *This* was the question I set upon, though it was the least of my interests.

Moa started gathering plates. "I can't do any more of this. I'll go get started on the dishes and send Jenny out for the rest."

"So Jenny is here?"

Moa huffed and pushed through the door.

"You'll have to give her some time," Wilson said.

A beautiful, dark woman came out from the kitchen, hair in braids to her shoulders. She looked like her parents, but only their best parts. "Jenny," I said, "you were just a little one the last time I saw you."

She looked to her father.

"It's all right, honey. Just clear the table."

It took her three runs to and from the kitchen to get it all. I didn't speak again until she was done. "Am I that awful?" "We aren't sure."

I pressed my thumb and finger into my eyes until I saw red sparks against the backs of my lids. The food turned against my insides, and I yearned for Kilby, for the ease of routine, the simplicity of my meals and lodging.

My stomach doubled over itself, and I pushed myself quickly from the table, overturning my chair. I didn't make it off the porch, but I got to the railing, and I heaved my dinner into the decorative shrubs that now lined the house. Maggie stood at attention on the walkway, unsure what to make of me. My body wouldn't stop until everything was gone. When I could stand, I headed to the pump by the shop, bringing water up first to wash my face and mouth. Pumping with one hand, I held my head under the spout, the cold water shocking me conscious. Water ran in and out of my mouth, down my cheeks and chin, soaking my collar. I filled a rusted bucket to wash away the mess I'd made of the bushes, and like Jenny and her dishes, it took three trips. Maggie trotted along behind me.

I told myself to write Taylor a letter thanking him for that dog.

Wilson came out on the porch once I'd finished. I was sure he'd watched from a window.

"If it's all right, I'll hear the rest tomorrow," I said. "I'd like to sleep now."

"Course. Help me pull a few things from the shop." Inside, Wilson threw a switch to cast the whole space with light, my thresher before us. "We're still using it. We've had electricity a long time now—legally, that is. There was a big push right after we went away to electrify us backcountry folks. They used your same route."

He was telling me how inequitably priced my project was, how much we'd lost for a gain we would've gotten just a little ways down the road.

Wilson pulled two oil lamps from behind a jumble of machine parts. "There's oil in that can behind you. The lines are in." I filled the lamps' bases. "We just haven't gotten them run through all the buildings. Could be something for you to do, if you want."

"Where am I sleeping, Wilson?"

He handed me one of the lamps and a box of safety matches, yellow and wooden.

THE trail from the house had grown over, the grass itchy through my trouser legs. I could see that walk I took out to the north field, excited to tell Wilson about my plans to electrify the farm. "I'll do this thing," I'd said, "or I'll leave." They had seemed exclusive—the doing and the leaving—but I know now that they had always been entwined. The doing set in motion the leaving, which I suppose set in motion the return.

"We've not had time to keep it up," Wilson said, as we emerged into the field where his old house stood. "But it's yours as long as you want it."

The brush had crept closer to the cottage, some of the old pines felled by hand or on their own. Creepers had taken over most of the siding, the few exposed planks closer to mulch than wood. New sounds ran their way around us—creaks and rattles, glass gone to shards in several of the windowpanes.

"Too much to do on the land," Wilson said. "Too much to do at the big house."

I was glad of the ruin, grateful to see something that had aged as much as I had. "Is there furniture?"

"Table and chairs. I won't make any claims about the cleanliness, but there are beds to sleep in, plenty to choose from."

The evening was bringing a chill, and I'd left my jacket in the big house. "There are blankets inside?"

"Plenty."

"Thank Moa for the meal."

"I will."

I watched him walk through the grasses and brush. I should

have called out, offered some sentiment about this place where we'd found ourselves. Instead, I went inside the cottage. The door latch was misaligned with the plate, unable to catch and hold. I would straighten it in the morning, drill new holes for the hinges, replace the rotted pieces of the doorframe.

"Come on," I said to Maggie. "It's not much more than your shed."

She curved her spine in nervousness, tucked her ears close to her head, the ends trailing down her neck.

"Come on."

She wouldn't come.

The gloom of evening was already thick inside the cottage, and I lit both lamps to fight it off. A long table and benches stood in the center of the main room, cupboards along one wall, a sink with a hand pump, ladder-back chairs, a blackened stove in the corner. Two small bedrooms were on the left—one for the parents and one for the children. The outhouse was around the side.

I hoped for food in the cupboards and was rewarded with a few jars of pickled beets, peaches, and a small sack of dried meat. The sack was mouse chewed, the meat gnawed, but it was enough to coax Maggie in.

Maggie didn't understand why she was in this house. She wasn't hunting anyone, wasn't working. She took the meat and chewed it slowly, her head hung with the effort. I closed the door behind her and sought out a broom in one of the cabinets. A dead mouse was in one of the corners, and when I opened the stove, I found three sparrows. They must've come through the chimney and gotten stuck inside, dying of thirst and starvation in that dusty tomb. I scooped them onto the pile I'd gathered and edged it all to the door. I again saw those chalky bodies drop from the hayloft of my parents' barn, and I thought of the comfort I'd taken in my sister's company. We'd shared our exile then, just as I was sharing it with Maggie now.

MAGGIE and I stomped around the cottage in the morning. We were both tired and cautious, neither of us having found much sleep. After nine years of the same noises and perpetual lights, the same smells and rough sheets and rougher blankets, it was hard to sleep in the quiet of a cottage in a stand of pines, with the rattle of broken glass and the shifting of branches, a down pillow and a thick mattress, old and musk soaked as they were. I'd eventually gotten down on the pallet that the children must have used, and on its thin mattress, just inches from the floor, I was able to sleep a bit.

Maggie and I circled out toward the fields to get our bearings, and we came to the power line. It ran straight from the big house, and it stopped just before the pines.

I figured I'd stay long enough to power the cottage, long enough to decide where to go. I'd never believed I would pass up electrical work were it to come my way. I'm sure my parole board didn't either.

I heel-toed my way back to the cottage, a little less than fifty yards. We'd raised poles every twenty-five yards or so along the roads when I was with Alabama Power, but this line was lower and would benefit from extra support along the way.

"Three poles," I said to Maggie. "We'll cut them from around the back of the cottage to let in a bit more light. All right, girl?"

She sat and whined.

"You're hungry."

I had no desire to return to the big house, but I knew I would need Wilson and Moa's help to live in the cottage, even for a short time.

They were on the front porch, sitting in the rockers, drinking from mugs.

"That dog's not welcome in the house."

"Wouldn't think of it, Moa."

"How'd you sleep?" Wilson asked.

"I didn't."

"Took me a full week before I could sleep in a bed at all."

"More than that," Moa said. "I'd find him curled up on the floor of the hall more times than not. Went on nearly two months."

"I'll see how the floor suits me tonight." Before the semblance of comfort was completely gone, I said, "I'm going to need a few things for the cottage. Tools, mostly."

"There's work for you to do there, sure enough," Moa replied. "Some of your things are in the closet off the kitchen. You best have a cup of coffee first. There's ham and biscuits, too."

"Wait—" But Moa was gone through the screen door, and Maggie was lying on the walkway as though my word were for her.

"There's all sorts of confusion," Wilson was saying. "All you can do is make sense of the pieces in front of you. It was the same when I got back."

"And when was that?"

"A bit ago."

"Marie was here?"

"Yes." He held the screen open for me. "Come on in and have some breakfast."

"Wait," I said, even though Maggie was already waiting.

The dining room was swept clear of any memory of our dinner, and the door to the kitchen stood open. The worktable was the only thing I recognized, though it was as shiny and polished as the rest of the house. An icebox thrummed loudly against the wall. The sink had a lever and a faucet. The electric cookstove had coiled burners circling round the black dots at their centers. New, white cupboards lined the walls, top and bottom, and several cooking gadgets sat on the countertops. I didn't even know what they were. Mixers? Grinders?

"Lovely, isn't it?" Moa said. "Marie had it done over like this for me, seeing as I spend so much time in here. She let me pick the paper."

There was only one wall of it—a pattern of lacy squares framing miniature men offering miniature women disproportionately large tulips. The women's faces looked out at the room, surprise on their features, the men in profile, expressionless. That paper still rings desperate to me, and pointedly sad.

"Mr. Roscoe," Moa said, "the closet is over here."

I remembered the closet, a narrow shaft of a room used for storage of strange or useless things, often with sentimental value. We'd rarely go in with the mind of taking something out, as opposed to putting something in.

It was packed tight with everything I once owned.

"Wilson's parked one of the wheelbarrows out the kitchen door for you to use for the hauling. I'll get you some breakfast. Suppose that dog'll need to eat, too." She dropped a pile of meat scraps into a metal bowl. "You can call it round back if you want."

Maggie and Wilson hadn't moved from their spots.

"Tried to call her up here, but she's not interested in listening to me. Figure she's used to treeing men my color."

"There weren't that many men your color at Kilby."

"Why put a man in prison when you can sell him to the mines for a few bucks."

I could only look at Wilson, his empty, pinned-up sleeve, the scars on his remaining hand, and imagine myself saying something that righted it.

"Once you take stock of what you have in the closet there, you let me know what else you need."

"Thank you. Come on, Maggie." I gave her the bowl to sniff, and she followed eagerly, sticking her nose into my leg a few times, nudging me.

Wilson laughed at us from his height on the porch. "I think that dog's got a good retirement in front of her."

I remember chewing on that word—*retirement*.

MAGGIE lay flopped on her side in the grass outside the back door of the big house while I sorted my belongings into piles on the lawn. I imagined Marie collecting the big things first—my toolboxes and my clothing—and the small pieces last. I could see the stages of stashing away. The first layer—the last Marie had added—was made up of items of questionable ownership. I found the ashtray her father gave me one Christmas, one of the only gifts I'd ever received from him. "It was his father's before it was his," Marie had told me, and not only had it belonged to her grandfather, it had been made by him, too. Her grandfather had been a silversmith, the house full of his platters and candlesticks, the family silverware, the tea service. Marie had a silver-handled hairbrush and hand mirror that he'd made for her when she was a girl. That ashtray was likely put in the final layer because Marie couldn't decide whether it was mine.

A framed photo of our wedding was stacked next to a painting done by my mother that Marie had admired, a silhouette in profile of my own head that Marie had commissioned and hung next to a matching one of hers, a small relief map of the state, hand-painted by the cartographer, a friend of Marie's father. I found a carving knife, also the work of Marie's grandfather, a silk handkerchief. Toward the back, I would find my electrical texts, but at the front I found an almanac from 1923 and a cookbook. I found a stuffed bear of Gerald's with blue button eyes and a red plaid jacket. I didn't know why these things were mine, but I sorted them all the same. Clothing and sitting-room things and trinkets and books. By the time I reached the back wall, I'd uncovered my rifle and three boxes of cartridges, all my tools, several jars of nails and screws, nine long coils of wire, and a remaining box of ceramic insulators.

MAGGIE was chewing on a bone when I carried out the last items.

"She's got that face," Moa said, hanging sheets on the line. "Puts those ears down and she can get 'bout anything she wants, can't she? Wilson got two deer last week. There's only so much stock I can make with the bones. Set you a bagful by your boots."

"Next thing you know, you'll be letting her in the house."

"Careful, Mr. Roscoe."

It was almost nice standing there, my dog gnawing a bone, the hint of humor between Moa and me, the warm sun, the leafy oaks, the fields stretching off behind them.

Moa took a clothespin from her mouth. "I'd like to see this lawn again before nightfall."

"Yes, ma'am." I'd never before said those words to Moa.

Maggie trotted along behind me as I pushed the first load to the cottage, the bone a prize in her mouth. She was already calmer than she'd been when we arrived, shrugging off that nervous need to run and sniff and hunt.

"Better not get too comfortable," I told her. "We won't be here long."

My arms and legs were worn-out by my second run, and I took a rest after the third. It was dusk, and the air was crisper, but my shirt was wet through with sweat. I still hadn't retrieved my jacket from the foyer. I pumped water at the sink in the cottage and filled a small cup. Maggie poked her nose into my knee.

"Thirsty?" I filled a bowl to set on the floor. She let the bone down gently and lapped at the water with her long tongue. She'd always been a dainty drinker. Even after a tough chase, she'd keep the same gentle motion, the other dogs nearly drowning themselves in their frantic thirst.

My jacket sat on a crate of jarred food in the yard, a towel-wrapped package on top of it. Moa had brought me dinner and something for the pantry. I loaded the painting and map and photo, the silhouette, the ashtray, the bear, having saved them for the end in the half hope that they'd disappear. I added my jacket and my food, and Maggie and I started for our home.

We'd already knocked the trail back down, the grasses flattened underfoot, but I wouldn't clear the brush or trim the branches. I'd rather duck to avoid those limbs overhead than open up a view to the big house.

Ten yards from the cottage, Maggie stopped, pointing as she'd been taught at the figure who ran toward us. Recognizing Wilson, she relaxed her pose and wagged her tail. He bent down to rub her head with his half arm, running it along the ridge of her skull. His right hand held an old thermos and a burlap sack.

"Moa thought you'd do for some coffee after your labors. Said you can keep that thermos. And there's beans in the sack there."

"Thank you."

"I think this dog's won Moa over. You have a good night, Ross."

"You, too."

I watched him start back toward the house, and I called out to him before he disappeared. "Wilson?"

"Yeah?"

"When will I know what's become of my family?"

He was quiet a minute. "Suppose when the timing's right. It's not much of an answer, but it's all I've got for you."

"All right," I said, though it wasn't.

At the cottage, I emptied the last load, tipped the wheelbarrow against the siding, and sat down at the table with Moa's food. She'd given me more ham and biscuits, enough for my breakfast, too. I pulled a jar of corn kernels out of the crate, loosened the ring, poked a hole in the lid with my silver carving knife, and pried off the top. Maggie settled back into her bone, and I poured myself a cup of coffee. A bird was singing a six-note whistle outside. "Do you know," I remember Marie asking, "what a group of warblers is called?" These were some of her favorite bits of knowledge, her students all experts on collective nouns.

"No. What is a group of warblers called?"

"There are options. You can call them a *bouquet* or a *confusion* or a *fall*, but my favorite is *wrench*. A wrench of warblers."

She'd told me that before we were married. These are the things I remember.

I lit one of the lamps and cleared away my crumbs, closed the remaining biscuits and ham inside a lidded tin to keep the mice away. I'd meant to fix the door, but it would wait.

In my pile of clothes, I found an old pair of pajamas, thin but soft. Pajamas were not part of Kilby's clothing allotment. The cold water from the pump felt good against my face and back and arms as I sponged myself clean at the sink. I'd found a bathroom in what I thought was a closet between the two bedrooms, all set with a basin and a chamber pot and a soaking tub. But that would wait, too.

I opened a copy of *Billy Budd, Sailor* that I'd found in the closet. Marie had left it for me in the first layer, one of her last additions. I'd already read it at Kilby—poor old Billy mistaken for a mutineer by his master-at-arms, the accidental death, the court-martial, the execution sentence—and I wasn't sure what Marie intended me to glean from it. Billy was wrongfully accused. Marie could be saying the same was true of me, that the trial, the conviction, the time at Kilby, had all been a mistake. But her silence had left me to assume that my guilt was absolute in her eyes. Maybe she'd wanted me to look only at the sentencing, Billy's execution a parallel for my own rightful end. I could still hear the young version of her telling me to claim Stevens's death and walk myself to Yellow Mama.

Marie had written in the front cover, *Dear Roscoe.* Those words in Marie's hand were the start of every letter I'd wanted her to write.

Dear Roscoe, Gerald and I hope you enjoy this book upon your return.—Marie

Dear Roscoe. Dear Roscoe. Dear Roscoe.

What would I have had her write?

Dear Roscoe, Gerald and I look forward to reading this with you upon your return.

Dear Roscoe, We miss you terribly.

Dear Roscoe, Welcome home.

Dear Roscoe, For you, a book, with love, from your wife.

The young version of Marie had been right—she'd had nothing to say to me.

I'd thought I'd read the book again, but I wasn't interested in

Marie's written words or the typed ones she'd gifted me—messages for a man she no longer cared to know.

THE trees around the cottage were straight and tall, and it took two full days to fell and strip one—work that would've taken a quarter of the time back when I had full use of my right arm. The poles didn't need to be perfect, but I wanted them to be smooth like the ones I'd raised for the power company. I'd found my drawknife in the closet, and I sharpened it with my file, holding it up to the sun to see the flat spots I'd missed. The beveled edge pulled the bark off in bits and pieces and then the pale wood off in strips. The motion was methodical, like mucking stalls in the dairy barn or filling tins with dog food, and my mind moved back to my old cell, Ed still there, dusty with sanded wood, tired and bitter about his chair. "Yellow!" he shouted. "They're covering that beautiful maple with highway paint, the bastards! Painting wood is a disgrace. You hear me? They're disgracing my profession in this bloody place."

"I won't paint this pole," I told him.

We weren't in our cell. We were in that small clearing by the cottage.

"That'a boy, Ross."

He looked stronger, thicker in the arms and neck.

"You visiting me now?" I asked.

"Suppose."

"Did you come here?"

"I told you I would, didn't I? Hell, I told the State I'd build them an electric chair, and you didn't see me backing out of that promise, did you? Paying a visit's an easy enough commitment to see through."

"What did Marie say?"

Ed was hesitant. "I tell you, Ross, your Marie is a fine cook. Made me a hell of a meal. But there wasn't much said, you see."

"You said she wasn't home."

"Easier that way."

"You lay with my wife, Ed?"

"She wasn't your wife, Ross. Hadn't been for a while."

Like my young Marie, this new Ed was my own making. I remember knowing that then. His words were mine—words I was putting in his mouth.

"She stopped being your wife when she lost all those future children." He was right. Even in the good times after the power first came, Marie had remained a ghost, a hollowed-out tree, something waiting for its escape.

"Why am I here?" I asked Ed.

He shook his head—about all anyone could do for me those days. I'm accustomed to the quiet that rises now, the lack of words that comes from comfort and stillness, but in that field with Ed, all the silent head-shaking built upon itself like the frustration that drove bruises into Gerald's arms and threw insults at Reed. I pulled the drawknife, anger wobbling my grip on the handles, the blade sloppy across the pole, my knuckles against the rough bark. I didn't register the skin coming away, the red imbuing the pine.

I pulled Marie into my anger, and I wanted her there to answer for herself.

Maggie whined at my side, her nose against my knee.

"Back!"

My blood would stay in the grain of the wood even after I'd scraped it again. Only one strip was left. Maggie nosed me again, and I kicked her fiercely in the chest.

"Back, goddamn it! Back!"

Then, just as quickly, I was on my knees, crawling to her as the coward I was, as the coward I fear I still am, at least on certain days. She let me grab her round her neck, press my face into the soft fur of her chest, pull on her ears like chords or ropes, like things to climb.

"Good dog. Good. You are a good dog."

She tried to lick my hands, but I lifted them out of her reach and went inside to get her a fresh bone. She took it, but dropped it immediately, watching me go to the basin where I pumped water into the bowl, setting my hands in it to soak. They ached. The water clouded pink.

I ripped strips from an old shirt to use as bandages, and when I gripped the drawknife again, pain seared up my arms. "You know this," I told my hands. "Go through the movement." I gripped and pulled, and blood crept through the layers of cloth. Still, I struggled against the pain, against myself, against Marie, the cottage, Kilby, even the village there on the Coosa—against everything that had brought me to that pole in that meadow.

WHEN it was time to start digging, I went to the big house to borrow a shovel.

"Help yourself to anything in the shop," Wilson told me. It was morning, and Moa and Wilson were on the porch again, a couple taking a moment to enjoy the start of the day.

"Not *anything*," Moa added.

"Just a shovel, Moa. I promise."

The thresher greeted me in the musty shop—intimate, but also distant. I felt nervous, the way I would should Marie appear. I placed my hand on the machine's metal, cool there in the dark, and I saw it moving with its electric engine, turning power into food into sales into salvation. I should have felt guilt. I should have hated that beast of a machine. But I was still proud. I could still recognize the accomplishment, and I wanted—right then, more than anything—to be acknowledged for the success I'd brought.

I picked out a narrow-bladed shovel with a thin shoulder.

The muscles of my left arm took the bulk of the digging, my bad shoulder weak and useless in this task. The hole needed to be deep. The cloth around my knuckles kept my hands from blistering too badly, but nothing saved my thumbs. They opened into sores before I'd finished, and I had to stop to soak my hands in cold water again. Maggie followed me inside.

I made more bandages from the same shirt, my hands so thick with cloth that I could barely operate my fingers. If my hands would just do this last bit of the first hole, I'd go back inside and eat an entire jar of peaches. I would lie down on the thick mattress and try to sleep. I would give my body anything it wanted.

When I finally finished, I let out a cry that brought Maggie to my side. My thumbs had bled through, and the scabs that had formed on my knuckles were broken open.

Inside, I built a fire and set pots to boiling on the stove. Wilson and Moa must have added the bathing room during their time there, and I gave them my thanks as I lowered myself into the hot water. My hands burned and then went quiet, like the muscles in my arms and legs, my shoulders and neck. The steam from the water felt warm and good in my lungs, and I listened to my breaths, each a *Dear Roscoe*, the *Dear* strung longer than the *Roscoe*. *Dear* coming in, and *Roscoe* going out. I could hear Marie's voice, there in that tub. To Ed she was saying, "Oh? You shared a cell with Roscoe? Come in." She was saying, "Come." And to me she said, "Dear Roscoe. Dear, dear Roscoe. I've been canning like mad this season. The harvest was grand, and we had money for more peaches than we knew what to do with."

Then I heard my young Marie come, not in person, but in a voice just slightly off from her older counterpart's. "Take the blame. Get yourself a permanent place here in Kilby. There's nothing for you when you get out."

The water went cold before I left it, my body turned to a shriveled kernel. The cottage towels were on the thin side, but still thicker than anything we saw in Kilby, and I rubbed myself dry before pulling on my same pajamas.

Maggie was by the stove when I came into the main room, her body hot to the touch. Kilby had given her a rusty pen, long hunts in the woods, the onerous strain of whelping, where here she had bones and ham scraps, grass and floors to lie on, stoves, pallets. There was nothing of conflict for her in that new life of ours.

I pulled her a foot away to keep her from catching on fire.

I hung my washed bandages across the back of a chair and blew out the lamps. I went to the thick mattress in the bedroom, but it took only a few minutes of shifting and turning to drive me to the pallet, and then just a few minutes of cold to drive me to the stove. I dragged the thin sleeping pad out, with its sheets and blanket and pillow, and I slept on the floor with my dog.

MAGGIE had curled herself against my legs in the night, her body up on the pad. I reached down to pet her when I woke and then rose to work on my throbbing hands. I was anxious to start the wiring and even more anxious to start the leaving, sure that my time there was temporary, a stopover while I waited to hear my real sentence.

Maggie lay close by in the grass while I worked. Toward evening, she lifted her head at the sound of footsteps as Jenny emerged into our clearing. "Dinner." The girl lifted the bundle in her hands. "I'll leave it by the door." Jenny hadn't visited before.

"Thank you."

"Thank my mama."

"Thank your mama for me, then."

Maggie wandered over to sniff at the hem of Jenny's skirt, and the girl crouched down to pet her.

"Mr. Roscoe?"

"Yes?"

"There's a favor I need to ask of you."

The sentence startled me. I didn't seem the type to grant favors. "What can I do?"

"Papa hasn't told you because he's ashamed, but Charles was—" She scanned the trees as if looking for words. "He was—incarcerated? Like you were. Sent to prison? And, well, we don't know where he's been sent. Papa thought you might have some connections at the prison and could do some asking round. We'd be awful grateful."

"What did he do?"

Jenny twisted the fabric of her skirt. "He drank too much and he—assaulted a man?"

"Do you know what that means?"

She nodded quickly. She must've been twenty, maybe nineteen, and I found myself growing angry with Wilson and Moa for making her deliver this request.

Now, of course, I understand why Jenny was given the job.

"I'm happy to do you the favor, Jenny, but tell your parents they're welcome to ask anything of me, too."

"Yes, sir."

"Don't call me *sir*."

"All right." She crouched back down to pet Maggie. "I wish people would stop leaving," she whispered.

"Where's Henry?"

"He's married." She smiled. "And he has a little girl that he named after Mama. She's six months old and the most beautiful thing. He's sent a photograph."

"And where is he?"

Her face returned to its quiet melancholy. "They're in New York City. Mama and Papa are very proud. Ms. Marie helped him get into college, like Gerry, and he has a real job there as a teacher. Ms. Marie sent us all up on the train to see his graduation."

That would've been about a year before.

"And why haven't you left, Miss Jenny?"

"I'm not book-smart like Henry. I like this work." She reached again for Maggie's ears.

"Listen, next time you bring my supper, bring some paper and a pencil, too. I know who we can write to at the prison to find out about Charles."

"Thank you, Mr. Roscoe." She kept herself back for a moment and then stepped over Maggie to give me a wide embrace. I hadn't held a woman of any color or age or size for nine years, and I didn't know what to do with my body. She pulled away as quickly as she'd come forward. "I'm sorry," she said, smoothing out her skirt. "Will you stay? Will you stay here until we find out?"

"Yes, of course."

"Good. I best get back, now. I'll bring that paper and pencil as soon as I can."

"Jenny," I said before she started off, "do you know why I'm here?"

She was quiet as her father had been when I'd asked a similar question, and I expected her reply to be vague and hazy, but instead she said, "I suppose it's because this is your home, Mr. Roscoe."

She headed down the trail toward the big house, and just before she vanished, she yelled, "What would you like for supper tomorrow?"

I was thinking about homes. "Anything. Anything you and your mama want to cook."

INSIDE the cottage, my body was all memory. I couldn't recollect the specifics of Jenny's touch, only the roar of it. I wanted that girl's arms around me again, and then once more every day after. I didn't know how much I'd needed a simple embrace.

That feeling has finally lessened some.

Ashamed, I unwrapped our supper package and scraped Maggie's portion into the pie tin that served as her bowl. Then I fell to my own dinner, not realizing my hunger.

I dug my holes, all three, and I bolted the crossarms firm in their notches.

"You'll need help," Wilson told me the morning I planned to put the poles up, surprising me with his appearance in the meadow.

"What are you doing here?"

"Jenny's been giving us updates."

"She your spy?"

"She speaks highly of you, Ross."

"That's kind of her."

I'd numbered my poles and laid them out in order, each gently decreasing in height as it neared the cottage. Wilson joined me at the first and said, "You take the arm. I'll get the end. I'm the one holding it up, though. No way I'm packing in the ground."

"I have braces. They can hold it while I tamp."

He lifted his end and anchored it against his side. The ghost of his left forearm and hand reached forward, sliding down. "Get your side."

Wilson had been my woodworker when we raised poles along the north field. He'd felled the trees and stripped them, cut the crossarms, notched the poles, bolted the arms in place. I'd held the poles while Wilson filled in the dirt.

"Already leaning to the right," Wilson said. "Too far left. Just a bit now. Too much again."

"We have time for final tweaks."

"You're the one who wanted them straight at the start."

"Yes, I remember."

That was all we said about it.

He held the pole, his left arm applying pressure from the front while his right hand wrapped round the back, and I settled into a quick rhythm—six shovelfuls, then tamping two times round the circle. Shovel, tamp, again. When the hole was half-full, the pole stood on its own.

Wilson stepped away. "Looks plum. Straighter than the tree it was before."

Filling the hole wasn't as bad as the digging, but the tamping jolted my weak shoulder. The next two would leave me broken by the day's end.

"You act like you know what you're doing, Ross." Wilson leaned against a pine. "You dig some holes at Kilby?"

"None this deep."

"How's it you knew how deep to make these ones?"

In between blows with the bar I said, "I'm a keen observer."

Wilson chuckled. "The tamping wasn't mine to do at Flat Top. Powder was the property of the white folks. Couldn't trust none of us with the explosives. I'd drill their holes, get it all good and ready, but then some fellow from ground level would come running down with his fuses and cotton and charges. We weren't far up the shaft when those charges would go."

I had been waiting for this, for Wilson to show me his time underground. "How long were you in the mines?"

"Just under three years."

Wait, my mind said. *Wait.* We'd been convicted in '22, and the leasing stopped in '28. I'd pictured Wilson working or dead in those mines for at least six years, sitting with the knowledge that I'd put him there, that I'd written him those long, dark days. My guilt had let me live a bit easier with Marie's silence. I'd cost a man his family. What right did I have to one of my own?

But he'd been gone only three years, a third of my time.

"I met a fellow who was over in the Peerless mine when it blew," Wilson was saying. "Sparks from a saw set that one off. His name was Conrad, and he was hoping on a homeward ticket, what with his burns, but they just patched him a bit and shuffled him off to Flat Top. It's only if you can't do the work anymore that they let you go, and only then if they don't have the papers to hold you."

I rested the bar against my chest and looked at him.

"Best finish that hole off. Got two more, if I counted right."

"That's right." I was nearly done. *Scoop,* I told my arms. *Pitch. Scoop.* And then, *Set the shovel down. Grab the bar. Hold it firmly, damn it. Hold it. Now, strike. Again.* Even with Wilson there, it was just work—work like any other, like milking and cleaning stalls, building pens and running dogs, rolling carts down narrow aisles, organizing cards, memorizing numbers. It was picking at coal veins on your side and breathing rushes of coal dust, awaiting explosions, lifting and loading. It was tamping and shoveling and pitching. And work is measured in time as much as it is measured in pay. I am uncertain how many hours of running equal a man's hand, his wrist, and forearm and elbow. How many books must be stacked in exchange for one finger? How much milk driven into a pail? How many holes dug, how many dogs pulled from the ground and then buried back even deeper? How many wives and sons?

I am still unsure of my debts.

I finished up and moved to the second hole. Wilson was talking now, more than I'd heard. "There are these stories that are passed round the mining camps." We walked with the second pole. My right arm was battening itself down, the shoulder tightening its leash. I wouldn't be able to turn my head the next day. "All the stories from all the mines that've come and gone. All those men bought from the State. It's like ghost stories. Watch that stump there. That one of the ones you cut down?"

I shook my head and stepped around it.

"Like the Banner mine," he said.

I'd been the first person to tell Wilson about the Banner mine, passing it along as the curse it was.

I turned the pole over to Wilson and set to shoveling. Our shared knowledge of Banner didn't have anything to do with the time Wilson and I had served or the new time we were serving together, there on the farm.

"You ever been in a tunnel sucked clean of oxygen, Ross?"

"You know I haven't. If I had, I wouldn't be alive. Why'd you make Jenny come with your request about Charles?"

"You telling me to shut my mouth?"

"Yes."

He smiled at that. "It's good having you here. Moa and I both feel that way. It's surprised her."

I threw my own silence into the mix of communication.

The ground firmed up round the pole. "Thanks for your help," I told Wilson. "The last one's shorter. Imagine I can get it in on my own. Gotta wait till tomorrow anyway."

"You sore?"

"I am."

"Hard work, setting poles."

I moved past him, and he followed me awhile before turning toward the big house. I felt him at my heels. I heard his breathing and the fall of his steps in the dirt and grasses, not so different from Taylor on his horse.

I had just lowered myself into the tub when Maggie let loose with whines of excitement. *Visitor,* she said. *Someone at the door.* I still hadn't fixed its slant.

It was hard to leave the hot water. I'd been boiling potfuls for the past hour.

"Quiet."

Maggie shushed and sank to her haunches. I'd wrapped a rough towel round my waist, expecting Wilson, ready to talk more. I knew I would listen, just as I would listen again while he held the third pole the next day. I'd listen with my head down and my arms and hands aching, both my arms, both my hands. He'd tell more ghost stories of black damp and cave-ins, and I'd think about Stevens's side blown to bits from Hughes's shotgun or that single piece of shot in Jennings's kidney that had poisoned his blood.

"Mr. Roscoe?" It wasn't Wilson's voice, but Jenny's. "Am I disturbing you, Mr. Roscoe?" The door creaked open.

"A minute!" I shouted. "Wait outside just a minute, Jenny." I went back to retrieve my clothes, the same filthy ones from the day's labors, stiffened a little from lying on the floor. I felt damned by the warmth in my stomach.

It's nothing, I whispered. I'd been naked and ready to bathe and then a young woman had come to my door. Of course I was shaky. *Quiet, now.*

I remained barefoot, my hair damp.

"I've disturbed you," Jenny said when I opened the door. "You were settling in for the night. My apologies, Mr. Roscoe. I have dinner and the writing supplies you requested."

Jenny had been so small before I left, Moa and Wilson's young-est, a child who played with Gerald at times. I had so few clear memories of her alone—chasing the chickens and then, outside this same cottage, festooning a tree with ribbons. Now, she was my only visitor with a history that didn't indict me directly.

"I'd rather eat than settle in. I'll light some lamps."

Jenny closed the door as best she could behind her.

"You have a pencil?"

She handed me a yellow stick worked halfway down, likely sto-len from her daddy's workshop. I dulled the point quickly etching *Fix* into the wood of the door.

"Now you'll always think it's broken." Jenny set food on the table, enough for two, even three. "Figure you could use a little extra." She dumped meat into Maggie's pie tin, tugging one of Maggie's ears as the dog set to eating.

I could remember the feel of Jenny's arms around me.

I started swallowing down Moa's beans—not so good as Marie's, but good all the same—and I called for the paper Jenny had brought.

"We'll write to the deputy warden, Taylor. He's the one who gave me the dog."

"Papa thinks ill of you getting a dog on your release."

"I worked those dogs for years," I told this girl who has no busi-ness hearing, who had no guilt to own, no part in Kilby or Flat Top.

Jenny set her hands flat on the table. "I'm sure you know what to say in the letter, Mr. Roscoe. Charles Emit Grice. That's his full name. Papa gave him Mr. Emit's name in the middle there. You probably already knew."

"No."

"It was so hard to lose Mr. Emit, but Mama always says every hardship has its blessed side, and she knew it was the truth because you and Ms. Marie came then, with little Gerald. She tells such stories from those days. Corn reaching to the tops of the pecans and the peanuts growing three and four to the pod. Everyone growing bellies, and the farm growing taller and wider every season—"

"That isn't true. The farm struggled until we got electricity."

We sat quiet for a moment, Jenny's lips shining in the weak light of my lamps.

"Charles Emit Grice," I finally said. It was only Jenny and me there in her parents' old cottage, this girl and me and my prison dog. *Dear Deputy Warden Taylor,* I wrote. I was polite and direct, stating our request simply. I said *please.* I was asking for a favor, and I treated it as such. Just before I signed my name, I wrote, *Thank you for sending Maggie with me.* I signed *Roscoe T Martin,* and only upon seeing my own name in print did I realize I'd written a letter to an illiterate man.

I couldn't tell Jenny. I couldn't tell her I had failed in this endeavor before we'd even handed the letter to the postmaster.

I'd memorized the prison's address from all the letters I once sent, and it was strange to switch the numbers and roads, to send from here to there. The letter I wrote with Jenny was the first Kilby'd seen from that house.

"I'll take it to the PO in the morning," Jenny said. "Papa is going into town."

I had a hard time giving the envelope away, a sad-sick murmur in my gut. It might go unanswered, an old, gnawing fear.

"It'll be a little while before we hear back, don't you think?" She seemed as scared as I was. "You said you'd wait until we hear. Even if it's weeks, right? Months even?"

"Yes, Jenny. I'll wait." With the poles in, it was good to have another excuse. Though I'd thought about Jenny's idea of this being my home, I was still convinced that I couldn't stay.

"Thank you, Mr. Roscoe."

I anticipated her walking round the table to embrace me in gratitude, but instead, she moved toward the door. Over her head I read, *Fix.* The light outside was still enough to catch her figure through the windows, that letter bright white in the dusky air.

ɪ feared I'd forget pieces when I started working on the lines. The power flowing in came in alternating currents at a higher voltage, and the company's new transformer on the main line from the road stepped down that voltage for domestic consumption, bringing it to another that lined up with my new poles.

Wilson took me to town for supplies, straight to Bean's Hardware. Electric lamps hung from the ceiling.

"Wilson." Bean paused on my face before slowly drawing out my name. "Roscoe T Martin. I'll be damned."

"Bean."

"Welcome back." He came round the counter to shake my hand. "Was a real shame how everything happened."

"I see you relented." I nodded toward the ceiling lights, their solid glow.

"Hah!" Bean laughed. "You remember how dead set I was against all that electrical nonsense of yours. Well, when they brought power to the block, suppose I just couldn't hold out any longer."

"How's it treating you?"

"Still makes me nervous as hell, but I'll admit to the ease it brings. What is it I can do for you gentlemen?"

"Insulated copper wire," I told him, "five hundred yards' worth, and fifty of sheathing."

Bean looked to Wilson.

"It's all aboveground now, Bean. Honest work. Ross here is electrifying the cottage, doing some fine improvements to the property."

Bean clapped me on the back. "Just have to check, son. Can't have you heading back out so soon after you've arrived. You boys'll have to help me with the rolls."

I saw Bean on the stand again, telling the jury that I'd made good on my debt to him. I saw those detailed bills he'd sent me, subtracting my payments, and then the final note, which read, *Paid in Full. Thank you for your business.*

We loaded everything into the pickup bed, and Wilson told Bean to add it to the account.

"Is that Marie's account?" I asked in the truck on the way home.

"It's the land's account. When you're ready for light fixtures, you'll use the same one."

Wilson helped me carry the wiring back to the cottage. "Need anything else?" he asked when we were done.

"No."

"Holler when you do."

It was strange to be hollering for Wilson when I needed material things, shovels and wires and fixtures. Before, he'd provided the labor—welding those cores, digging and filling holes, harvesting and planting. I thought again of his replacing rails on that fence, both his arms pulling the rotted pieces loose. He hadn't needed it, but he'd asked for my help that day I sought his support for the lines. He would always need assistance with that work now, and I wondered whether it was my responsibility to give it, to stand in for Wilson's lost arm, my presence there one of necessity. It seemed clean, like Bean's columns of payments applied to debts, something near balance.

I took time weaving the copper together—eight strands of it twisting over and past themselves. The wires already had a thin layer of insulation, which worked with their twisted positions to force a more equal current through the total cross section of the strand.

I finished the weaving in a week and slid the bundled wires into their coats. As much as I hated to enlist him in the same endeavor, I called upon Wilson to help me set the lines in their porcelain insulators. He held the coiled length while I strung it, three lines on the poles to distribute the current in case of surges or lightning before they came together at the service conduit I'd cobbled together on an eave of the cottage. The lines went in the steel pipe from below, up and through a U-joint curve, before they came out inside. On their own, wires can withstand water just fine, but stick them in a contained space with a puddle, and there's promised damage. Water is a beast in captivity, father to rust and mold and rot. Give it a bit of air, though, some sun, and it goes on its way quiet enough.

"Another couple yards," I shouted to Wilson. We were on the last line of the last pole, those twisted copper wires hidden away under their black coat, the thick cord settling into the shining brown of its insulator as if lying down to bed. All of the pieces were so beautiful together—snug and purposeful and poised—and I let myself feel the inherent magic I'd always felt for the work. The power I'd soon feed into those wires had its home in water, far back at the start of the transmission lines I'd run from the dammed-up Coosa. We made this fierce, blazing force out of something wet and fluid. We changed it completely, but it still behaved the same.

"That's all I have," Wilson said.

We walked together to the company's transformer perched high overhead. Wilson held the base of the ladder as I climbed. "Don't even have to knock down a tree this time," he said. Alabama Power had taken care of that, the current severed until it was asked to work.

I attached my wires and flipped the lever on.

The moment lacked the thrill of our first, but still I wished Marie were there to see it, to see me legally running electricity onto her land, improving it as I said I would.

ELECTRICITY hummed through the cottage, wires in white coating running their way across walls and ceilings through small, white insulators I'd ordered from Bean. I knew people were starting to hide the wiring inside walls, but I will always prefer it exposed.

The new lights were bright, and I found myself lighting the oil lamps instead. The cottage looked better in the lamplight, like the upstairs library, I suppose.

The door hung straight on its hinges, a new frame running round it. Scraping the word *Fix* off had set me to scraping the entire thing, and I'd taken the wood down a few grains before polishing it with linseed oil. It had become a handsome entrance.

I'd replaced the broken panes in the windows, too.

Three weeks had passed since Jenny mailed the letter, and we hadn't received a response. She didn't linger when she brought my meals.

Summer struck out hot and humid, but the cottage stayed cool in its shade. The oaks had been dropping their leaves on the roof so long, it'd become a mess of mulch up there. A leak near the stovepipe had grown, warping the ceiling planks, dripping loud into the pot I kept stationed underneath it. The summer thunderstorms set it streaming, so I climbed to the roof to begin replacing it. The shingles had rotted to the consistency of leaves, everything sloughing loose against the flat edge of the shovel. I pounded a few spikes into the slope to help station myself, and I scraped all the junk toward one corner of the house, pushing it over the eaves, where it littered the ground in great brown clumps. When I got to the planking underneath, it was like exposing treasure, the flat, smooth boards so stark against the pulpy roofing. The cottage had been built well.

My hands no longer blistered against the handle of the shovel.

I raked leaves and shingles out wide in the meadow, a single layer so the sun would parch them. If the sky could give me two days without rain, they'd be dry enough to scrape back into a pile and set aflame. Wilson had given me a roll of tar paper, and I'd intended to get it up that same day, but the wood needed drying time, too. I asked the sky to stay clear.

"Who're you talking to?" I imagined my father asking. "You a praying man, now?"

My young Marie said, "You shouldn't be here, love. You should be waiting on Yellow Mama."

Ed might say, "Fastening that farmer's coat tight, aren't you, brother?"

"Come out," I whispered to the timber, my eyes on the low holly and the middling dogwoods, the heavy oaks and tall pines, the nubby grasses. Birds were in the branches making their noise, wind scratching through. The day's work ran in sweat down my arms, dampening the wood of the rake handle. Its teeth were rusted a dark red-brown. "Ed?" I questioned. "Pa?"

Maggie lifted her head from the shade where she rested and let out a low growl. Footsteps followed the sound, and a figure I didn't recognize appeared from the bushes and trees. He was tall and heavy, comfortably thick about his middle. His cheeks were pudgy and his chin gave a small sag, his face childish in a sad way, like a boy on the verge of crying.

Maggie stood and barked, and the man's face twisted into a fear I recognized. Gerald—my son. What life had given him the time and food and lack of work to become so large about the middle and face? I remembered him as an active boy, alongside his reading. Sword fights and tree climbing and races through the stalks and furrows.

"It's all right," I said to Maggie. "Down."

She gruffed once more and flopped back down, too hot to put up a fuss.

"Gerald?"

"Hey, Pa."

Was he eighteen? Nineteen? I didn't know. Either way, I'd been younger than him when I met his mother.

He put his thick arms around my back, squeezing my body against his own, crushing between us the rake still clutched in my hands. "Pa."

"Gerald?" The question was a muffled whisper I doubt he heard.

The embrace ended before I'd had time to process my response to it. We were nearer than we'd been since the day Sheriff Eddings had come for me. We'd joked over dinner about the knock at the door—a pirate come to steal our treasure. We were planning a sword fight. I'd tousled his hair on my way out, promising to be back before bedtime.

"I got news of your release. Moa told me you were here."

"Oh?"

He looked toward the trees. "I wanted to visit you while you were away," he said eventually.

"Why didn't you?"

This was my question—the only one I cared about—and the conversation was his to make or abandon. I watched his teeth bite at the inside of his cheek, a habit I'd seen in him as a child—gnawing away at himself when he was thinking, eating himself into an idea. He'd bitten his nails then, too, and I saw that his nails were still rough, the skin around them torn and red.

"Mother convinced me you were to blame. For everything—Wilson and our back payments and the years we struggled after what happened. The death of that man." Gerald raised his hulking shoulders up to his ears. "I guess I just got tired of fighting her. But then I got that call from Moa, telling me that you were here, and I—I had to come." He brought a thumb to his mouth, but there was nothing to chew or clip.

I couldn't tell whether it was a good thing to see him, or whether it was awful. He had been my boy for those good years, and I had known what fatherhood could be, but then he'd disappeared. I had disappeared. I didn't know I would stop being his father that day Sheriff Eddings came. Gerald didn't either. And now he was telling me he might have been my son these nine long years, had his mother let him.

I tried to figure out how to start that process—parenting. I could invite him inside, offer him a glass of water to stave off the heat, maybe a jar of peaches to quench his chewing and distract his hands. The words were ready in my mouth, clear in my mind. *Come in,* I would say. *Come inside out of the heat. Let's sit down and talk awhile. We have a lot to catch up on.* I would put my arm around his shoulder, though he'd grown taller than me, making the gesture awkward, but no less heartening. *Come inside, Son. I've missed you.*

And I had. I did. I do still. I miss the nine-year-old version, the ten-year-old, and the eleven-year-old, too, and I wanted that child to translate into the stranger in front of me, with his meaty face and messy hands. I wanted to know how to be his father.

"I'm sorry. I'm so sorry, Pa."

For a moment I could see us together—on a walk out to the lines, in the shop watching the thresher, pushing out to the south woods in the fall, rifles on our shoulders, venison steaks on our minds. I had taught him to shoot.

"I should've gone against her earlier."

I let the rake fall to the ground and reached for him with my good arm. He was so tall and so thick. He hadn't even begun the route to manhood when I left, hadn't grown any hairs or inches, and I found myself imagining every one of those moments I'd missed—the first beard and mustache, the first shave, the drop in voice, the thickening of the legs, the hair growing in dark and thatched, covering his body. He would always be a man, now, and I had missed him become one.

I did ask him inside, but he declined quickly. "I can't stay. I didn't even know I was coming today—I just got in the car. I have to be back for a shift in the library."

"I worked in the library at Kilby."

"Mom told me. She never showed me your letters, but she gave me updates sometimes."

"So she read them."

For a moment again neither of us spoke.

"Could I come again? Maybe this Saturday?"

"Yes. Please."

We shook hands—right hands, and he looked at the reduced height of my arm. "Is that from the fight you had with another inmate? I remember getting word about that."

Wilson had told me the same.

"It's a different injury. Later, from a guard, not an inmate, but it's fine." I held on to his hand. "Did your mother visit me when I was injured that first time? Did she come to the hospital?"

Gerald looked caught, a trapped thing. "We'll talk about it next time I see you, all right?"

So Marie had come. Those flimsy visions in the hospital had

been grounded in at least some truth. She'd said something, and we'd been together long enough for her to put something in my hand before Nurse Hannah chased her away. Crows in flight, pecking and shouting.

"Next time."

"Good-bye, Pa."

He walked toward the trail, the back of him holding up greater than the front. His hair needed a trim, and there were sweat rings under his arms, but I could appreciate his stride—quick and long. Still, I admit to wanting his appearance to be like so many of my other imaginings, a shaky reality, untenable and flawed. I was afraid after Gerald left the clearing. My rake was at my feet. Maggie lay in the shade of the cottage. A bird let go a song, steep-noted, unique. I should have known what it was. I could name all the plants around me, the trees and shrubs, flowers and grasses. I could raise poles and wire an abandoned cottage. I could strip a roof and stand in the midst of years of rot, willing it dry enough to burn. But I didn't know if I could be a father to a son.

GERALD didn't come that Saturday, but Jenny did, an envelope in her hands. I was outside the cottage, and she walked toward me slowly.

"What's that?"

"It's come. Word from Kilby."

The look of my name on the paper scooped some great dormant need out of my stomach. I'd waited for my name in that location for nine years, *Kilby Prison* in the upper left, with its address there on Wetumpka–Montgomery Highway. I didn't recognize the writing, a blocky print, a bit too big for the space. Someone had written my name on that envelope and put it in the mail, and a man had delivered it to the big house, where Marie had received the letters I sent. Her handwriting was much lovelier than the writing I held, but she didn't once turn that writing into words and send those words to me. Few things go freely through the walls of Kilby, but letters are one of them. *Just one letter, Marie. One envelope with my name in your hand. Roscoe T Martin.* Only four weeks had passed before Kilby answered mine.

"I don't know that I can open this." My fingers had already left brown smudges on the paper that I would have liked to wipe away. It was too perfect a thing, that envelope.

"You best," Jenny said. The mulch was thick at her feet, and her hands worked at the fabric of her skirt, wringing it to wrinkles just as she had when she'd first asked me to help with Charles.

The flap gave way easy enough along the glue, the paper inside thin and folded into thirds.

"What does it say?"

The message was short, the writing even bigger and sloppier. "Nothing."

"Nothing?"

And so I read the unfamiliar writing aloud: " 'Martin. You no beter an to ast me the foks past threw here. Hows that dog?' " After the question mark, the writing changed to form one new word: *Taylor.* It was practiced, that word, the only one he really needed. The rest of the letter must have been turned from Taylor's speech into words on a page by one of his new trustees. This one didn't look to be taking out books from the library or ordering up articles on whelping.

The letter was short, but I could hear Taylor's voice in it. Those few words were communication from him to me. I'd written a letter to Taylor, and he'd written one back. He even asked a question.

Hows that dog?

Maggie lay in the shade of the cottage, on the side farthest from the roof debris. She was deep in the thick grass, her head cradled in her front paws, her ears dribbling onto the ground. *She's good,* I wanted to tell Taylor. *The best dog. The best gift.* She was a gift. I could see that then. I see it now.

I never again wrote to Taylor, though.

"What does that mean?" Jenny asked.

I folded the letter along its creases and tucked it into its envelope. "It means he only notices the boys he has working for him or the ones he's tracking down. It sounds like Charles isn't one of them."

"Well, it's disappointing." She broke into a determined smile and pointed to the roof. "But that's sure to take a while."

"No more than a week." Then I would leave. There would be a dam near the ocean somewhere, lines to run, forces to capture and convert. I would go and work as I once had. Maggie and I could find ourselves a small house in a village, and I might even meet a nurse like my Hannah, maybe even have a child or two. I'd forget I owed Wilson the work he could no longer do, forget I'd seen my grown son, forget that all these people existed this many years after my memories of them stalled.

"I'll go get your dinner." But Jenny didn't move.

"What is it?"

"Just—" She didn't look at me. "I don't know why it feels so wrong, but I have—I have. They have. I mean, they—" Her eyes trained themselves on some high branch far off to the right of her vision. "It's theirs to talk about. That's what I mean. And they don't want me saying anything, which is why they put me here in the first place. You asked that, and it was all I had in me not to answer truthfully. They wanted time to pass, you see, wanted everything to get settled, wanted—"

"What are you saying?"

When she spoke, the words were mousy and skittish. "They figured the bit about Charles would keep you occupied. They had all kinds of talks before your release, and you have to believe that this was only a backup in case it seemed like you weren't going to stay at all."

"Where is Charles, Jenny?"

She looked over her shoulder toward the big house.

"Where?"

"He's in New York."

"And Henry?"

"Oh, that's true, Mr. Roscoe. Henry's in New York, too. They're all there. Mama and Papa are awful proud."

"Why did you choose Charles?"

"I'm sorry?"

"Why'd you all decide to make Charles the criminal? Why not Henry? Hell, why not Gerald, my own son?"

"Daddy remembered the times you'd seen him lose his temper out when he was helping you two with the thresher and the crops."

Of course. I had seen Charles slam his closed fist into the unforgiving wall of the shop, ripping his knuckles raw, and all because his count was off—not as many shucked ears in the bucket as he'd anticipated. I had seen him shout and kick, and I hadn't thought to question a moment of violence that could send him to prison. They'd been smart in their planning.

"The *they*"—I stepped closer to the girl who'd so blatantly deceived me—"the *they* who orchestrated this—I assume you're talking about Marie?"

She shook her head.

My anger paused, confused. I was set to add this injustice to Marie's register. She'd ignored my letters, forgotten our marriage, stolen my son, and then settled me into the help's quarters. It made sense to blame her, and I wanted to. I wanted to loathe her charity and pity and condescension.

"Who then?"

"You need to talk to Mother and Father and Gerald. I know he's visited, but there's more he needs to tell you."

"He was supposed to come today."

"Yes, I know. But then the letter arrived."

"And your time was up?"

"I suppose that's it."

We stood staring at each other for what seemed a day, a week, nine years.

Finally she said, "I'll get your dinner, Mr. Roscoe." She walked toward the trail, fading and fading until there were only woods and grass and the power line sloping from the third pole to the conduit on the house.

THE next morning, the Grices found me on their porch when they returned from church. Maggie lay at my feet.

Jenny and Wilson stood at the bottom of the steps, but Moa strode up next to me. "Least you can do is wish us good morning."

"Good morning."

"That's better. Now, come inside and have some lunch. Best invite that beast in, too." Moa was trying to soften me, and I should've declined in order to keep my solemnity. *No thank you,* I should've said. *Maggie's comfortable out here.*

But I couldn't deny Maggie a bowl of scraps inside that fine house, and Moa knew it. She's still the smartest of us all.

Jenny helped me up from the rocker I'd chosen hours earlier, and we walked into the house hand in hand behind her father. Maggie brushed by us, trotting toward the kitchen as though she'd been there innumerable times. She was spoiled, that dog. Still is.

The squirrel wallpaper confronted me in the foyer, and I fought to keep my eyes trained away from that whimsy. Like the layers I'd seen on my son, those squirrels were products of ease and time. I'd have longed for extra pounds in Kilby—a few to fill in my face, raise my eyes, cover my ribs. I'd have longed for images that meant nothing, there only to see, to lighten the scene like Chaplain's flowers. Instead, I'd grown used to efficiency and precision. What wasn't necessary was relinquished. Whoever I'd been when I came to Kilby, I'd left condensed, only the core of me surviving, the part that worked, the part that ate and slept in order to continue.

Wallpaper and fat had no place in that life.

Moa was already at the stove in the kitchen, the kettle nearly boiling, the table laid with biscuits and spreads. "Sit down, Roscoe. Help yourself."

She fed Maggie by the back door, and the dog fell to the food quickly, wolfing it down as though those other prison dogs were still pushing at her sides, trying to get their piece—a dainty drinker and a ravenous eater.

I was hungry, too, but I didn't follow her lead. I'd been sitting on the porch for hours, hunger sharpening the words I planned to say. I didn't want to feel full.

"You'd like us to start, I imagine." I looked to Wilson, who was pulling up a stool across from me. "You know about our deception, and I apologize for it. You have to know that we did it out of true concern for you. We needed you to stay, and we couldn't think of another way to do that."

"Why did you need me to stay?"

"We needed to get a sense of you," Moa said.

"And," Wilson added, "we wanted you to have some time to figure out a place for yourself."

"I don't think that's happened."

Wilson shook his head. "You're wrong about that. Look at all you've done—the power and the poles and wiring, the improvements to the cottage. It's work you can do, Ross, work you're good at."

"For better for worse," Moa added.

"Moa."

She looked at her husband. "I'm allowed my doubts, Wilson."

I still think about those words of hers.

I ran through uncertainties of my own. I'd seen myself working, as Wilson had said—and with power, the electricity that had first awoken me to inquiry and pursuit and knowledge. It wasn't dogs and it wasn't musty books, not reading to men from a Bible. It wasn't dairy cows, pails of milk, calves mewling. It was work I knew and loved, but it was here, on Marie's land, with its memory—the haunted familiarity of the shop and the trail, the cornstalks and that line of fence where I'd first told Wilson the idea, the house I was sitting in, with its new wallpaper and residents, my family still gone.

"How could I stay here?"

I watched a look pass between Moa and Wilson, another between Jenny and Moa.

"Will you excuse us, Jenny?" Moa asked.

I was proud of the girl when she said, "No." She'd grown brave in the short time I'd been there—courage building with every meal she brought, every lie she told.

"Please excuse yourself," Moa said. "I know we've put you in the midst of all this, but we need to talk to Roscoe alone for a moment."

"I know everything there is to say."

"Listen to your mother," Wilson said. "Go on now."

"Yes, Papa."

I remembered Moa's words eliciting quick compliance in the past, her directives always followed. Wilson had been the softer of the two. But their roles had clearly swapped in my time away, and I resisted the envy that rose in me for two people together long enough to become each other.

Jenny nodded at me out of support, I chose to think, and then she left the room. The stairs creaked under her feet as she climbed to the second story. We listened to her footsteps move down the hall, the doorknob turn, a few more steps, the firm latch of the door closing.

"Seems she's gone," Wilson said, but Moa shushed him.

After a few more steps, the scratch of a record floated down to us, one of Marie's. The notes slid right into their slots in my memory.

"Come here," Marie had said. We'd been in our tiny sitting room—I'd just come home from a day topping poles—and she'd taken my hands. "Isn't this the very best music you've ever heard?" We'd danced round that small room, to this very song, and she'd rested her head against my chest, just as she was supposed to.

"It's called 'The World Is Waiting for the Sunrise,'" she told me. "Can you hear the longing in it?"

"Yes."

I can hear it.

I imagine Jenny hearing it, too, listening to it right now.

Maggie had long finished her food and lay chewing on a bone over by the stove. Moa poured our coffee. "Jenny's right that she knows most everything we're about to tell you. I just didn't want her to see your reaction, which is me asking you to keep as calm as you're capable of while we give you the news we've got to give. Can you do that?"

"Yes, ma'am."

"Thank you, Ross," Wilson said.

Trouble was growing in me.

"Now, you'll have to go through this whole thing again with Gerry when he visits next, but I suppose it's best you hear it from our mouths so you have a chance to calm down before seeing him. He's missed you, Roscoe, and he wants you in his life."

"All right."

Wilson took over. "Whether the blame of our hardships fell squarely on you or not, Marie put it there, and she did her best to get Gerry to put it there, too."

Moa was nodding. "Wilson tried to talk to her about it a couple times. Imagine you know as well as we do how stubborn Marie can be. There was no budging on this particular matter. But I bring this up only to assure you that none of this is Gerry's doing."

"You're making me nervous, Moa."

"Hell"—Wilson chuckled—"me, too."

Moa held tight to her mug with both hands. She took a breath that seemed to last minutes, the inhale draining all the air from the room, the exhale bringing it back. "Marie's divorced you, Roscoe. It's been years now."

I expected anger, a great circulating current. I waited for it, clenching my fingers round my mug, readying to throw it against that damn wallpaper, splattering those tiny people with their huge flowers, a great stain to mar that shiny room.

Moa and Wilson watched me.

But my hand couldn't bring that mug high enough to throw it. Instead, I took a sip of the coffee Moa had brewed for us. Coffee was a treat still, having been gone for so long. I worry that I've grown too used to some comforts now, coffee just a part of my life like sleeping in a bed and waking in a room and working my own hours. All these things are privileges.

"Ross?" Wilson asked.

"Just taking it in." Then I found a question. "How?"

"She got your signature on the papers the one time she visited," Wilson said. "You were injured. She told us you were fully conscious and in agreement, but I recognized the lie in that the day I picked you up—asking me about whether she'd visited at all."

"Why didn't she just ask me when I was awake?"

"We can't answer that, Ross."

"But there are things we can tell you," Moa assured. "It's this next part that we wanted the time for—the time with you here." The swiftness in her speech felt like panic. "Once Marie paid off the power company and we got back the electricity, the farm did well. We all did well. Six months after Wilson returned, Marie chose to leave, though. She moved down to Mobile for a teaching position. She took Gerald, against his wishes, and she insisted we move in here to keep up the maintenance. A little over a year later she came back with a lawyer who'd drawn up a bill of sale for the house and property."

"She sold it to us for a hundred dollars," Wilson said.

"A hundred dollars we'd already given her—taken from wages. She wouldn't let us argue."

I was thinking of the divorce, trying to see it, to place it within the time I'd known in Kilby. Marie had been absent, but she had played the role of wife in my mind, a silent wife, an absent wife, even at times a figment of a younger wife, but she was still—always—the woman I had married, the woman I was married to still.

"Ross?"

"It's a lot to take in," Moa said.

I traced the story they'd given me—from my furtive divorce to the lawyer's visit. "This is yours? You own the land?"

"Yes," Wilson said.

"And you chose to bring me back here?"

They nodded, and I looked between them, a foreignness settling around me. Marie's father's land handed over to the people hired to till it, and those people my new custodians. I was in the cottage because of them, because of the mercy they'd shown.

"You'll have to forgive me," I told Wilson and Moa, a desperation stirring, a need for escape so fierce I couldn't finish the thought. I couldn't even say I was going before I was moving away. I paused only for a moment—there at the door, long enough to call Maggie to my side.

I spent the next days burning the old roof mulch and laying tarpaper across the dry planks. Twice, I'd packed and then unpacked a bag. The second of those times, I'd left, making it to the original power line running along Old Hissup Road, belongings on my back, dog at my side. My transformers stopped me, all three of them there, rusted, quiet ghosts of the creations they'd been. The combination sent me back to the cottage, unsure of the part that was mine—the wires with their live currents or the broken-down transformers that'd long been replaced.

Then Jenny arrived. "Will you come up to the house? Gerald's here."

I'd slept fitfully since my talk with her parents, questions keeping me awake, wispy things, crippled and dark.

I let Jenny lead us into the meadow, the grass crumpled, the burned mulch a dark circle, and then the big house came into view, its glinting windows and bright siding.

I stopped at the porch steps, Maggie's nose in the pits of my knees.

"Come on," Jenny said, but I didn't know that I was ready for another conversation about my former wife and her property.

Finally, Jenny took my hand.

My toes caught on every stair, and only Jenny's grip kept me from stumbling. We climbed for hours, it seemed, though there were only six steps. The porch, too, had grown. Its planks stretched far away to the front door, a mile at least.

"I can't make it," I told Jenny, but she pulled me forward. Maggie lay down on the brick walkway without being told. The heavy oak door was open, as it was every day of every summer I had lived here. Even the lightest hint of a breeze helped in fighting the heat. People were in the front sitting room, taking me in. My trousers were gritty, my hands calloused. My shirt hung loose, the cuffs ratty and threadbare. My nose and forehead were burned red by sun, and the beard I'd finally grown to cover the slack skin of my cheeks hung uneven off my chin. I still have that beard, though there are patches along my jaw that will never grow.

Jenny brought me into the room where Moa and Wilson stood with the stranger I now recognized as my son. I was surprised again by his appearance—his height and thickness and clothes.

"Hey, Pa."

Next to him stood a man closer to my age. His suit was dark blue, his tie gold. His hair was gray at the sides, but dark on top and greased back from his forehead.

"Mr. Martin." He lifted an enormous hand in my direction. "Good to meet you." His voice was like Ed's, something foreign to it. "My name's Robert Hill. Gerald's retained me to help with your situation."

"We'll go through it all," Gerald said.

"I'm staying." Jenny settled herself into a chair, and no one argued.

Gerald reached for me, and I allowed myself to grip hold of him.

Moa passed me a glass of iced tea, cold and slick in my hand. Wilson and Gerald took the chairs on either side of Jenny, leaving Moa and Robert Hill and me the sofa to share. We squeezed ourselves onto our own cushions. My glass poured its sweat into my hand.

Sips were taken. The house creaked in the walls with the breeze outside.

I wondered again how old my son was—eighteen? Nineteen? His birthday was in March. Maybe March 16? That didn't sound right. Marie's birthday was July 16. Mine is September 10. I would turn forty that coming fall. I feel like an old man.

"I know Moa and Wilson have talked to you about their owner-ship of the land," Gerald said, "and the state of your—" He looked to the Grices for help.

"Your marriage," Wilson said. "Yes, Moa and I told him about the divorce."

"We didn't know what to do," Gerald said, pleading in his voice. "I hope you understand—we just didn't know how to fight Mother, or whether we should, or what to do when you were released. We needed time to figure it out, time to get to know you again, and I know I haven't done that, but I'm going to try, and I trust Moa and Wilson and all they've told me about your time here."

"Gerald, honey," Moa said, "you've nothing to apologize for. Just tell your father what we're doing."

He sucked in a thick breath. "Mr. Hill is here to help you fight the divorce."

The lawyer must have sensed my astonishment. "Mr. Martin, we're all quite certain that your marriage was dissolved without your consent."

"Yes."

"And that is against the law. Your former wife has divided her assets as she sees fit, but were you married—as the law would dic-tate—all of her assets would be as much yours as they are hers."

"But she's already given you the land," I said to Moa.

She nodded, but Wilson spoke. "You don't deserve to be cut out of it entirely."

"There are a few options you can take," Robert Hill said. "You could fight the divorce, which would be the longest route. It'd require witnesses from the prison hospital testifying to your mental state when your wife visited. You could also sue her for half of her current assets, which are significant—Gerald shared her will with all of us, and it's clear she's done well. She put her returns on this property toward investments her father had started, as well as other properties, like the one in Tuscaloosa, where Gerald currently resides. She has assets to distribute, quite certainly."

"And if I'm not interested in either of those options?"

That damn iced tea felt dainty in my hands, a false thing that said we were the type of people who had time to sit around drinking iced tea through the afternoon. I set it on the table.

Robert Hill reached down on his side of the sofa and returned with a sheaf of papers.

"Take a look."

The words were jolting, sharp-ridged things. *Last Will and Testament of Marie Dawson Martin.* It was strange to see Marie's full name attached to that other phrase. We'd never made a will.

Custody of Dependents read, *Preceding March 15, 1932, custody of Mrs. Martin's son, Gerald Roscoe Martin [heretofore referred to as the* Dependent*], goes to Mr. and Mrs. Wilson Grice.*

March 15. How could I have forgotten the middle of the month? The ides of March?

"Would the State have let you be his legal guardians?" I asked Moa and Wilson.

"Marie's lawyer was ready to fight the Jim Crow laws," Moa said. "I thank God nearly every day that we didn't have to go through that."

After Gerald's care, I found a list of assets, long and staggering. The house and land weren't there, as I knew they wouldn't be, but there was an address in Mobile and one in Tuscaloosa. There were accounts I didn't know, investment descriptions that didn't make sense. Marie's mother's silver was listed, alongside several pianos and two cars, a fur coat worth a small fortune, and a set of china. *Collection of books* held its own line, its worth *unknown*. There was a diamond ring and *Other Jewelry*, two paintings by Eileen Agar. Who was Eileen Agar? Furniture was separated out by type— dressers and wardrobes, dining tables, a sideboard, lounge chairs, sofas, chaises, beds. When had Marie gotten all of this?

Beyond the assets, I found the *Division of Assets*.

"I imagine that's the part that'll interest you most," Robert Hill said.

The smaller assets went first—the furniture and books and clothing—and they went mostly to charities. I was somewhat con- fused by the diamond ring that went to Gerald, but realized it was intended for his future bride. The rest of Marie's jewelry went to Jenny.

The house in Tuscaloosa was the first property to be designated, and Marie left it to Gerald, as well as the house in Mobile.

"None of this is mine," I said.

"A part of it is," Wilson said.

"Is it?" *Wilson's arm is gone,* I wanted to tell them, and his time was both shorter and longer than any I did. I stood up, unclear of my intentions.

"It's all right, Pa. You don't have to do anything, if you don't want. Mr. Hill has something else to tell you."

I dug the heels of my hands into my eyes, rubbing fiercely, willing the room gone, those damn roses on the walls, the damn people on the furniture.

"It's all right, Roscoe," Moa said. "Sit down."

I sat, that prison part of me still moved by someone else's re- quests.

"All right, now," Robert Hill said. "Those first two options I mentioned still stand—they're independent of what I'm about to tell you, and as your counsel, I encourage you to pursue one of those paths. You'd have a strong case either way. What we have here"—he tapped a new set of papers in his lap—"is something Mr.

and Mrs. Grice recently put together with the support of Gerald. It'd be easiest just to let you read through it."

The first page described a small structure on a parcel of land, a quarter section, 160 acres, mostly agricultural, with a few acres of woods. The structure was *wood construction on a pier-and-beam foundation with no modern amenities*. The following pages added in legal talk of fences and taxes, easements and county lines. The words were familiar—Coosa County, Old Hissup Road bordering the north and Jacks Creek bordering the west. It was Marie's land, but it didn't make sense to me, this fraction of it. The farm was two sections—more than 1,200 acres—and it'd never been subdivided. "Land's not for cutting up into tiny pieces," Marie's father had said. "You want yourself a bit, then you move into a township and buy yourself a street-side lot."

At the end, I found a deed transferring ownership of the property.

"I don't understand."

"It took a lot of convincing," Moa replied, "and I'm still not altogether convinced. But Wilson believes you deserve a home, and you've done enough to convince me you deserve a chance at least."

"You've done good work here, Ross."

"It's your home, Mr. Roscoe." Jenny smiled. "Like I said."

Moa offered her seat to Gerald, who squeezed himself against me like a child. "Mother took us away from each other," he whispered, warm and moist against my ear. I fought revulsion. He was my son, but he was too soft a man. I should've been able to welcome his need, to hear in his words my own misfortune and loss. But instead, I heard an educated man, fed and clothed and housed in ease and comfort, his only handicap self-imposed through the biting of his nails and cheeks—I heard this man lamenting his years of privilege, years without a father, but still years of ease. I knew it was unfair to compare our time. I know it still. When I see him, I remind myself that my punishment came from a choice I'd made, and that his was out of his control. I try to talk to him about his life over there in Tuscaloosa, full of dinners and fancy dress and occasional ladies, though he still hasn't married.

"It's all right, Son," I told him.

Moa had gone to stand between Jenny's and Wilson's chairs. They were all so strong—the three of them—strong and whole enough to be able to offer a part of their lives to me. I didn't want half of Marie's assets. I didn't want to fight the divorce. But I wanted to stay. I hadn't before that moment, before seeing Moa and Wilson and Jenny across from me. I wanted to stay close to them. I wanted to stay because the deed was theirs to transfer.

I wanted to stay because they believed I should.

I was freshly bathed and sitting down to breakfast when the knock came on the door. I pictured Jenny out there, my regular visitor. Only a week had passed since the meeting with Robert Hill, and she'd come every day. At first I thought it was out of guilt, but I was growing to see that ours was a friendship. We are currently exchanging lessons—she's interested in the workings of electricity, and I'm learning how to use the herbs she's cultivating in the meadow.

"Coming," I said, pulling a thin undershirt over my head, maneuvering my right arm through the sleeve. I would spare her the sight of my stomach and shoulder.

Jenny wasn't at the door.

Goddamn it, Marie.

Her dress was blue, like the one her younger self had worn, but the Marie that stood before me wasn't young. The evidence of her age was everywhere—the thinning and graying of her hair, the webs of lines at the corners of her eyes, the veins and spots on her hands. It could've been her mother there in front of me, that long-dead woman I'd never met.

"You have a dog." Her voice was unchanged.

Wind was in the trees outside, shaking the branches. The leaves slipped together like whispers.

"May I come in?"

I stepped aside, regretting my shirt. Jenny didn't deserve to see the ruin of my body, but Marie did.

She took a seat at the table, and I closed the door.

I sat down opposite her.

Maggie followed behind, a rumble filling her throat. "Down." She dropped to the ground, whining once.

"I heard an eastern phoebe on my walk over."

I didn't respond.

"Roscoe."

The woman before me was a mess pieced together from fragments that sat ill and wormy in their current grouping. I couldn't place her face, at once so familiar and yet completely unknown. She was the young woman I'd met in the village on the Coosa, and she was also the woman who'd sat next to me in my hospital bed asking me to sign away my past. She could have been a teacher coming home from her schoolhouse, and I could've been an electrician coming home from my dam. Her belly could've been rounding with its second pregnancy, Gerald a sweet toddler nannied by Nettie Williams. But she was also that broken woman, bleeding and pale, on her way to the hospital in Birmingham, where the parts of her that grew babies were removed, along with her compassion and her hope. She was mother to a son who fed on the milk of the woman three doors down. She was the daughter of a dead man who'd left her his land, a landowner who'd given her land away, the mother of a resentful son, a wife no longer married.

The sun had changed its slant outside.

"Roscoe."

"Why are you here, Marie?"

She cast her eyes around that meager room. She sighed, and the breath was ugly—deeply worried and aged, but familiar. Even when she was young, it held those same tones.

"You're thin."

"Prison will do that."

"It fits you."

She stared at me, and I made myself focus on her face—the light eyes with their new lines, the graying hair, the thinned lips and widened nostrils, the pronounced cheekbones. Though her body was wider, her face was gaunt and pale.

"I didn't expect you to be here."

Again, I didn't offer her a response.

"I didn't expect you to get out so soon, and when you were released, I expected you would go someplace new. All this"—she motioned around the room—"surprised me. Gerald let me know you were here. He says you're going to fight for your *rightful* share of the property, that you've already retained a lawyer. I suppose that's my main reason for coming. I've given the land to Moa and Wilson. It's theirs, Roscoe, and that's as it should be. For all we've taken from them, it's only right. It was the only way I could think to start repaying our debt. Wilson suffered all that hardship—his family suffered all that hardship—because of our mistakes."

"*Our* mistakes?"

She dropped her gaze and pinched the bridge of her nose. "I have plenty to own, too. You think I'm not willing to admit that?"

"I don't know what you're willing to do, Marie."

She nodded as though I'd asked her a question. *Yes,* her nod said, *that's right.* "Did they tell you?"

"About what?" I wanted her to admit her treachery, her dishonesty and manipulations. She could've said so many things.

I'm sorry, Roscoe.

I could nearly see the letter she could've written.

Her eyes came to rest on the pallet by the stove. "Are you sleeping there?"

"Sometimes."

I came round to her side of the table. "Take off my shirt."

"I'm sorry?"

"Stand up and take off my shirt."

"Roscoe, I'm not comfortable with that. I— You must not know. It's—"

"Take off my shirt."

She took a deep breath, pulled herself free of the bench. Her hands were itchy at her sides, flighty and quick. They moved toward me, then away, and then back to the hem of my shirt. We were in that room together. *Put your hands on my body, Marie.*

She did, and her fingers were cold where they brushed my skin. I lifted my left arm, but my right wouldn't rise, and she accommodated it, sliding my shirt free of that low limb.

She stared at my body and brought a finger to the line on my stomach.

Sun was outside the window, trees and sky. Maggie was there, her head on her paws. Marie's touch was torture against my skin.

She made her voice as small as possible when she said, "We are no longer married, Roscoe."

That's right, Marie. We aren't.

Her hand lingered. "It's easier for everyone."

"Easier?" Anger was upon me fearsome and hurried, and with it, the words I'd been willing myself to speak since first recognizing her face at the door. "Is it easier for Gerald? For Moa and Wilson and Jenny? Is it easier for all of them to take on the burden of me?"

My voice brought Maggie up, and she stood behind my knees. I could so easily have torn a piece off the hem of Marie's dress and held it down for Maggie to smell. *Got it?* I could have said. *This is what we're after.*

Why are you putting that dog on me? Marie would yell.

Maggie here can smell the wrongs in a person.

Or I could have told her she was simply a convict, a criminal, and that we—this dog and I—were in the habit of catching those types.

I could see her climbing a tree, her blue dress snagging on its branches and bark, the hem torn to her knees and then her thighs, her skin seeping small scratches. Maggie would haul me up to the trunk, barking at my ex-wife, treed like any other escapee.

Easy. Easier. There was no such thing.

My hands found themselves on her shoulders, just the height my right arm would allow. The bones of her collar lurked there beneath the layers of fabric and skin. *You were once so beautiful, Marie.* I pushed her back against the wall, my elbows finding their way to her chest, my forearms on either side of her aged face, my hands in her graying hair. My shoulder fought me, but I forced it to listen.

Tears seeped from her thick-lidded eyes. "Roscoe."

Her hand was still on my stomach, that long scar.

I pressed against her, against her face, against the trail she'd planted to that spot, and as I pressed, I saw them—my people—Ed and Chaplain, Taylor and the warden, even Beau and the remains of Stevens. They had all built my story, and I followed the routes they'd given me. Even George Haskin was a trap I'd been set to release. I had been Taylor's dog boy and Chaplain's reader and Ed's friend, and before that I had been Marie's salvation as well as her disappointment, and before that—long before—I had been her husband and an electrician running power from the banks of the Coosa, and a father if only for those few moments I held the infant version of our son, offering him my knuckle to stanch his crying.

And now I was a landowner, living off the kindness of those I'd harmed. I was the things around me—an old cottage fed by new power, a hound bred to run and tree men, lazy by a woodstove. I was a child's pallet on the floor, as close to a prison cot as I could get. I was rafters and roof shake, a burned circle in the grasses. I was the poles I'd raised—trees stripped bare, reappropriated, renamed. I was Wilson's lost arm.

And given the choice, Marie would have had me back at Kilby, or walking a road toward somewhere unknown. She would have had me disappear.

I kept my hands in her hair, my arms on her shoulders.

Her fingers dropped from my stomach. "Roscoe."

Gerald was in her, the soft man he'd become and the smug son he'd once been. I had left marks on him and would leave marks on

Marie—all my anger and ruin squeezing itself against her, into her, through her. I could see Yellow Mama welcoming me in, my conjured young Marie right after all, Yellow Mama my resting place, all this electricity leading me to her seat, her wires, her current.

But I had chased after Hughes. I had thrown my lot in with the warden and Taylor and Rash and Chaplain, and because of those particular loyalties, I had escaped—escaped Yellow Mama and her guards, Kilby and its wall, the hospital and solitary. I'd escaped and been offered a place—here, a home.

I wouldn't let Marie steal that. I wouldn't let her send me back.

I pressed down, leaving just the briefest bruises on her papery neck—reminders of what I'd done and what I still could do. Then I stepped away, the feeling of her drying up like the anger, a frail, parched thing.

Her hands were at her throat, her fingers exploring, her eyes wet and wide.

"Roscoe," she said, as though it were the only word she knew.

"Did they tell you? About this place? Do you know that I own it?" Her face told me she didn't, and I welcomed the chance to surprise her. I stepped forward, and she shrank from me, her body begging access to the wall's plaster so she could slip away. I wouldn't touch her—not ever again—but she didn't know that. "Moa and Wilson signed it over to me—the cottage and a quarter section of land. This is my home, now." My voice was calm, more fearful than my shout, possibly more fearful than my grip on her neck. "I won't fight you for your remaining assets, Marie. This place—the cottage and the land—it's welcome because it's not yours."

Maggie pushed her nose against my palm. I didn't tell her to sit down. Instead, I pulled on one of her ears, both of us eyeing Marie, holding our line. I would've welcomed Taylor in that moment, high on his horse, shackles ready. *Let's lead her in,* he'd say, once Marie's hands were bound. *She's a tricky one. Best keep that dog on her.*

I could see Marie out in front of us, her shoulders hunched, her feet shuffling her toward whatever confinement she'd created for herself, whatever her life had become.

She should go. She should stay gone.

"I don't want to see you again." I bent to collect my shirt from where it'd dropped to the floor. Maggie stayed standing, her attention on Marie. I went to the table, where my breakfast had gone cold. Marie had to see the deep scar along my back from the dog belt.

"All right," I heard, her voice a quiet mewling.

She squared her shoulders and held her hand out toward Maggie, her face nearly the one I'd known before. "Will she bite me?"

"Easy," I said to Maggie. And to Marie: "No."

Maggie held herself rigid. "Easy, girl. It's all right."

Marie's hand reached the dog's head, her fingers around the back of Maggie's skull, the nails starting to scratch—a spot Maggie loved. The stiffness went out of her quick, all her muscles releasing, her tail wagging.

"You've gone soft," I scolded, though it was hard to mean it, knowing I had, too.

Marie knelt, her face level with Maggie's muzzle. "I didn't know what to expect from this. This moment here, this morning. I wanted to convince you to go, but I wanted you to try some convincing, too. Silly, isn't it? I even imagined you courting me again. I saw us taking a walk around the cottage here, out past your new lines. I imagined you telling me about all the plants again, and I'd tell you about the birds—the eastern phoebe I heard on the way over and the bay-breasted warblers that I started noticing right after you left. They're called a *confusion* of warblers, or a *bouquet*. I was thinking about telling you all those collective nouns." Her hands stroked Maggie's ears. "But then my own anger comes again, and all those fantasies go away. I remember how distant you became after Gerald's birth, and then your reluctance to come here. I see those lines you raised and the lies you told me, lies I believed and spread. I see that boy's dead body, all burned and blackened, and I see Wilson in those coal mines. I see his arm, Moa's pain. And you—I see you spending all that time in prison, and I'm angry for that as well, angry at you for doing it to yourself, for leaving us."

She stood slowly, her joints audibly complaining.

"I know you have your own list, Roscoe, all the ways I've disappointed you."

She smiled, and I could nearly see myself loving her.

"Walk me out?" Bruises were bluing up on her neck.

I pulled my shirt over my head, tired of my demonstration.

"I don't know that it's good for you to be in Gerald's life, but will you please try—try to make it good." We were at the door.

"I will." I am trying.

Marie nodded, and we stood there facing each other, Maggie between us like a pastor overseeing a ceremony, presiding over our good-byes. I want to think Marie and I felt the same, that we both wanted to hold each other, to bring our mouths together once more, to possibly even take each other's hand and walk into the bedroom to lie once more as husband and wife on that old mattress where I rarely slept, that we wanted those things alongside the clenched fists, and the thrown books, the clawing fingernails and bruised skin. And because we wanted both the tenderness and the violence, we could do nothing but stand that short distance away from each other, quiet and still.

After days or possibly months—dust having gathered on our shoulders, birds having nested in our clothes, our skin sallowed and dry, our eyes turned to glass—I finally opened that handsome door I'd stripped and oiled myself and held it wide. Marie walked under my arm, and neither of us spoke. Outside, the sun shone its slanted light, the breeze swung the needles and the leaves of the trees, the grasses sprouted through the blackened patch, tiny threads of green. Marie walked away, but I am still there, standing in the doorway of my home. Maggie stands next to me, an old dog now. Jenny's garden is tall, and electricity runs through the lines over my head.

ACKNOWLEDGMENTS

I would like to thank my parents, John and Debbie Reeves, for raising me in a house full of books. You started this whole thing. I thank my sister, Annie Shaw, for her inspiring brilliance and individuality. My grandparents, Jim and Terry Reeves, introduced me to Alabama. Thank you, Bam, for keeping that door open. I wish Paspa were here to celebrate with us. My aunt Terrie and uncle Wil have been unflagging in their support and love throughout my writing career. I am fortunate to have Art and Linda Compton and Dick and Rita Swenson in my corner. They are family in all the right ways.

This book would not exist without the open arms of the Michener Center, specifically Jim Magnuson, Michael Adams, Elizabeth McCracken, Marla Akin, and Debbie Deweese. The idea for this novel was born in a history writing course with H. W. Brands. My cohort at the Michener Center remains a fierce force of greatness. Extended thanks go to Ben Roberts, Carolina Ebeid, Kate Finlinson, and Shamala Gallagher. Mimi Chubb was an early reader, and this book is better for her comments. Kevin Powers helped me bring my work to a bigger audience, and I am grateful for his support.

My colleagues and students at the Khabele School have been instrumental in the creation of this novel, offering feedback, encouragement, and accountability. I finished this novel with my students. Tyler Clayton asked me every day if I'd worked on the book. In response to an early draft, Atticus Tait suggested I spend more time with Marie; her sections stemmed from his advice.

The amazing Mauro clan gave me a beautiful, quiet space to finish my revisions. Eric and Jaclyn Mann, Kelley and Nate Janes, Ryan Phillips, John Mulvany, and Ashleigh Pedersen are the best fan club anyone could ask for. They're damn good friends, too.

My agent, Peter Straus, is an incredible editor and advocate, and he's responsible for reviving my own belief in my work. My editors at Scribner, Nan Graham and Daniel Loedel, are not only brilliant but delightful to work with. I am so fortunate to reap the benefits of their keen observations and insights.

My thanks go to Maggie McCall, whose loyalty and strength are alive in her namesake. Bethany Flint's morality and resilience flow through the pages of this book.

I became a writer under the mentorship of the poet Loren Graham, and he remains one of my most valued readers and friends. Special thanks and love to Fiona McFarlane, the perfect guide to this adventure and the most wonderful person I know.

And lastly, I thank my family. Margot, thank you for your inspiring discipline, your unapologetic and rigid morals, and your tremendous encouragement and love. Hannah, you are mature and wise beyond your years, and you've woven your way into the heart of this book in more ways than even I know. And finally, to Luke Muszkiewicz, my greatest and oldest advocate. You have been challenging and supporting me since I was nineteen, and you have never wavered in your faith in my work. I am here because of your trust, love, and patience. Thank you.